SUPERNATURAL™
MYTHMAKER

SUPERNATURAL™

MYTHMAKER

TIM WAGGONER

SUPERNATURAL created by Eric Kripke

TITAN BOOKS

Supernatural: Mythmaker
Print edition ISBN: 9781783298549
E-book edition ISBN: 9781783298556

Published by Titan Books
A division of Titan Publishing Group Ltd
144 Southwark St, London SE1 0UP

First edition: July 2016
10 9 8 7 6 5 4 3 2 1

To receive advance information, news, competitions, and exclusive
offers online, please sign up for the Titan newsletter on our website:
www.titanbooks.com

HISTORIAN'S NOTE

This novel takes place during season ten, between
"Hibbing 911" and "The Things We Left Behind."

ONE

Beads of sweat dotted Renee Mendez's forehead as she worked. She'd been holding the brush for so long—several hours at least—that the muscles in her right hand burned like fire. Her back and shoulders ached, as did her feet, and her stomach gurgled painfully. She couldn't remember the last time she ate. This morning? Yesterday? She wasn't even sure what day it was.

She stood in front of a canvas on a wooden easel, to her right a small bench upon which rested a collection of brushes and tubes of paint. She used a piece of old plywood as a makeshift palette, and it was covered with small globs of paint squeezed from the tubes and mixed as needed. Her studio, such as it was, occupied a corner of her parents' garage. Her father had cleared the space for her when she started taking art classes at Eldridge Community College after graduating from high school. It was cramped—if she backed up too far while she was working, she'd bump into her mom's car. If she stepped too far to the right, her elbow would hit the garage wall, too far to the left, and her foot would touch a leaf blower propped against the wall. But she appreciated her parents allowing her to work here. It saved her from having to drive to the college and use one of the equally cramped studio spaces reserved for students. Here, she could work whenever she wanted, day or night, and she could do so without distractions. Both of her parents were good about leaving her alone when she was painting. They might occasionally sneak a peek over her shoulder if they were in the garage, but they never tried to engage her in conversation, never asked her what she was working on or how it was going. She deeply appreciated that.

Her mother worried about her sometimes, though, especially lately. *Are you getting enough sleep? You look so tired, and you barely touched your dinner.* Renee was nineteen, and while her mother's concern irritated her—she wasn't a child anymore—she also knew it meant she cared. And on some level she knew her mother's worries weren't without justification. Renee had loved art since she was old enough to hold a crayon, and she'd rather draw or paint than do anything else. But the last several days she'd been especially prolific, completing one painting after another in a white-hot frenzy of inspiration. She'd never experienced anything like this before. It was like she was caught up in a tidal wave of artistic energy, unable to do anything but hold on tight and let it carry her wherever it would. The experience was equal parts amazing and frightening, but she couldn't stop if she wanted to. She *had* to keep painting.

She wore her long black hair tied back in a ponytail to keep it from brushing against the canvas, and she had on an old T-shirt and ratty jeans, both of which were covered with paint splotches. She positioned her face close to the canvas as she worked, not because she had poor eyesight but so she could better focus on the small details. She was almost finished with this painting, and it was now just a matter of adding a few final touches. Normally, she liked to draw and paint images based on real life—flowers, birds, trees, people... But lately her mind had been filled with fantastic characters: men and women with strange, unearthly appearances and abilities, like creatures out of fantasy novels or comic books. This current painting was of a cruel-faced woman whose waist-length hair, flawless skin, and sleeveless floor-length gown all appeared to be made of the same silvery metal. An oversized metallic gauntlet covered her right hand, the fingers tapering to sharp claw-like points. There was something missing, though, and Renee couldn't put her finger on what it was. But then it came to her. She dabbed her brush in white, then blue, and with a couple of quick strokes the woman's eyes now appeared to be crackling with electric energy. Perfect.

She lowered her brush and stepped back to admire her work. But as she did so, the colors that comprised the silver woman began to fade, and within seconds she was gone, the canvas blank once again.

This should have struck Renee as strange, but it didn't. After all, the same thing had happened to the last dozen or so paintings she'd produced. Why should this one be any different? She sighed, selected an image at random from the dozens swirling in her mind—a man wearing a white lab coat and holding a strange object: a golden rod with snakes intertwined around it—and lifted her brush.

"In the end there shall be One," she murmured, and began a new painting.

"I can't believe this."

Geoffrey Ramsey walked along the sidewalk of downtown Corinth, Illinois, his friend Jimmy Reid at his side. Well, maybe *friend* was too strong a word. *Temporary companion* was closer to the truth. Geoffrey had been homeless for almost three years now, and he found it easier not to get too close to anyone. You had to look out for Number One on the streets, even if those streets were located in a small Midwestern town instead of some big city. In a lot of ways, being homeless in a small town was worse, Geoffrey thought. At least in a city there would be more places to hole up for the night where the cops would leave you alone, and more places where you could find an odd job or two to score some cash to buy food. Not in Corinth, though. He and Jimmy had been going from business to business all morning, and so far they hadn't found a single bit of work. No trash to take out, no floors to sweep, no heavy boxes to carry... Usually they could find *something*. But not today.

"It's just the way it goes sometimes," Jimmy said.

Jimmy always had a good attitude, regardless of the situation. It was a quality that irritated Geoffrey to no end.

"Yeah? Well if it keeps on going like this, you and I will go to sleep with empty bellies tonight."

Jimmy shrugged. "Wouldn't be the first time."

Geoffrey sighed. "True enough."

The two men continued walking, and Geoffrey tried to think of other places they could look for work. It was the second week of December, and there were several inches of snow on the ground. Despite this, the sun was warm, the sky cloudless, and the air still. But Geoffrey knew the weather would be taking a turn for the worse soon. He wore a thin brown jacket over a flannel shirt and two T-shirts. It was all about layers when you were homeless. This jacket wouldn't see him though another Illinois winter, though, but right now it was the heaviest coat he had. His sneakers were shot, too. He could feel cool air filtering through the numerous holes, and when it rained it didn't matter how many pairs of socks he wore, his feet got soaked.

The state of Jimmy's wardrobe wasn't much better. His blue windbreaker was even thinner than Geoffrey's jacket, his jeans had holes in both knees, and his old, broken-down work boots had been repaired with duct tape so many times that almost none of the original material remained. Both of them were going to need to get hold of better clothes, and soon. But that was a worry which could be postponed a little while yet. The first thing they needed to do was eat.

Clothing aside, the two men were a study in contrasts. Geoffrey was black, Jimmy was white. Geoffrey was a stocky man of medium height, Jimmy was thin and six-and-a-half feet tall. Geoffrey was in his fifties and had a beard that held more salt than pepper, while Jimmy was in his thirties, with a thin patchy beard and shoulder-length blond hair. And of course, Geoffrey tended to look at the negative side of things while Jimmy preferred to focus on the positive. And right now, Geoffrey was definitely in a negative frame of mind.

Downtown Corinth was a collection of two- and three-story buildings that had been erected in the forties and fifties, narrow structures of red brick and gray stone. Businesses came and went as the years passed, and right now the buildings housed coffee shops, restaurants, antique stores, secondhand clothing stores, funky art galleries, used bookstores, and the like. The old-fashioned architecture should've clashed with the bohemian vibe of the businesses, but somehow they complemented each other. The small business owners that struggled to make a living downtown were normally sympathetic to the town's homeless population, but during the holiday season they became more focused on their own needs. Geoffrey couldn't blame them. If they didn't make good money this time of year, more than a few of them might end up having to close their doors for good. And the last thing customers wanted to see was two homeless guys hanging around, trying to pick up a couple bucks. Geoffrey had hoped they'd have a week or so before Jimmy and he became *personae non gratae* downtown, but from the response they'd gotten in their quest for work today—or rather lack thereof—it seemed the holiday season had already kicked into high gear in Corinth. He and Jimmy probably wouldn't be able to find odd jobs to do until after New Year's.

Peace on Earth, goodwill to men, Geoffrey thought bitterly.

It wasn't noon yet, but there was a steady stream of traffic, and most of the parking spaces in front of the businesses were taken. There weren't many pedestrians, though. People in Corinth tended to drive straight to their destination, take care of whatever business they had there, and then leave. They didn't window-shop much.

Geoffrey had worked as a machinist for twenty years before the factory laid off all its workers and closed down. He drew unemployment while he looked for work, but one night— after he and Ellen were coming back from a late movie—a drunk driver ran an intersection and hit the passenger side of the car head-on. Ellen was killed instantly. Geoffrey wasn't so lucky. He sustained numerous injuries which required multiple surgeries. He had so many pins and rods in him that he'd set off an airport metal detector if he came within fifty feet of it. His medical insurance had lapsed when the factory closed, and he'd used what savings he had to pay for Ellen's burial. He couldn't pay his astronomical medical bills, and because of this he lost their house. He and Ellen had never married or had children, and what little family he had left lived in the Chicago area. So once his house was gone, instead of looking for a new place to live, he hit the streets and he'd been on them ever since.

"It's kind of weird, huh?" Jimmy said.

The question pulled Geoffrey out of his glum thoughts and he turned to look at Jimmy.

"What?"

"The decorations."

Geoffrey turned away from his friend and examined their surroundings. At first, he didn't know what Jimmy was referring to. The downtown businesses always decorated for the holidays—normally well before Thanksgiving—and this season was no exception. Wreaths hung on doors; cardboard figures of snowmen, Santa, Jack Frost, and even a few dreidels hung in windows. But the longer Geoffrey looked, the more he understood what Jimmy was talking about. The usual holiday decorations were out in abundance, yes, but there were other decorations too, all of them strange and unfamiliar. A music store across the street called Tune Town had a black spiral pattern painted on the inside of its display window. A couple buildings down, a pawn shop called Cash Bonanza had a straw figure hanging on its front door. The figure was roughly human-shaped, but it had two heads and four arms. And on their side of the street, only a few doors down from where they stood, an antique store called Treasures and Trinkets had a small sign out front on the sidewalk, red letters painted on a wooden board. But instead of advertising the business, it read ALL HAIL ARACHNUS! complete with thin strands of webbing drawn between the letters.

Geoffrey frowned. "What the hell?"

"Pay no heed to the signs of false gods," said a steely voice behind them.

Geoffrey and Jimmy spun around to see a woman standing on the sidewalk. Geoffrey hadn't heard her approach, and his first thought was that she'd somehow appeared out of thin air. He knew it was a crazy idea, but he couldn't shake it. The woman was silver from head to toe, both her skin and her gown, and Geoffrey wondered if she was some sort of street performer one of the businesses had hired to attract customers. But her skin didn't look as if it were covered with makeup or body paint. Her hair resembled finely wrought strands of metal and her eyes shimmered with unearthly blue-white light. The fabric of her gown appeared to be made from some combination of metal and cloth. It hung on her stiffly when she remained still, as if it were some sort of armor, but when she moved, it shifted with her, suddenly soft and pliant. She wore a large metal glove over her right hand that stretched halfway up her forearm. No, not a glove, Geoffrey thought. There was a better word for it. A… gauntlet, yeah, that was it. The gauntlet was the same silvery color as the rest of her and so highly polished that it gleamed in the sunlight. The gauntlet's fingers ended in wicked-looking claws, the sight of which made him shiver. He imagined those claws slicing into flesh, needle tips parting skin and muscle with the ease of a hot knife cutting through warm butter. The image nauseated him, but at the same time it gave him a thrill to think of the damage the gauntlet could do.

What the hell's wrong with me? he thought. He wasn't a violent man, had never raised a hand against anyone in his life. But he couldn't take his gaze from the gauntlet and its deadly fingers.

The woman's height added to her otherworldly appearance. She stood over seven feet tall, taller than Jimmy by at least six inches, giving her a commanding presence. But beyond her size, she exuded an aura of strength, of *power*. It radiated from her in waves that Geoffrey could almost feel physically, and he thought he could hear a slight hum in the air, as if he were standing close to a powerful machine that had just been activated.

"I am Adamantine," she said. Her voice was cold and

unemotional, with a hollow, echoing quality that made the hair on the back of Geoffrey's neck stand up. "I have Manifested."

Geoffrey exchanged glances with Jimmy, but Jimmy only shrugged. Geoffrey faced Adamantine once more, but he didn't look directly into her eyes. He couldn't bring himself to gaze into the light that shone from them. He tried to speak, but nothing came out. He swallowed once then tried again.

"We don't understand," he said. His voice was hushed, almost reverent, and he felt a near overwhelming urge to kneel before this strange woman. It took an effort of will, but he remained standing.

Adamantine ignored his comment. She took a moment to look around at her surroundings, and Geoffrey had the impression she was taking everything in, as if it was all new to her. Traffic continued at a steady pace, and while most drivers were too intent on where they were going to notice Adamantine, those who did see the tall silver woman gaped at her as they drove by.

"It's a modest place," she said at last. "But I suppose it will have to do." She turned to look at Geoffrey and Jimmy once more, her silver lips stretching into a smile. "What are your names?"

Neither man answered at first, but then Jimmy told her his name, as did Geoffrey.

Adamantine inclined her head, as if giving them some sort of official acknowledgement.

It's like she's royalty or something, Geoffrey thought.

"Today the two of you have the great honor of becoming the first of my worshippers. Kneel before me, accept me into your hearts, and I will lead you to glory."

As Adamantine spoke these words her presence, already far stronger than anything Geoffrey had ever experienced, intensified. He felt her power reach out and envelop him, call to him, tell him that he could be part of something larger than himself, that he would no longer have to live on the streets and seek out the most menial jobs just so he could put a few crumbs in his belly. If he went with her, he would eat and eat well.

He opened his mouth to speak, but before he could say anything, Jimmy shook his head back and forth rapidly, as if trying to clear his mind. Then he looked at Adamantine and laughed.

"I don't know what you're on, lady, but whatever it is, it's got to be pretty damn strong. Do you want us to take you to the free clinic? It's only a few blocks away. Or we could stay with you until you come down, make sure you're okay."

Adamantine's smile had remained in place as she made her offer, but now it fell away, and her brow furrowed in anger. The humming noise that seemed to emanate from the air around her grew louder. She turned to look at Jimmy, the light in her eyes glowing with increased intensity.

"Do you mock me?" Her voice was soft, but the anger in her tone was unmistakable, at least to Geoffrey. He tried to catch Jimmy's attention, wanted to signal to him to cool it before he got hurt. But Jimmy ignored him.

"Maybe just a little," Jimmy said. "But you have to admit, that's one wild costume you're wearing. You do know that Halloween was like, two months ago, right?"

Adamantine regarded Jimmy for a moment, and then she stepped toward him. She didn't run, didn't seem to move fast in any way. But within an instant she stood directly in front of Jimmy, a hair's breadth between them. Before Jimmy could react, she grabbed hold of his throat with her gauntlet, and the humming noise grew so loud it hurt Geoffrey's ears. A crackling sound filled the air as thin bolts of electricity coruscated across the gauntlet's metal surface. Jimmy's eyes flew wide and he screamed, his body jerking all over, as if some invisible force was shaking him. *No*, Geoffrey thought. As if he were being electrocuted.

Jimmy reached up to grab hold of the gauntlet and tried to pull it off him, but either he was too weak or Adamantine was too strong, and he couldn't budge it. Wisps of smoke began curling upward from both his hands and his neck, and the skin that was in contact with the metal began to blacken. Jimmy no longer screamed. Instead, he was making *uh-uh-uh* sounds, his voice pulsing in time to the electric current running through him. Sparks began to shoot off his body, and tendrils of smoke rose from his head, arms, torso, and legs. Geoffrey feared that his friend would burst into flames, but then his body stiffened all over, and then his head lolled to the side and he fell limp.

The humming diminished, and while Jimmy's body—his *dead* body, Geoffrey thought—was still smoking, it no longer emitted sparks. Adamantine continued to hold onto him for a moment longer, looking at him with a detached curiosity, before finally releasing her grip. Jimmy's body fell to the sidewalk and lay still, smoke continuing to curl upward from his form, the skin on his neck and palms charred black.

Adamantine then turned her attention to Geoffrey.

"And how do *you* feel about my more than generous offer?" she asked.

Geoffrey glanced sideways at his friend's smoldering corpse. He was horrified by what had happened to Jimmy. He was a good guy and hadn't deserved to die like that. But... he *had* mocked Adamantine. Hadn't he been able to feel the power radiating from the woman? You didn't make fun of that kind of power. It demanded respect. And if you respected it, maybe you could share in it, even if only a little.

Geoffrey got down on one knee and bowed his head.

"My lady," he said.

The gauntlet was still warm when Adamantine placed it gently on his head. He felt that warmth spread through his body, and he trembled with the joy of it. He'd never experienced anything so wonderful.

"I'm sorry."

Lena Nguyen finished speaking and clasped her hands in front of her on the top of her desk. She always did this whenever she delivered bad news to a patient, although she wasn't sure why. A self-comforting gesture, perhaps. Oncology wasn't the easiest field to work in, especially when you cared for your patients as deeply as she did. She was used to delivering bad news—too used to it—but that didn't make it any easier.

A couple sat on the other side of the desk, two men in their forties. They both had short hair flecked with gray and neatly trimmed goatees that looked the same. One of the men was thinner than the other, and Lena knew his appearance wasn't down to choice. The men held hands, and while the heavier of the two had tears in his eyes, his husband's expression remained stoic. Lena had seen that look on patients' faces many times before. He was stunned by the news he'd just received, and it hadn't fully hit him yet. But it would, sooner rather than later.

Thomas Rosenman and his husband, David, had first come to her three years ago. Thomas had been having trouble breathing, and his doctor scheduled a battery of tests for him. The result: several suspicious masses were found in his right lung, and they proved to be Stage Three cancer. Ironic, considering the man had never smoked a cigarette in his life. But cancer was like that. Sometimes it had a clear cause, but all too often it was random, like being struck by lightning. It just happened.

Lena had been brought onto his medical team after that. She prescribed surgery followed by aggressive chemotherapy. The surgery went well, and while the chemo was rough, Thomas endured and made it through. Thomas had gone through more tests afterward, and it looked like he was free of cancer. Of course, when it came to cancer, "free" really meant "free for now." There was always a chance it could come back, and that's what had happened to Thomas. Two years without a sign of recurrence, and now his latest CT scan revealed his lung had several tumors, all of which had grown so rapidly that Lena knew Thomas had little chance of survival this time. She hadn't put it that way to him, of course. She'd talked about immediate surgery, followed by more chemo. She'd tried to sound positive, even upbeat about his chances, but neither Thomas nor David seemed to buy her sales pitch. Maybe she hadn't been as convincing as she'd hoped. Or maybe they'd simply been through so much already that they didn't have the strength for another fight.

Neither Thomas nor David spoke for several minutes, and Lena sat silently as well, hands still clasped on her desk. It was difficult to sit and observe their pain without doing something—anything—to relieve it, but she knew from experience that there was nothing she could do right now, other than give them more time to absorb the news they'd received.

Lena's office was small, but since she used it primarily as a consulting room, its size didn't matter much. What did matter to her was that it didn't look like just another cold, sterile examining room. She wanted it to be warm and comfortable, a place where her patients could relax—at least as much as possible, given their reason for coming to see her. To that end, she had the walls covered with wood paneling, and she'd installed cream-colored carpet. The chairs were plush leather and extremely comfortable to sit in. There was a wooden bookcase behind her filled with medical texts, and paintings of soothing landscapes—a mountain range, a forest, an ocean beach—hung on the walls, along with her framed diplomas, honors, and awards. She'd brought plants into the office too—a Boston fern, a peace lily, and a philodendron. Not only did they scrub the air, they helped create a calmer environment. Or so she hoped. Aside from a phone and a laptop that usually remained closed, there was nothing to clutter the surface of her desk. There were fluorescent lights on the ceiling, but she left them off, preferring to use a floor lamp whenever possible, or the softer, natural light provided by the room's lone window. But no matter how hard she worked at making her office comforting, in the end she knew it only helped a little, if at all.

Lena was a short woman, barely over five feet, with a round face, shoulder-length black hair, and glasses. She thought the latter gave her an air of seriousness that helped counter her height. When people first met her—especially if they didn't know she was a doctor—they tended to treat her like… not a child, exactly, but not like a full adult either. It was for this reason that she kept her glasses instead of switching to contacts. She wasn't sure if it really helped, though.

Thomas stared at the wall the entire time the three of them were silent, but at last he turned to meet Lena's gaze and spoke.

"If I don't do anything—no surgery, no chemo—how long will I have?"

She wasn't surprised by the question. She'd gotten it from patients before, but it was one she never liked answering. She didn't believe in giving up.

"Six months," she said. "Maybe as long as a year. But you'll be in a great deal of pain for much of that time, and toward the end you'll be hospitalized." She paused. "Or in a hospice, depending on your choice."

"Whatever you're thinking about, Tom, you can stop it right now," David said. Lena could hear the fear in his voice, but his manner was firm. "We're going to fight this just like we did last time, and we're going to beat it."

Thomas gave his husband a sad but loving smile.

"The odds—" he began.

"I don't care about the odds," David snapped. "I only care about you."

Lena found the man's love touching. Her own marriage had ended in divorce several years ago. It had been amicable enough, but they'd had no children, and while she'd dated on and off since, she'd never gotten close to anyone, let alone fallen in love.

Conversations like this were the worst part of her job. She'd become a doctor and specialized in oncology after losing her mother to breast cancer when she was in high school. And while she wasn't foolish or arrogant enough to believe she could single-handedly cure cancer, she'd dedicated her life to fighting it and, more importantly, giving people hope. But she had no hope to give Thomas and David, and she hated it.

She was about to make another pitch for treatment, even if the chances of success were low, but before she spoke, the office door opened, and a man in a white lab coat entered.

Lena's breath caught in her throat when she saw him. He wasn't just handsome, he was *beautiful*, in the same way that an ancient Greek statue was. He had curly black hair, high cheekbones, a strong chin, full lips, and the most startling blue eyes she'd ever seen. They were so bright they seemed to gleam with internal light. The effect was so powerful that she could only look at his eyes for a few seconds before experiencing a strong urge to turn away. His lab coat was so white it practically glowed, and a name was stitched onto the left breast in blue thread the same color as his eyes, one word: *Paeon*. The name struck her as familiar, but she couldn't place it. He wore a white shirt under his coat, along with a red tie that had a design made from a collection of medical instruments—stethoscopes, hypodermics, tongue depressors, thermometers, and blood pressure cuffs. Black pants and shoes completed his outfit, so dark they seemed to draw in and swallow the light around them.

He was tall, but more than that, his entire body, facial features included, was larger than an average man. It was almost as if he belonged to a different species entirely, or was a more highly evolved form of human. A word came to her mind then: *god*. His appearance was only part of what created the impression of otherworldliness, though. The man—Paeon— exuded an aura of strength and power which filled the room, a raw energy like the way the air feels before the arrival of a massive thunderstorm. The sensation didn't provoke fear, but rather a feeling of vitality. Lena felt alert, bursting with energy, as if she could go outside and run a mile—no, *five* miles—at top speed without getting winded or becoming tired.

She'd never seen this man before. She definitely would've remembered if she had.

It took her a moment to find her voice, but when she did, she said, "I'm in a private consultation with a patient at the moment. If you'll go back to the reception area, I'll be with you as soon as I can."

It took an effort of will for her to get the words out. The last thing she wanted to do was send him away, but she had to think of Thomas first.

Paeon gave her a warm, caring smile.

"That is why I am here."

His rich tenor was like honey in her ears. He held her gaze for a moment before turning to Thomas. He lowered his gaze to the man's chest, eyes narrowing, as if he were peering inside his body.

"You are ill," he said to Thomas. "Gravely so." He lifted his gaze and smiled. "It is most fortunate for you that I Manifested in this place."

Paeon reached inside his lab coat and withdrew an object from an inner pocket. It was ten inches long, too large to conceivably fit inside the pocket, and it appeared to be made from gold. It was a rod with a pair of intertwined serpents wrapped around it and two small wings protruding from the top. Lena recognized the object, although she'd never seen a three-dimensional version of it. It was a caduceus, an ancient symbol that the medical profession had adopted as its emblem. And when she saw it, she remembered where she'd heard the name Paeon before. In mythology, Paeon was the physician of the Greek gods.

Paeon held the rod in his right hand and extended it toward Thomas.

"I can banish the foul corruption from your body. Is this something you desire?"

Thomas looked up at Paeon, doubt and confusion in his eyes. But there was also a glimmer of hope.

"Yes," he said.

Paeon smiled. "Good. And in return for this gift, you must swear allegiance to me and come to me when I summon you. Are you willing to do this?"

David put a hand on Thomas's shoulder.

"I don't think this is a good—"

"I am," Thomas said.

Lena could sense there was more behind Thomas's answer than a dying man's desperation. She felt power emanating from Paeon. It was as if he had *willed* Thomas to agree. She wanted to tell him to stop it, that no patient should ever be coerced into treatment, but she couldn't make herself speak. Despite her objection, part of her was glad that Thomas had agreed to Paeon's terms.

Paeon nodded, clearly pleased, and then he stepped forward and touched the tip of the caduceus to Thomas's chest. The rod glowed with golden light, and Thomas drew in a gasping breath, his eyes widening.

Lena rose to her feet, afraid that the caduceus was hurting Thomas somehow, although she knew instinctively that it wasn't.

This can't be real, she told herself, but she knew it was. More, she *hoped* it was, for Thomas's sake.

Paeon held the caduceus to Thomas's chest for several seconds before pulling it away. The instant the rod was no longer in contact with Thomas's body, its glow began to diminish and quickly faded to nothing.

"How do you feel?" Paeon asked.

Thomas drew in a deep breath, held it, and then blew it out in a burst of air.

"I feel…"

Lena and David leaned toward him.

"Great!" Thomas finished and grinned.

* * *

Both Thomas and David thanked Paeon profusely, and David also accepted the caduceus's touch in exchange for his "allegiance." The couple then left, all smiles and laughter, pledging to go forth and tell everyone they met about Paeon's miracle cure. Paeon seemed satisfied by their promise, as if he wanted them to go out and drum up more business for him.

"Do you really expect me to believe that you can cure lung cancer with a touch from your magic wand?" But even as Lena spoke these words, she knew she *did* believe, such was the man's strange power over her.

Paeon gave her a tolerant smile and sat in one of the leather chairs. "You are a physician, Lena. Skepticism is one of your most important tools. But I assure you that man is free of his illness."

"Next you'll tell me that he'll live forever."

Paeon grew thoughtful. "I'm not certain how long my servants will live." He smiled. "I'm still very new at this, you know."

She *didn't* know. She had a dozen questions for him. Two dozen. But right now, she could only think of one that was important.

"Can you heal *any* illness with that?"

He still held the caduceus, and Lena nodded toward it.

"Yes."

There was no ego or arrogance in his answer. He spoke the word as if it were a simple statement of fact.

"Then I've got patients for you to see," Lena said. "A *lot* of them. Are you willing to help them?"

She didn't know exactly who or what this man was—or

if he was even human, as crazy as that sounded. But if he could heal people—especially people like Thomas, who had been given a death sentence by their bodies—then that was all that mattered.

"Of course," Paeon said. "That is, after all, why I'm here. But I will require payment for my services. They will have to give me their *allegiance*."

"Why?" Lena asked. "What could they possibly have that someone like you—with all your power—might need?"

Paeon's smile fell away and his too-blue eyes literally darkened, as if thick shadows fell over them.

"There's a war coming to your town, Lena. A war in which there can be but a single victor. I intend to win this war, and to do so, I'm going to need all the... allies I can get, as quickly as I can get them. I've already got Thomas and David." His eyes brightened and his smile returned. "Would you like to join them?"

He'd first referred to those his caduceus touched as *servants*, but then—as if realizing how that might sound to her—he'd instead used the word *allies*. There was a world of distinction between the two words, and she knew which she preferred.

He held the caduceus out over her desk, and its golden surface began to glow. She could feel warmth emanating from the metal, and in response she experienced a sensation of well-being and contentment. The caduceus was so close she could reach out and touch it. And she wanted to, *needed* to.

He's making you feel this way, she told herself. She wasn't certain, but she thought maybe the caduceus was doing it. Perhaps the object could perform other wonders besides healing. However it was being accomplished, she knew that Paeon was manipulating her. But the healing power of the caduceus was amazing, and she had to be a part of it, even if only as one of Paeon's *allies*. And if she ended up being a servant, what of it? Hadn't she dedicated her life to serving her patients? How much better could she help them by serving a being like Paeon?

Despite her misgiving, she reached out and slowly, almost timidly, wrapped her fingers around the caduceus. When it was finished and she let go of the object, Paeon smiled.

"Now let's get to work," he said.

And Lena smiled back.

TWO

Dean would've preferred to wait for nightfall, but Sam had argued it would be better to approach the farm in daylight.

"Ghouls aren't nocturnal," Dean had argued back. "They eat whenever they get the chance, day or night."

"Yeah, but they tend to do their dirty work after the sun goes down, right? Easier not to get caught that way. There's a good chance they're resting now. They won't expect anyone to come after them in broad daylight." Sam had grinned then. "Who'd be crazy enough to do that?"

"Us, apparently," Dean had said.

In the end, Dean had agreed, and now here they were, on a farm outside McCormick, Missouri, sneaking through a cornfield that had long ago been harvested. The empty stalks were dry and most were bent over or broken. They made rustling, rattling noises if you brushed against them; crunching noises if you stepped on one. The few stalks that remained fully upright weren't all that high—four feet, five at the most—and they didn't provide much cover. The sky was overcast, so at least they weren't walking around in bright sunshine, but even though they walked hunched over to decrease their visibility, Dean felt awfully exposed.

Sam sighed. "All right, I admit it. This wasn't the best idea I've ever had."

"Hey, I'm not the kind of guy to tell you I told you so."

"But?"

Dean smiled. "Told you so."

The brothers continued making their way slowly through the cornfield. Neither suggested turning back or trying a different approach to the farmhouse, or waiting until dark, as Dean had originally suggested. They'd committed to this strategy, and Dean judged they were more than halfway across the field by now. Besides, the brothers knew from long experience that it was usually better to keep moving forward and adapt for any mistakes than to abort a hunt and start again. There was always a chance that despite their precautions, their target knew they were coming.

The creatures that inhabited the dark corners of the world and preyed on humans were experts at remaining hidden. If they were discovered, they were just as likely to abandon their lairs, get the hell out of Dodge, and set up shop somewhere else as they were to lay in wait and attack anyone who came after them. Maybe it would be safer if Dean and Sam tried a different approach, but it could mean losing their chance to clean out this nest of ghouls. And while ghouls fed on the corpses of the dead, they weren't always picky about where their meals came from. Sometimes they waited for people to die a natural death before grabbing their knives and forks.

But all too often they would kill people and devour them afterward, after they'd aged a bit. And once or twice the brothers had encountered ghouls that preferred to chow down on the living. Regardless of what type these were, the brothers couldn't afford to risk them escaping. Not because they were eager to spill the monsters' blood—though Dean had to admit that was one of the job's perks—but because they wanted to prevent the ghouls claiming any more victims. That's what it was all about when you were a hunter: protecting others.

Dean felt—or *thought* he felt—warmth on the inside of his right arm, precisely where the Mark of Cain was. He figured the sensation was due to his imagination, and *not* because the Mark was eager for the battle to come. He told himself this, and he believed it. Mostly.

The early December air was chilly, and without any direct sunlight to warm them, it felt even colder. The brothers both wore light jackets, flannel shirts, jeans, and boots. No gloves. Gloves made it more difficult to maintain a grip on weapons, and the last thing any hunter wanted to do was risk losing a weapon in the middle of a fight with some fanged and clawed nasty looking to gut you and feast on your innards. Speaking of weapons, both brothers carried guns as well as machetes, cutting edges honed to razor sharpness. Decapitation was the best way to slay a ghoul, although a hard enough blow to the head would do the job too. Right now the machetes rode in leather sheaths on their belts, and their guns were tucked into their pants against the small of their backs.

They had a good view of the farmhouse from the cornfield:

white, two-story, black roof, black shutters. It looked to be in good condition, at least based on its outward appearance. The lawn was neatly kept, and there were two vehicles parked in the gravel driveway—a pick-up and an SUV, both of them not more than a couple years old. There was a barn on the property too, not far from the house and painted a stereotypical red. It could use a fresh coat of paint, but otherwise it appeared to be in decent condition as well. Some monsters liked to make their homes in dark, dank, decayed places such as forgotten cemeteries, abandoned factories, deserted houses… the gloomier and more rundown the better.

But other monsters—too many—preferred to hide in plain sight among the humans they preyed upon. These monsters worked hard to remain below radar and not draw attention to themselves. The more normal they came across, the better. It was this second type of monster, which Dean thought of as *passers*—as in passing for human—that was the most dangerous. Not only were they harder to track down, they were used to being sneaky. Sneaky equaled unpredictable, and Dean *hated* unpredictable. He liked it best when monsters behaved exactly like they were supposed to. It made everything easier and kept things neat and tidy. Unpredictable meant messy. And when it came to hunting, Dean hated messy more than anything else. Messy got people killed. The brothers had saved many people over the years— the whole damn planet, really—but it was the ones they couldn't save which haunted Dean.

It's just a nest of ghouls, he told himself. *It doesn't get much simpler than that.*

Sam and Dean had first gotten wind that there might be ghouls living in McCormick when reports of missing townspeople began surfacing on the Net. There were two main types of news stories the brothers searched for: strange phenomena and missing persons. Sam had set up accounts for several search engines to email him links to any such stories, and he received dozens each day. He and Dean spent hours going through them, searching for any hint of supernatural activity. Most of the time they didn't find anything, but every once in a while they got lucky. The reports from McCormick had caught their attention because there had been a spate of missing person reports combined with a number of funeral home break-ins. And when the brothers broadened their search, they discovered a number of additional incidences of both within a thirty-mile radius of McCormick.

They might've thought they'd stumbled across an ordinary human serial killer at work, except the victims varied in age, race, and gender. The only common quality they shared was that none of them were over fifty, and most were in their twenties and thirties. So the brothers hopped in the Impala and took a trip to Missouri. Once in town, they did their usual poking around, posing as FBI agents, asking questions of local law enforcement and relatives of the missing people. They'd learned nothing useful until, by chance, one of the local cops mentioned an employee who'd been killed during a break-in at one of the funeral homes in town. No money or equipment had been stolen, but whoever had broken into the building had cut open the corpses stored there and taken their organs. And while different monsters—not to mention warlocks and witches—would have use for the organs, when it came to dead flesh, ghouls were always the primary suspects. Once the Winchesters began looking into the murder and organ theft, it didn't take them long to become suspicious of one of the funeral home's recently hired employees, a young man named Phillip Carson who lived with his parents Darrell and Kate on a farm outside town—the very farm they were currently heading toward.

Dean heard a sound then, a muffled *mmmpf*, off to their left, and the brothers froze.

"You hear that?" Sam asked softly.

"Yeah," Dean acknowledged, keeping his voice low. "Sounded like someone trying to talk through a gag."

"That's what I thought."

The brothers headed toward the sound, doing their best to avoid making any noise of their own as they went. A cluster of dried cornstalks higher and straighter than the others rose from the bare soil in front of them. The brothers continued toward the stalks, and as they drew closer, Dean saw they were bound to short wooden poles with lengths of thin wire. The sound came again and Dean knew he had been right: it was a human voice. And from the strained, muffled sound of it, whoever it belonged to was not exactly having a good time.

The Winchesters stepped toward the wire-bound structure, exchanged glances, and then in unspoken agreement, they slowly pulled their machetes free from their sheaths. Dean knew they should take a couple minutes to make sure the structure wasn't booby-trapped. Supernatural creatures, at least the more humanlike ones, weren't averse to using technology, and there could be motion detector alarms or even explosives rigged to blow if anyone got too close. Hell, you didn't need modern tech to make traps. There were plenty of low-tech ways to hurt someone who was putting their nose where it didn't belong: snare traps, spear traps, stake pits... But when the muffled voice sounded again, this time louder and with a tone of desperation, Dean forgot about being cautious. Someone was inside the makeshift enclosure and needed their help.

Dean started hacking at the dry cornstalks with his machete. An instant later Sam joined him, and within moments the brothers had cleared away a four-foot section, giving them an unobstructed view of what lay inside. Six people were buried up to their heads in the cold earth, mouths sealed with silver duct tape, eyes covered with strips of black cloth tied around their heads. Four males, two females, ranging in age from early teens to late forties. Two of the men were black, and one of the women was Latina. The rest were Caucasian. Their noses and ears had been damaged by frostbite, and none of them moved. Their heads lolled on their necks, tilting forward, backward, or to either side. Dean couldn't tell if they were alive or dead, but at least one of them must still live, for someone had made the sounds that had drawn them here. The six were arranged in a circle, buried so that they faced one another.

The Latina woman, who looked to be in her mid-thirties, started moving then, shaking her head back and forth slowly, as if trying to get their attention. She attempted to speak, but all that came out from her tape-covered mouth was a strained *mmmmm*. None of the other prisoners made noise or moved, and Dean feared the woman was the only one who remained alive. He gripped his machete tighter and stepped through the opening they'd made and entered the enclosure.

"Don't worry," Sam said. "We're here to help you."

The brothers took up positions on opposite sides of the circle, crouched down, and began checking the ghouls' prisoners for pulses. Dean first checked the woman who'd made the sounds that had drawn them here. She calmed when he touched her, and he found her pulse weak but steady. When he pulled his hand away from the woman's neck, she gave a muffled grunt of protest, as if she feared she was being abandoned.

"Hold on," Dean said. He removed her blindfold and gag, and then checked the next person—a man—to the woman's left.

When the brothers finished checking the remaining prisoners, they knelt next to each other and compared notes.

"I found two weak, but alive," Sam said. "You?"

"Just the one," Dean said. "She's not in great condition either, but I think she'll make it—*if* we can get her and the others to a hospital."

Dean tried not to think about the three dead people in the circle. The brothers had left their blindfolds and gags in place, more so the survivors wouldn't have to see the lifeless eyes of their companions than anything else. There was nothing he and Sam could do for the dead now, and the brothers had to stay focused on the living if they were to have any chance of saving them. Dean was good at compartmentalizing his feelings at times like these, but that didn't mean he liked it.

Dean turned to the Latina woman. "How long have you been out here?"

She frowned as she struggled to answer. "I don't know. A week, maybe?"

"They could've been here even longer if the ghouls have been giving them water," Sam said.

"Like they're livestock," Dean said, anger rising. "Or worse, some kind of crop."

"Yeah."

Dean still held his machete, as did Sam, and he jammed the tip of the blade into the ground and twisted it back and forth a couple times. The ground was hard, but far from frozen solid. Good thing too, or there would be six dead bodies in the circle instead of three. Dean figured that he and Sam should be able to dig out the survivors without much difficulty. Of course, their shovels were back in the Impala. One of them should stay here and guard the prisoners while the other went to get the shovels. Dean didn't like the idea of splitting up—especially not when they were right in the middle of ghoul territory. But they could hardly leave the survivors alone, even for a short period of time. What if the ghouls returned while the brothers were gone and decided to kill the three living prisoners rather than risk losing them? It was a chance they couldn't take.

"You go get the shovels," Dean said. "I'll stand guard here."

His fingers wrapped tighter around his machete's handle, and Sam noticed.

"Maybe I should stay," Sam said. His tone was neutral and revealed nothing of his feelings, but Dean knew exactly what he was thinking.

"Yeah, I'm angry at what the ghouls have done to these

people, what they did to our family, but I'm fine. *Really*."

The Mark of Cain sparked a lust for violence within the one who bore it, and that spark could quickly become a raging inferno if the Mark's bearer lost control. Dean had experienced that rage before, had been overwhelmed and swept away by it, until he'd become little more than a fury-driven killing machine. But it was precisely because he'd experienced that level of rage that he had learned how to try to resist the Mark's influence so it would never control him again. He hoped.

Sam looked into Dean's eyes, as if searching for any indication that his brother was lying or was mistaken about his condition. But he saw nothing that immediately worried him, and he nodded.

"Okay. I'll be back as soon as I can."

He started to rise, but wind rushed into the clearing, rattling the dry cornstalks and ruffling the buried victims' hair. An instant later four figures stood shoulder to shoulder at the opening Sam and Dean had cut into the circle. Ghouls could move inhumanly fast when they wanted to, and given the amount of wind they'd kicked up racing toward the circle, it seemed these were especially fast for their kind.

One of us should've kept watch for them, Dean thought. *Getting sloppy in our old age.*

The quartet consisted of two males and two females. One couple appeared to be in their fifties, while the other looked to be in their twenties. They wore jackets, jeans, and boots, and the older male also sported a green trucker cap. All four were armed. The older male held a double-barreled shotgun, and the older female gripped a hand scythe. The younger male held a hunting knife, while the younger female carried a 9mm. Both the shotgun and pistol were aimed at the Winchesters. Ghouls might be faster, stronger, and tougher than humans, Dean thought, but that didn't mean they were dumb enough to go up against a pair of hunters unarmed. Too bad. Dumb monsters were easier to kill than smart ones.

The older male spoke first. "Looks like we got us two more for the garden."

With the ghouls' arrival, the woman whose muffled cries had first alerted the brothers to the circle—or rather, the ghouls' grotesque *garden*—began shaking her head back and forth and making sounds of distress. Dean didn't blame her. Right now, things didn't look too good for Team Human.

His hand tightened on the machete's handle, and the Mark of Cain burned.

Attack now before it's too late.

He couldn't tell if the thought was his or if it originated from the Mark. Either way, it was a stupid idea, and he wasn't about to try it. As fast as the ghouls' reflexes were, the ones with guns would be able to fire before either of the brothers could stand and raise their machetes. Hell, given the crouching positions they were in, an ordinary human would've been able to get a shot off before the brothers could reach him or her.

"These are hunters, right, Dad?" While the other three ghouls were thin, this one was on the chunky side. Not fat, but definitely well-fed.

Dean figured that this must be Phillip, the one who worked at the funeral parlor. Where else would a ghoul want to work? It would be like a human working in a candy store.

Too bad he couldn't keep his hand out of the cookie jar, Dean thought. If he had, the brothers never would've known about this nest of ghouls. *Just goes to show that overeating is bad for you in all kinds of ways.*

The older female, who Dean presumed was the younger man's mother, Kate, answered before the boy's father could speak.

"No, Phillip," she said, sarcasm dripping from her voice. "They're carrying machetes because they love to collect dead cornstalks."

The younger woman snickered. "They probably use them to make crafts, like little cornhusk dolls."

Phillip shot the younger woman—his sister? His wife?—an angry look.

"Shut up, Lori."

The father, Darrell, kept his gaze trained on the Winchesters as he spoke to two of his companions.

"Phillip, Kate—get their machetes. Lori and I have them covered. If their hands so much as twitch, they're dead."

"Damn straight," Lori said.

Phillip and Kate stepped into the circle, Phillip looking considerably less thrilled than his mother. Phillip took Sam's machete, and Kate took Dean's. The Mark of Cain sent a momentary jolt through Dean's arm as the older woman pulled the machete from his hand, as if protesting the weapon's loss. *I know how you feel,* Dean thought.

Phillip and Kate stepped back out of the circle, knelt, and stabbed the machetes into the ground. Then they stood and gripped their own weapons tighter.

Dean had to keep from smiling.

Mistake one: They should've thrown the machetes as far away as they could. Mistake two: They should've searched them for other weapons. Both brothers still had their guns, along with knives sheathed against the sides of their legs, hidden by their pants. *Looks like these ghouls aren't so smart after all,* Dean thought.

"So you're Phillip Carson," Dean said to the younger man. "I'm not surprised you're overweight. Bet you were snacking on all those organs you stole from the funeral home. What's wrong? Don't like the way free-range carrion tastes?"

Phillip bared yellow teeth, raised his knife, and took a step toward Dean. His mother grabbed hold of his shoulder and stopped him.

"My son strayed from the path," Darrell said, "but he has renewed his commitment to our ways, haven't you?"

Phillip glared at Dean, but he sounded calm enough when he answered, "Yes, Father."

"Why did you bury these people out here?" Sam asked. "To make their… *meat* taste better?"

Dean knew Sam was stalling for time. No matter how intelligent supernatural beings were, they tended to be more basic than humans, almost elemental, like wild animals or forces of nature. They focused on one thing—whatever they fed on in order to prolong their unnatural lives—and that focus was often so intense it bordered on obsession. And while these ghouls were different than any the brothers had encountered before, they remained ghouls, which meant that filling their bellies was all they truly cared about.

"The meat tastes best when it dies a natural death," Darrell said. "No disease or trauma. Plus, leaving them exposed to the elements *seasons* them. It gives them a nice outdoorsy taste. And this way, they get some of the toxins out of their systems before we feed. Alcohol, caffeine, drugs—both prescription and illegal—junk food… All of them spoil the flavor of the meat."

"Meat must be untouched and must die of natural causes," Kate said.

"Sounds like the ghoul version of kosher," Dean said.

Dean caught his brother's eye and gave a slight incline of his head toward the Latina woman. Sam gave an equally slight nod back. Message received.

"We'd prefer to plant you with the rest of our crop," Darrell said. "But I think the two of you will be a lot less trouble if we just go ahead and shoot you. We won't be able to eat you then, but that's the way it goes. You can't always have your meat and eat it too." Darrell grinned. "Ready, Lori?"

Darrell glanced at Lori, and she glanced back at him—and that's when the brothers made their move.

Dean dove forward at the same instant that Sam dove backward. Dean twisted in the air, pulled his gun from his waistband, and fired at Darrell as he hit the ground on his back. The round struck the ghoul in the middle of his chest, and he staggered backward from the impact, although he managed to maintain his grip on the shotgun. Dean knew Darrell wouldn't go down. Ghouls weren't only stronger and faster than humans, they were more durable too. It would take a lot worse than a single bullet to the chest to slow down a ghoul for any length of time, and no amount of bullets would kill a ghoul. Only decapitation could do that. But Dean wasn't trying to kill Darrell. Not yet, anyway. He was trying to buy his brother time.

Dean didn't wait to see how Darrell had reacted to his attack. Still lying on his back, he swung his gun toward Lori and fired once more. His aim was a bit off, and although he was aiming for the woman's core, the round struck her right shoulder. She jerked back, but she didn't stagger. She did, however, drop her 9mm, which was good. If he could grab hold of it, he would be able to fire with both hands, John Woo style.

But Kate and Phillip didn't stand by motionless while Dean attacked their family members. They lunged toward him, Kate wielding her hand scythe, Phillip his knife. But before either of them could strike Dean, Sam shouted, "Don't move or the meat gets it!"

All four ghouls froze, and Dean turned his head to look at his brother. Sam was crouched next to the Latina woman, the barrel of his 9mm pressed against the side of her head. The woman gasped and began whimpering.

"*The meat gets it?*" Dean said.

"Shut up," Sam muttered, his gaze fixed on the Carsons. Both Darrell and Lori were bleeding from their wounds, although not as much as might have been expected. Neither seemed concerned that they'd been shot, though. They, along with Kate and Phillip, were staring at Sam with wide-eyed horror.

Dean knew Sam would never hurt an innocent, but he didn't need to—all that mattered was that the ghouls *thought* he would ruin their "food," at least long enough to give Dean a chance to act.

With the ghouls' attention focused entirely on Sam,

Dean dropped his gun to the ground, moved swiftly into a crouching position, and launched himself between Kate and Phillip. He grabbed the handle of the machete Phillip had taken from Sam and yanked it out of the ground. Once he was behind the ghouls, he turned and reached for the second machete, which was stuck in the ground between Darrell and Kate. He took hold of it with his free hand and rose to a standing position, now armed with both machetes.

The ghouls realized what was happening, but they reacted too late. Fast as they were, they only managed to turn halfway around before Dean swung the machetes, the Mark singing in his blood. A few seconds later, the ghouls lay on the ground, bodies and heads separated. Dean wasn't even breathing hard.

Not bad, he thought. The cuts were clean and straight, and he'd put the ghouls down before Darrell could fire his shotgun. And as fast as he'd taken them down, it might just be a personal record.

"Dean?"

"Hmmm?" He didn't take his gaze off the dead ghouls right away. Sam had to speak his name a second time, louder and more forcefully, before he finally turned to look at his brother. Sam's concern was written all over his face, and Dean had to work to keep the irritation out of his voice as he said, "Don't worry. I'm not going to go into berserker mode. Like I keep telling you, I've got it under control."

But even as he spoke these words, he felt the Mark pulsing. His head throbbed in time with the pulse, and accompanying the throbbing was a word, repeated over and over.

More.

THREE

Normally, the Winchesters avoided calling the authorities for help. The police, firefighters, and paramedics were not trained to deal with the sort of threats that were part of what Sam often thought of as "the family business," and they tended to ask a lot of questions the brothers found more than a little uncomfortable to answer. But with the three surviving prisoners in such bad shape, Sam hadn't wanted to risk digging them out and driving them to the nearest hospital—which, according to his phone, was thirty-six miles away. Dean agreed, and Sam called 911, gave the dispatcher a very truncated and heavily edited version of the situation at the farm, provided the Carsons' address, told her to make sure someone brought shovels, and then disconnected. The brothers then buried the ghouls' remains and waited until they saw the lights of emergency vehicles and police cars approaching. They then headed back across the field the way they'd come—but not before assuring the woman who'd first caught their attention, the only one of the survivors who was fully conscious, that she was going to be okay.

Now the brothers were once more in the Impala, driving on Route 70 toward Kansas and the Men of Letters Bunker, which these days served as their base of operations as well as their home—in many ways, the only real home they'd had since they were children.

Dean sat behind the Impala's steering wheel—as usual—and stared out at the road rushing toward them.

Sam wanted to ask Dean how much the Mark had influenced him during the encounter with the ghouls, but he wasn't sure it was a good idea right now. That it had influenced him to some degree, Sam had no doubt. Magic that powerful couldn't be denied simply by force of will, not entirely anyway. He thought of the way Dean had killed the four ghouls. Dean was a highly skilled fighter, as he damn well ought to be after a lifetime of hunting and killing monsters. But the speed and savagery with which he'd slain the ghouls had been frightening, but not as frightening as the smile on Dean's lips as he'd decapitated the monsters in record time. Dean insisted he had the Mark under control, and while Sam had his doubts, he'd seen no evidence to the contrary.

"I wonder what the town's medical examiner will think if the bodies of those ghouls ever turn up," Dean said.

Sam shrugged. "The same thing they all think. Whoever it is will note the anatomical anomalies in their report, consider writing a scholarly paper about the discovery, before eventually deciding their colleagues will think they're crazy and then they'll forget about it. Or at least try to."

One of monsters' greatest advantages—perhaps the

main one—was that people didn't want to believe in them. So whenever someone encountered a supernatural being and lived to tell the tale, no one in authority would credit their story and they found themselves ridiculed at best or institutionalized at worst. Most witnesses kept their mouths shut and did their best to sleep at night, knowing what they now knew. And if they felt compelled to tell their stories, they did so in tabloid newspapers, on paranormal websites, or on their own blogs. Leaving behind the ghouls' remains wasn't going to result in a worldwide realization that monsters were real. At most, it would lead to a few puzzling comments on four autopsy reports that a handful of people would read and everyone would ignore.

Dean turned on the radio and Molly Hatchet's "Flirtin' With Disaster" blasted out of the speakers. Dean bobbed his head in time with the music and pounded the steering wheel as if he were playing drums. Sam settled back against the passenger seat, looked out the side window, and ignored the music while he thought.

During the encounter with the ghouls, Dean had made a joke about their dietary practices being a monstrous version of the Jewish concept of keeping kosher. There had been no indication that the ghouls' preference for meat that died a natural death had any religious basis, but he supposed it was possible. Not long ago, the Winchesters had learned that some werewolves worshipped Fenris, the giant powerful wolf of Norse legend. Maybe it wasn't as uncommon for monsters to have their own religions as Sam and Dean had thought. After all, a lot of monsters mimicked humans or had once been human. Why shouldn't they long for the guidance, approval, and especially the love of some higher power?

Humans had invented hundreds, maybe thousands of religions throughout history, and many had centered on the worship of powerful monsters who styled themselves as gods. These monsters used their worshippers as nourishment, whether physically, mentally, or a combination of both. Sam and Dean had encountered numerous "gods" during their careers as hunters, and although they were a hell of a lot harder to kill than garden-variety supernatural entities, they *could* be killed. The closest thing to a true god the brothers had ever encountered was *the* God—the Judeo-Christian-Islamic one—and even then they'd only encountered His servants, the angels. Hell, Castiel—the brothers' closest friend and ally—was an angel. Not only were angels real, so was Heaven. The Winchesters knew this because they'd visited Heaven on several occasions. But the Big Man Himself was missing and had been for thousands, maybe millions of years. But both Sam and Dean weren't sure how to view God. Was He the supreme being, the creator of the universe, as advertised? Or was He something else?

One night, not long after the angels had been cast out of Heaven by Metatron, he and Dean had been up late drinking and trying to figure out how to deal with the whole mess. At one point, Dean had mused that if gods with a lowercase G were in reality monsters, maybe God with a capital G was simply the first and biggest monster of them all. Sam had not found the thought especially comforting.

Sam's thoughts continued along these lines for several more

minutes, and before he realized it, he found himself falling into a memory of the first time he and Dean had encountered a god—although at the time, they hadn't realized what it was.

"Make yourselves at home, boys."

Sam and Dean exchange glances before giving the woman a pair of smiles. Sam adds a "Thanks" for good measure. The woman smiles back, but her gaze is measured, assessing them. Sam remembers their dad once telling them that you can always recognize hunters by their eyes. *Hunters are always watching*, John Winchester said. *They never let their guard down, not all the way.*

Julie Underwood definitely has a hunter's eyes, Sam thinks, and the intensity of her scrutiny makes him uncomfortable. It isn't as if she's seeing them for the first time. She met them at the hospital and drove them here to her home. But she always seems to be judging them, as if she doesn't quite trust them. Maybe it's his imagination. Dad said she was a friend, not to mention a hell of a good hunter. He said they'd be safe with her, and Sam has no reason to doubt him. Still, he doesn't like meeting her gaze.

Julie is in her early forties, not much over five feet tall, with an unruly nest of short brown hair. She has a round, kind face—except for those eyes. She wears a brown flannel shirt unbuttoned over a light gray T-shirt, jeans, and brown boots. No make-up or jewelry, not that she needs any. Sam thinks she's pretty without them. Sam and Dean stand just inside the doorway of Julie's home. Her living room looks ordinary enough, Sam thinks. Couch, TV, a couple of chairs, curtains for the windows, carpet on the floor. At least, he thinks it's normal. It's not as if he and Dean have spent a lot of time in people's houses, and they don't really have one of their own. They're on the road with their dad part of the year, which means they spend a lot of time in hotel rooms. Sam's seventeen now, and the nomadic aspect of the hunting life—most aspects of it, really—is starting to wear more than a little thin for him.

Each brother carries a threadbare knapsack that contains extra clothes and toiletries. The bags—which are far from full—hold all the possessions the Winchester boys have in the world.

Julie doesn't live alone. She has two children, both roughly the same ages as Sam and Dean. They stand in the living room, looking at the new arrivals with a mix of curiosity and mild suspicion. They don't have hunters' eyes, not quite. Dean has them, has for quite a while now. Sam wonders if he does too. He's not surprised to find himself ambivalent about the thought. He's had mixed feelings about hunting as long as he can remember, and those feelings have only grown stronger the older he's gotten. Neither Stewart nor Gretchen Underwood resemble their mother much. Both are taller than she is, and each has blond hair. Like their mother, they both wear their hair short. Stewart wears glasses, but Gretchen doesn't. Their faces are narrower than their mother's, their features sharper. Sam figures they favor their father, but there's no sign of him around, not even any family photos framed and hanging on the walls, at least not in this room. Maybe their dad is out on a hunt, or maybe he and Julie are divorced. But Sam thinks it's more likely the man is dead. Hunters tend not to die of old age. While most people consider it polite to ask about the health of family members when talking with a friend, such questions are considered rude and insensitive in hunter culture. All hunters suffer loss and the last thing they want to do is reopen old wounds. Sam understands this well. Even though he was only an infant when it happened, he doesn't like talking about how their mother died. He doesn't even like *thinking* about it. So he's not going to worry about what happened to Mr. Underwood. If Julie, Stewart, or Gretchen wants him and Dean to know about it, they'll tell them.

Stewart wears an AC/DC T-shirt, which Sam knows Dean will approve of, and Gretchen wears a long-sleeved white shirt, the neckline low enough to reveal a portion of her chest but not so low as to show any cleavage. Gretchen is pretty in a different way than her mother, and it's a way that he likes

All three of the Underwoods have trouble standing still. They shift their feet, reach up to touch their faces or brush back their hair, cross then uncross their arms. They're so full of energy that they almost seem to vibrate. Sam thinks that if he closes his eyes and listens closely, he'll hear an electric hum coming from them. They speak a bit too fast, their eyes wide, and they blink too often. It's like the whole damn family has downed massive quantities of coffee and are suffering from a caffeine overdose. Sam doesn't bother looking at Dean to see if his brother has noticed the Underwoods' strange behavior. He knows he has.

Julie turns toward her children.

"Kids, this is Sam and Dean Winchester. Their father, John, is a friend of mine."

Stewart and Gretchen both frown at their mother's use of the word *friend*, and Sam doesn't blame them. Mary Winchester has been dead a long time, and while John hasn't shown any interest in remarrying, Sam knows his father is no saint. This is something else he doesn't like to think about, but he's glad to see the idea that John and Julie might have been lovers at some point bothers Gretchen and Stewart as well.

"John came to West Virginia tracking a pack of werewolves that left their hunting grounds in Ohio. Why the idiot didn't call me for help with the wolves, I don't know."

"Maybe it's because he's a badass," Dean says defensively.

"A badass who ended up in the hospital," Julie says.

Dean scowls at this, but Sam can't help smiling. John Winchester insists on doing as much as he can on his own, and while Sam knows he does this to protect others—especially his sons—it's gratifying to see it irritates someone other than him.

Julie continues, "Anyway, he found the pack and managed to kill most of them, but in the process he got himself clawed up pretty good. Luckily, he wasn't bitten, so he'll be back on his feet after a couple days in the hospital."

More like a week, Sam thinks. That's what the doctors said. But as hardheaded as their dad is, he'll probably check himself out early, whether he's recovered enough or not.

"They're going to be staying with us a few days while John rests up," Julie finishes.

Sam expects Stewart and Gretchen to react to the news

without enthusiasm. No one's thrilled to hear they're going to have surprise houseguests. But the Underwood kids smile and step forward to shake the brothers' hands. Sam doesn't expect such a formal, not to mention adult, greeting from the other teens, and he feels awkward as he first shakes Stewart's hand, then Gretchen's. Her hand is warmer than he expects, but not unpleasantly so. Her grip is strong, but her skin is soft, and without intending to, Sam continues holding onto her hand after they're done shaking. When he realizes what he's doing, he pulls his hand away from hers too quickly, reddening in embarrassment. Gretchen smiles, amused, but there's kindness and sympathy in her gaze.

Dean leans close to Sam's head and softly says, "Smooth."

Sam feels an urge to punch his brother on the arm, but he doesn't want to look more childish than he already does.

Stewart looks at Julie. "Are they going to help us?"

"If they want to," Julie says.

Dean frowns. "Help you with what?"

"Hunting, of course," Stewart says.

Gretchen smiles.

"You boys ever heard of Sheepsquatch?"

Sam was pulled out of the memory by the sensation of his phone vibrating in his pocket. It only buzzed once, which meant he'd received a text or email. He slipped the phone out of his pocket, swiped his thumb across the screen, and saw the email notification. He had one message waiting. He opened the email and started reading silently.

After a minute, Dean asked, "Anything good?"

"Just the daily news of the weird," Sam said. "I've been checking out the links, but so far I haven't…" A new item came up on his screen, the headline written in large capital letters. CULTS CONNECTED TO KILLINGS? *This sounds promising.* Sam quickly read the article, and when he was done, he summarized it for Dean. When Sam finished speaking, Dean thought for a moment before responding.

"The town's named Corinth? Like in rich, Corinthian leather?"

"Corinth is a Greek city," Sam said, trying not to sound exasperated. Dean might be joking, but then again, he might not know about the original Corinth. "The town this article talks about is Corinth, Illinois. This Corinth's got a couple problems. In the last two weeks, it's had an explosion of religious cults, dozens of them. And in the last few days, several dead bodies have been discovered. The deaths are bizarre, too. People whose lungs are filled with water in the middle of a bone-dry street or who are struck down by multiple bolts of lightning."

"Real wrath of God stuff, huh?" Dean said.

"More like *gods*," Sam replied. "The article says there are fifty-three separate and distinct cults in Corinth, some only consisting of one member while others have a dozen or more."

"Did anyone investigate the cults?" Dean asked.

"If they did, the article doesn't say. Reading between the lines, I get the sense that as much as the town paper would like there to be a link between cults and deaths—"

"Sell a lot more issues that way," Dean said.

"—there isn't any compelling evidence for a connection."

The brothers fell silent for a time while they chewed over what Sam had discovered. Eventually, Dean sighed.

"I don't know, Sammy. Seems pretty thin to me."

"Weird deaths are always worth a look," Sam said. "Besides, we don't have anything else on our plate at the moment."

"True." Dean glanced at the rearview mirror, and Sam knew he was looking at the trunk's reflection. "Unless you count dropping by the Bunker to put Iggy into storage."

Sam smiled. "So first stop, the Bunker—"

"—and next stop, Corinth," Dean said.

"What do you think?"

Geoffrey stood next to Adamantine, but not *too* close. After watching Jimmy get electrocuted by the silver-skinned woman's touch, he'd become determined to remain out of her reach at all times. Adamantine sat at a metal café table on the sidewalk outside a frozen-yogurt place called Chill Out. A cardboard bowl with the store's name and logo emblazoned on the side sat in front of her. Inside the bowl was a pinkish coiled mound that looked like something that had come out of the south end of a northbound dog whose last meal had been soaked in pink food coloring. Geoffrey decided to keep this observation to himself, though. He didn't want to upset the woman who could electrocute him with a touch. Besides, from what she'd said, this was the first food—and he used the term loosely—that she'd ever had, so why spoil it for her?

It was early evening, but this time of year, that meant it was full dark. A nearby streetlight illuminated the table where Adamantine sat, and her silvery skin gave off an unearthly glow in the fluorescent light. The effect was eerie, but beautiful in its own way, Geoffrey thought. People stared at the odd-looking woman as they passed by, but no one approached her. Geoffrey didn't blame them.

Adamantine held a plastic spoon with a glop of yogurt on it up to her face. She stared at it as if she were assessing it down to the molecular level. Who knows? Maybe she was. So far, all she'd done was briefly touch the yogurt to her tongue, she hadn't actually eaten any of it yet.

"I am… uncertain," she said.

He didn't want her to think he was mocking her, but he couldn't stop himself from smiling.

"It's just a dessert. It won't bite you."

Adamantine looked up at him with a puzzled expression.

"Of course it won't. It has no mouth, let alone any teeth." After looking at him a moment longer, she returned her attention to the yogurt.

Geoffrey wasn't a big fan of frozen yogurt. He preferred ice cream, but he'd rather not eat either on a chilly December evening like this one. Just seeing Adamantine hold the yogurt—the *frozen* yogurt—on her spoon made him shiver. But the cold didn't seem to bother Adamantine. So far, nothing seemed to bother her. After killing Jimmy and taking on Geoffrey as one of her *followers*—the only one, so far—Adamantine had commanded him to show her around Corinth. *I would like to become better acquainted with the domain I shall soon rule,* she'd said. And so Geoffrey had taken her for a tour of the town, such as it was. Corinth, despite its classically inspired name, wasn't anything special to look at. But since it was the only town Adamantine had ever seen, he supposed it looked good enough to her. Her head had swiveled back and forth as she took in everything around them—pedestrians, street traffic, shops—her expression giving away nothing of what she was thinking or feeling. *Maybe she's not doing either,* Geoffrey had thought. *Maybe she's just experiencing.*

Something about the yogurt store had caught her eye, and she'd stopped in front of it and demanded to know what its purpose was. Geoffrey tried to explain frozen yogurt, but she had trouble grasping the concept of food, let alone treats. She'd ordered him to go inside and "procure" some for her. His empty stomach had gurgled painfully as he stepped inside, and he got an empty bowl from a table next to the dispensers, chose strawberry, filled the bowl and—since he had no money—went up to the counter, took a spoon from the container next to the cash register, and then headed for the door. There was no one behind the counter. The teenager working the register tonight was helping an older customer operate one of the yogurt dispensers. There was a handful of other people in the store, some of them sitting at tables and eating, others standing in front of the dispensers, trying to decide what flavor to get, but all of them ignored him as he made his escape. Geoffrey disliked stealing, but he liked the idea of the employee stopping him from leaving, causing Adamantine to come inside to see what was taking him so long, even less. She'd get angry, start throwing around electricity, and probably fry everyone in the place. He'd been relieved when he'd made it outside without anyone noticing.

Adamantine hesitantly brought the plastic spoon toward her mouth again, and this time she actually took a taste. She didn't eat much, just a tiny smattering, but it was enough. Her mouth pursed and she shuddered.

"This is a most unpleasant sensation."

She dropped the spoon into the container, stood, and walked away from the table.

Geoffrey followed, but not before snatching up the frozen yogurt and wolfing it down, shuddering as the cold substance slid down his throat. Waste not, want not. He finished quickly and tossed the empty bowl and spoon into a trash receptacle and then hurried to catch up to Adamantine. She continued looking around as they went, and Geoffrey had the impression that she wasn't taking in the sights anymore, but rather looking for something—or someone. He was about to ask her what she was searching for when she abruptly stopped and turned to face the street. Standing on the sidewalk on the other side was a strange woman—stranger even than Adamantine—accompanied by five men and women. The woman and her companions stood still and all of them stared across the street at them. *No*, Geoffrey thought. *They don't give a damn about me. They're staring at Adamantine.*

The woman was taller than Adamantine by at least a foot, which made her seem like a giant compared to the people standing around her. Her arms and legs were thickly muscled, her shoulders and chest broad. She wore a brown leather vest, armless and with a laced, closed-in back. Her shorts were made of the same leather and ended halfway down her thighs. In her left hand she carried a white spear that looked as if it had been carved from bone. All of that would've been strange enough to see on the streets of Corinth, but the woman was covered with golden fur from head to toe, and her hands and feet ended in wicked-looking claws. Her head and face looked more catlike than human, and the only hair she had was the fur that covered her skull. Geoffrey thought she looked like a lioness that had suddenly decided to start walking on two hind legs. But again no one dared approach the strange woman, or stopped to snap a photo on their phone.

Suddenly Adamantine's eyes glowed and sparks of electricity danced across the silver surface of her body. The cat-woman glared back and began growling deep in her throat. She took hold of her spear in both hands and stepped into the street. When a couple of her companions attempted to follow, she looked back and snapped at them.

"Remember your place!" Her voice was low and guttural, but the words were clear enough. The two stepped back onto the sidewalk and lowered their gazes, chastened.

Adamantine left the sidewalk and started walking toward the cat-woman. Adamantine gave no indication of whether Geoffrey should follow her or stay where he was, but since the choice seemed to have been left up to him, he remained on the sidewalk. It was obvious that the cat-woman was a being like Adamantine, and from the less-than-friendly way they'd reacted to each other so far, he thought it would be best to keep well away from them.

Cars stopped to avoid hitting the women and scared, angry drivers blasted their horns. Neither woman looked toward the upset motorists, didn't seem to be aware of them at all.

Their gazes were locked on each other, and at that moment it was as if nothing else in the world existed except the two of them. They stopped in the middle of the street with less than five feet between them, illuminated in the wash of headlights.

"I am Adamantine."

"I am Wyld."

These words came out stiffly and without emotion, as if they were part of a formal ritual of some kind.

"In the end there shall be One," Adamantine said, and Wyld echoed her words.

The women fell silent then and peered intently at one another, as if trying to take the other's measure. And then, without warning, Wyld attacked. She swept the tip of her spear upward, angling it toward Adamantine's throat, immediately going for a killing strike, but Adamantine blocked the spear with her gauntleted forearm before the sharp tip could cut into her neck. Bone raked across metal with a loud scratching sound, but the spear left no mark on the gauntlet. Adamantine struck out with her left hand, slamming it palm-first into Wyld's chest, releasing a burst of electricity as she did so. Tendrils of power spread swiftly outward from Adamantine's hand to wreathe Wyld in a cocoon of dancing silver energy. The cat-woman's body stiffened and she roared in pain, the sound so loud Geoffrey winced and slapped his hands over his ears. The cat-woman's followers did the same, as did the drivers closest to the two women. Headlights popped and windshields cracked, and Geoffrey gritted his teeth. It felt like white-hot blades had been jammed into his ears, and a moan escaped his lips as he fell to his knees. Through the pain, he wondered if the roar was Wyld's version of Adamantine's electricity, a sonic power she wielded that was more devastating than her spear could ever be. He felt warmth trickling from his ears and nose, and he knew he was bleeding. He feared that if this noise kept up much longer, it would puree his brain.

Wyld's deafening roar affected Adamantine as well. She yanked her hand from the cat-woman's chest, and turned away, clapping both hands over her ears. The instant her flesh was no longer in contact with Wyld, the electricity coruscating across the cat-woman's body winked out, leaving behind patches of singed, smoldering fur and a black scorch mark in the shape of a handprint burned onto Wyld's leather vest. The cat-woman stopped roaring then, her voice cutting off with a wet click, and she grimaced and swallowed. Geoffrey wondered if using her sonic power had resulted in damage to her throat. He wouldn't have been surprised, loud as her roar had been. His ears hurt like hell and they were ringing so loudly, he couldn't hear anything.

There was nothing wrong with his eyes, though, and as he removed his hands from his ears and straightened, he saw Adamantine standing with her back turned to Wyld, hands still covering her own ears. She might be stronger than a human—maybe a *lot* stronger—but she'd been standing closest to Wyld, and thus had caught the worst of the woman's sonic attack. Wyld took advantage of Adamantine's distraction. She spun her spear around to get a stronger grip on it and then lunged forward, clearly intending to plunge the tip between Adamantine's shoulder blades. But

Adamantine, sensing the attack, spun around and swept her gauntlet upwards in a swift, vicious arc. The claws of the metal glove smashed into the spear and knocked it aside. Wyld maintained her grip on the weapon, though, and the impact caused her to almost lose her footing. She staggered to her left, and Adamantine allowed the momentum of her strike to spin her all the way around so she could attack with the gauntlet once more, only this time she sank the sharp tips of its fingers into the cat-woman's left shoulder. Adamantine released a second burst of electricity, eliciting another ear-shattering roar from Wyld, only this one wasn't quite as strong as the first. It was still painful as hell, though, and Geoffrey once more covered his ears. He expected Wyld's followers to do the same, but this time they knelt on the sidewalk, hands clasped together in front of them, heads bowed, bleeding ears unprotected. At first, Geoffrey had no idea what they were doing, but then it came to him. They were praying. But were they praying *for* Wyld or *to* her? Maybe both, he decided.

That was the moment that Geoffrey realized what creatures like Wyld and Adamantine were, why they had such strange abilities, and why they sought out followers. They were gods, or at least beings so similar to gods as to make no difference.

I'm the disciple of a metal-skinned psychopath, Geoffrey thought. *Life sure is funny sometimes.*

Wyld continued roaring, her voice cracking, and blood began to trickle out of the corner of her mouth. She'd damaged something inside herself, Geoffrey thought, and he imagined her vocal cords tearing like strips of overcooked meat. Adamantine's teeth were gritted, and a dark silvery liquid he assumed was her body's equivalent of blood flowed from her ears and nose. She must've been in great pain, but if so, she ignored it and kept pouring electricity into Wyld's body. The cat-woman shuddered and jerked, tendrils of smoke rising from her fur and curling from her mouth, as if she were cooking inside. Her roar diminished until it was little more than a kitten's mewling. All the power was gone from her voice, and Geoffrey lowered his hands, the sonic bombardment over. Adamantine yanked her gauntleted fingers from Wyld's shoulder with a swift, savage motion, rending flesh and sending gouts of blood into the air. The electricity cut out, and Wyld's body stopped convulsing. She slumped to the ground and lay there, motionless and breathing hard, eyes half-lidded, as if she were only barely managing to hold onto consciousness.

Adamantine grinned as she gazed down upon her fallen opponent.

"Sorry, my sister, but as you know, in the end there shall be One."

She stepped forward, pulled the bone spear from Wyld's lifeless hands, took a two-handed grip on the weapon, and without hesitation plunged the tip through the cat-woman's chest and into her heart. Wyld shrieked and her followers cried in despair. Blood bubbled past Wyld's lips, and her clawed hands grabbed hold of the spear. She tried to pull it out of her chest, but Adamantine leaned forward, putting all of her weight behind the weapon, and there was nothing Wyld could do. A few moments later, her hands fell away from the spear, her eyes glazed over, and she stopped breathing.

Adamantine pulled the weapon free from Wyld's chest and held it over her head, blood dripping from the tip.

"I still stand!" Adamantine said.

As if in response to her words, a white light began to emanate from Wyld's body, growing stronger and more intense until the cat-woman's form was completely obscured by the energy. Then, so swiftly that Geoffrey almost wasn't able to detect it, the energy contracted into a sphere roughly the size of a soccer ball and shot toward Adamantine. It struck her in the chest, but instead of knocking her down, the sphere vanished, as if her body had absorbed it. Wyld's corpse was gone, and no sign remained that the cat-woman had ever existed, not even any splatters of blood on the asphalt.

Adamantine's eyes glowed a bright blue-white for an instant—even brighter than they did when she was angry—and when the glow diminished, Geoffrey saw that she no longer was bleeding from her nose and ears. In fact, all traces of her silvery blood were gone.

He wasn't sure what had happened, but it looked like Adamantine had killed Wyld and somehow absorbed the other god. Had she absorbed her power too?

Wyld's five followers, some of them wiping tears from their eyes, stepped into the street and walked toward Adamantine. When they reached her, three fell to their knees—two men and one woman—and bowed their heads. Two others—an elderly woman and a young man barely out of his teens—remained standing.

"Mistress," the three who knelt said in unison, voices hushed and reverent.

Adamantine looked at the two still standing. She stepped past their kneeling comrades until she stood directly before them.

"What of you two?" she asked. "Will you pledge yourselves to me as well?"

The older woman and younger man looked at each other, then turned to face Adamantine. Both looked scared—tears trickled down the man's cheeks—but they shook their heads nevertheless.

"We belong to Wyld," the woman said. "And we always will."

"Y-yes," the man said softly, the word little more than a sob.

"I appreciate your devotion," Adamantine said. "As well as your honesty. Rest now."

Her gauntleted hand flashed through the air, and the man and woman collapsed to the ground, heads nearly severed, blood pouring from their ravaged throats onto the street.

Adamantine returned to the kneeling men and woman, blood dripping from the fingers of her gauntlet. She gazed down upon the trio, as if trying to decide what to do with them. A spark of electricity glimmered in her eyes, and for a moment Geoffrey feared she might kill them as well. But then she stepped forward and without bothering to clean her gauntleted hand, placed it on their heads one at a time. When she was finished, she commanded them to rise and follow her. They did so without speaking, hair matted with the blood of their dead companions.

Adamantine returned to where Geoffrey stood on the sidewalk, spear in hand and new followers in tow. The two gods no longer battled in the street, but none of the cars moved. Many of the drivers were too injured from Wyld's sonic attack to drive, but others stared at the two bodies lying in the street, mouths agape, as if unable to believe what they'd just witnessed.

At that moment, Wyld's spear began to glow with the same white light that had consumed her body. Adamantine trained her gaze upon the spear and frowned in concentration. A few seconds later, the light dimmed and was gone, leaving the spear intact. Adamantine smiled and nodded once in satisfaction. Geoffrey thought there was something different about her, but he wasn't sure what it was. It had nothing to do with her appearance; she looked exactly the same as when he'd first encountered her. She projected a stronger presence now and waves of power emanated from her with almost physical force. She seemed more real, more *there*. And she was glorious.

Adamantine smiled. "I think I'll keep it," she said, nodding to the spear. "It shall serve as a reminder of my first victory."

"But far from your last," he said, and smiled back at his god. The three new followers stood back several feet, gazes lowered, as if afraid of Adamantine. Geoffrey didn't blame them.

"The Apotheosis has begun, Geoffrey," Adamantine said. "Do you know what that word means?"

He searched his memory but came up empty. "No, my lady."

"It's the process of being elevated to a divine state. New gods for a new age are being born, Geoffrey, but only one of us will survive to become permanent."

He remembered what Adamantine and Wyld had said before their battle: *In the end there shall be One.*

She continued.

"We fight one-on-one to the death, with the victor absorbing the power of the vanquished. The more battles we win, the more strength we acquire, until finally only the two most powerful remain. And whoever wins that battle claims the power of *all* the gods born during the Apotheosis and gains the ultimate prize: immortality."

She looked off into the distance then, electricity sparking in her eyes.

"That prize will be mine, Geoffrey, and I'll do whatever it takes to claim it."

Of that, he had no doubt. He thought of Jimmy and of the man and woman lying dead in the street. When the Apotheosis was finished, he wondered, would there be anyone left alive in Corinth—god or human—besides Adamantine? Or would she stride alone through streets filled with blood, the last god standing?

The electric light in her eyes dimmed, and she turned to Geoffrey.

"Now that I have won my first victory, it is time to take the next step."

"Which is?"

"Isn't it obvious? A temple must be built in my name."

Geoffrey looked at Adamantine's three new "recruits."

"I think we're going to need a larger workforce."

FOUR

Sam and Dean got into Corinth a little after 10 PM. Both brothers wore their FBI suits, their standard cover when embarking on an investigation. The suits, and the false IDs that accompanied them, usually worked wonders with local law enforcement, who were only too happy to have a couple of federal agents' assistance with whatever bizarre events were occurring in their town. Dean reached up and tugged at his shirt collar, trying to loosen it. He hated wearing suits—ties most of all—but the clothes were as useful in their own way as holy water and silver bullets, and for that reason alone he tolerated them. But he was always glad when an investigation was underway and he and Sam could get back into their normal clothes.

The outskirts of Corinth didn't look like anything special. Suburban neighborhoods, some higher up on the economic ladder than others, but similar enough for the most part. A thin layer of snow covered lawns, and a number of houses were decorated for the holiday season. Blinking lights hanging from roofs, Christmas trees placed before front windows, inflatable snowmen and Santas standing in front yards. But there were other less-recognizable decorations as well. One house had long strips of black cloth hanging from the large oak in the front, while another had a mound of rocks in the driveway topped by what looked like an animal skull of some kind, a raccoon maybe, or an opossum. And one house they passed had strange symbols, none of which either Sam or Dean recognized, painted on it in a variety of colors.

Dean turned to look at Sam.

"Maybe the town's having a decorating contest," he said. "First prize goes to the ugliest-looking house."

Sam smiled at the joke. "Whatever's going on here, it's widespread."

"Think the whole town is affected?"

Sam shrugged. "No way to tell for sure, but I'd guess not. Most of the decorations we're seeing are normal for this time of year."

"True."

Usually when the brothers investigated a case, only a few people were affected. Supernatural predators were careful to conceal their activities to avoid attracting the attention of hunters. This was why they tended to live in out-of-the-way places and tried to limit their killings as much as possible. Because of this, Sam and Dean were normally able to locate and nullify a supernatural presence before it had a chance to spread, like an infection. But some supernatural creatures weren't as cautious as others, or it was their nature to spread their evil as fast and far as they could. Dean hated cases like the latter. Not only was it more difficult to pinpoint the source of the problem, too many innocent people were affected, and the brothers could never save all of them. And from what they'd seen of Corinth so far, it looked like that was exactly the kind of situation they were going to be dealing with here.

Terrific, he thought.

Without realizing he did so, Dean scratched idly at the Mark, as if it were beginning to irritate his skin.

The Winchesters continued to drive toward the center of town, passing more oddly decorated houses as they went. Dean had been a hunter for the better part of his life, and it took a lot to creep him out. But there was something about these houses that did the job. Part of it was the number of them, part was their sheer strangeness, but he supposed the biggest part was that, despite their odd appearances, all the houses looked quiet and peaceful on the outside. But he couldn't help wondering what was happening on the *inside*. Whatever it was, he had no doubt it was bad. The question was how bad?

"Look at that," Sam said.

His brother's words pulled Dean out of his thoughts. He turned to Sam and saw he was pointing out the windshield. Dean looked in the direction Sam indicated and saw a synagogue. He pulled the Impala over to the curb in front of the synagogue and parked, engine still running. The building looked like it should've been part of an elementary school—two stories, simple rectangular construction, pale orange brick, glass doors with chrome handles. The name of the synagogue was spelled out in metal letters bolted to brick above the main entrance: Temple Beth Israel. At least, that's what Dean *thought* the name was. Several letters were missing, and those that remained were blackened and twisted. The brick beneath and around the sign was scorched, as if by fire, and chunks of brick were missing, as if they'd been knocked out.

Or blasted out, Dean thought.

There was another sign, this one made of wood and nailed to a post that had been sunk into the front lawn of the temple. Painted in red letters were the words HERALDS OF THE CRIMSON EYE and below it was a crudely rendered representation of an eye.

The brothers looked at the sign for several moments before Dean put the Impala in gear and pulled slowly away from the synagogue. They passed two more churches as they continued toward the center of town. One was a Unitarian church that, according to the letters that had been gouged into the building's surface, was now called the Hall of Despair, and the other was a mosque called the Corinth Islamic Center, which was covered with thick green vines. A single word was written in green paint on the walkway that led to the center's entrance: VERDANT.

"This is looking worse all the time, Sammy."

Dean scratched the Mark again, and this time Sam noticed.

"The Mark bothering you?"

"Huh?" Only then did Dean realize what he was doing. He stopped scratching at his forearm and put his hand back on the steering wheel. "I'm fine."

But now that Sam had drawn his attention to the Mark,

Dean realized that it was itching. Not any worse than a cluster of mosquito bites, but it was damn annoying. It seemed to be getting worse the farther into Corinth they drove, but he told himself it was his imagination. At least, he hoped it was.

At first glance, downtown Corinth looked like a lot of Midwestern towns the brothers had visited over the years, but a second glance quickly revealed its differences. Even though it was after 10 PM and cold, there were still a number of people on the sidewalks. Some were walking, clearly on their way somewhere, but the majority stayed where they were, talking in small groups or standing alone. The groups' conversations were animated, people speaking loudly, some almost yelling, and waving their hands in broad, angry gestures. Some of the loners stared into the distance, lips moving rapidly, as if they were speaking to themselves or to someone only they were aware of. Others stood with heads bowed and hands clasped, as if they were praying, and some held homemade signs with slogans like SUPPORT YOUR LOCAL GOD and THE END ISN'T HERE—*THEY* ARE! In addition, a number of downtown businesses had odd decorations in the windows, on the doors, or painted on the outside walls. Dean recognized some of the decorations from seeing them on the houses they'd passed on their way here, but many of them were unfamiliar.

"Looks like the whole damn town's been taking crazy pills," Dean said.

The brothers turned a corner and saw that the street ahead was blocked off by a pair of sheriff's cruisers, their rooftop lights flashing. A paramedic vehicle was parked in the middle of the street, and two more sheriff's cruisers blocked traffic on the other side.

Dean pulled the Impala to the curb and parked, then he and Sam got out and started walking. A female paramedic stood on the far sidewalk, talking with a man in a sheriff's uniform. A pair of bodies lay close by, an older woman and a teenage boy, both splattered with copious amounts of blood. One of the deputies was taking pictures of the bodies with a digital camera, recording details of the crime scene.

"Looks like we just missed out on the fun," Dean said.

Sheriff's deputies were interviewing witnesses, and two other paramedics tended to a cluster of people at their vehicle. Dean wasn't sure what had happened to the wounded, but he could see they were bleeding from their ears and noses. There were a dozen cars in the street parked outside the makeshift crime-scene barriers. Some of the drivers sat in their cars, but most were outside, talking with deputies or being treated by paramedics. Their expressions were blank with shock, and more than a few were crying.

"Whatever happened here, it looks like it was nasty," Dean said.

"Bold too," Sam added. "It happened out in the open, in front of witnesses."

"It's easier to gank whatever it is if it doesn't hide," Dean said.

"The more reckless it is, the more people will die," Sam countered.

"There is that," Dean agreed.

A deputy stood next to one of the cruisers that blocked off the crime scene. Before she could say anything, the brothers displayed their fake FBI IDs, and the woman let them pass.

"Sheriff Deacon's over there," she said, pointing to the man standing by the bodies.

Where the hell else would he be? Dean thought. But he thanked the deputy and he and Sam headed toward the sheriff.

The sheriff was in his late thirties, trim, with thick black hair and a mustache to match. *A seventies porn star mustache,* Dean thought. He wondered how he'd look with one of those. Probably as douchey as this guy, he decided. Like his deputies, the man wore a brown coat over his shirt, the logo for Allan County Sheriff's Office sewn on the shoulder. The paramedic he was speaking to was a tall woman with blond hair pulled back in a ponytail. She too wore a coat over her uniform—red-and-white stripes on the shoulder, medical symbol on the left breast—and she kept glancing at the bodies while she spoke with the sheriff.

As the brothers drew closer, Dean could see that the two victims' throats had been cut so deep their heads had nearly been severed from their bodies. Sometimes it felt to Dean like he and Sam had seen more bodies in their careers than a mortician, but they'd rarely seen wounds this severe.

Sheriff Deacon turned to the Winchesters as they approached, and Sam and Dean displayed their IDs.

"Agents Holly and Valens," Dean said.

The sheriff arched an eyebrow and smiled.

"You boys forget to bring the Big Bopper with you?" he asked.

The brothers kept their expressions carefully neutral, but inwardly Dean thought, *Great. We had to run into an old-time rock-and-roll fan.*

When neither brother responded, the sheriff's smile fell away.

"Guess you've heard that one before," he said.

"Actually," Sam said, "we haven't."

Next time we go with Coheed and Cambria, Dean thought. "What seems to be the trouble, Sheriff?"

"You're kidding, right?"

The paramedic standing next to the sheriff looked Sam and Dean over before turning to the sheriff.

"I'm not doing any good here. I'll go help with the injured drivers."

"Okay, Gayle. Thanks."

The woman—who Dean found attractive in an all-business, all-the-time kind of way—nodded and then walked toward the paramedic vehicle without giving either of the brothers a second look.

Dean watched her go and muttered, "I love it when they play hard to get."

"Excuse me?" the sheriff said.

Sam gave Dean a look, and he cleared his throat. "We've gotten word that there have been some strange deaths in your town lately." Dean nodded toward the bodies. "Case in point."

"Can you tell us what happened?" Sam asked.

Instead of answering right away, the sheriff told the deputy taking crime-scene photos to go help the others. The man nodded, took one last picture, and then headed off to do as he was told. The sheriff then turned back to Sam and Dean.

"A lot of strange things have been going on in town the last couple weeks," the sheriff said, "but they've gotten worse the last few days. Almost like..." The man trailed off.

"Like what?" Sam prompted.

The sheriff was clearly uncomfortable as he replied, "Like something is coming. And it's getting closer."

Dean exchanged glances with his brother. Some humans were more sensitive to the supernatural world than others, and they could sense—even if only on a subconscious level—when unnatural powers were at work around them. Maybe Sheriff Deacon was one of those people.

The sheriff then proceeded to fill them in on what had taken place here—or at least what witnesses claimed had taken place.

When he was finished, Sam asked, "Did anyone see where the silver woman went afterward?"

The sheriff shook his head. "So far, all we know is she walked off and a handful of people followed her. If they're smart, they got the hell out of town as fast as they could."

Dean highly doubted that had happened. Whatever was going on in Corinth, it was happening *here*, and this "Silver Woman" was part of it. She and her followers would stay in Corinth to the bloody end.

"How do you explain the powers the women were reported to wield?" Sam asked.

"Technology," the sheriff said confidently. "The cat-woman had some kind of long-range acoustic device, and the silver woman used some kind of souped-up stun gun."

"And their appearances were due to—" Sam began.

"Costumes," the sheriff said. "They aren't the first to get dressed up and fight on the street this week." He glanced quickly at the corpses. "Although this *is* one of the deadlier incidents. Usually bystanders aren't harmed."

"What do you think caused this level of violence?" Sam asked. "Some kind of gang activity?"

"Maybe a Halloween-themed fight club?" Dean added.

"Religious wackos," the sheriff said without hesitation. "They started establishing their own weird churches a couple weeks ago, even replacing some of the regular ones. At first, there were only a handful, but more popped up every day, like mushrooms after a rainstorm. I'm sure you noticed the weird decorations on the houses and businesses as you entered town. Well, the cults are the reason for the strange costumes, too."

The sheriff looked away from the brothers and toward a black van that approached the crime scene.

"Good. The coroner's here. Now we can get down to processing the scene properly. It's only a matter of time before some cultists show up to pray or chant or do who knows what over the bodies. I'd just as soon avoid that. Feel free to talk to any of the witnesses here, and you're welcome to stop by the station and take a look at the other incident reports whenever you like. I'll make sure to let them know you're coming."

"We appreciate that, Sheriff," Dean said, and then he and Sam turned away.

The sheriff remained by the bodies as the coroner and his assistant approached, and Sam and Dean walked to the paramedic vehicle. The female paramedic, Gayle, was taking care of an elderly man while the other two paramedics were helping people still sitting in their cars, people who Dean assumed were too hurt to move. The back of the vehicle was open, and the man sat on the back steps while Gayle leaned next to him. The man wore a brown sweater and jeans, and he had a deep gash on his forehead. Gayle worked on cleaning the injury with antiseptic wipes, the man drawing in small hisses of breath whenever she touched the wound.

The brothers stopped when they reached the vehicle.

"Do you mind answering a few questions?" Sam asked.

Gayle didn't take her eyes off the old man's wound as she answered, "As long as I can keep working, sure." She continued dabbing at the man's head.

"We know you weren't on the scene when the incident occurred," Dean said. "But anything you might be able to tell us will be a help."

"I don't know if there's anything more I can add to whatever the Sheriff told you."

She returned her attention to her work. She finished cleaning the man's wound, pulled some gauze out of a medical kit resting next to her patient, folded it, and pressed it to his forehead.

"Hold this for me, please," she said, and the man did so, freeing her hands so she could secure the gauze with strips of surgical tape.

Dean addressed the man. "What about you, sir? What can you tell us?"

The man scowled as he looked up at Sam and Dean. "Those two crazy women started fighting right in the middle of the street." His voice grew louder as he spoke, and he winced. When he resumed, he lowered his voice to just above a whisper.

"A bunch of us had to slam on the brakes to avoid hitting them. Unfortunately for me, I hit the windshield instead. No concussion, though. At least, that's what *she* tells me."

Sam and Dean thanked the man. They interviewed several more witnesses after that, but they didn't learn anything new, with the exception of one man who told them watching the strange women fighting was like "watching superheroes battle—or maybe gods." Superheroes weren't real—which was too bad, Dean thought. He loved to see women in spandex—but gods were real, as the brothers knew from unfortunate experience. And given the sort of power witnesses had said the two women wielded, Dean figured they might be gods, which sucked. He *hated* gods.

"Let's go to the sheriff's station and see what they have on the other murders," Sam suggested.

"Sounds good," Dean said.

The brothers headed back to the Impala, got in, and Dean pulled the car away from the curb. Sam used his phone's GPS to get directions to the sheriff's station. It was only a few miles away, and the drive would only take several minutes.

"So what are we dealing with here?" Sam asked.

"Weird religious cults, strange super-powered killers fighting in the streets… Sounds like we're dealing with some kind of god infestation," Dean said.

"Yeah, but the gods we've encountered are usually solitary creatures. Less competition for worshippers that way."

"You mean victims. They may call themselves gods, might even believe that's what they are, but the bottom line is they're nothing more than higher-class versions of the ghouls

he wielded was staggering, and she couldn't help thinking of the lives she could've saved over the years, the suffering she could've alleviated, if only she'd possessed that same power.

The girl raised her arm and looked at the cast, frowning as if she were trying to see through it and into the arm beneath. She wiggled her fingers and then smiled.

"It doesn't hurt!" She turned to her mom, but her mother continued looking adoringly at Paeon.

"You healed her," the woman said.

"Of course," Paeon said. "It is what I do."

He held out his hand and without looking at Lena said, "Doctor, would you mind fetching me some shears?"

Lena didn't appreciate his use of the word *fetch*, but she walked over to the cabinet and sink, opened a drawer, and found a pair of plaster shears. She walked over to Paeon and placed them in his palm, a bit harder than she needed to. Paeon didn't seem to notice. She returned to her station and leaned against the wall and folded her arms once more.

With precise, confident motions, Paeon cut through the cast length-wise. When he finished, he put the shears on the table, pried the cast off the grinning, wide-eyed girl, and deposited it in the trash can near the door. He took a moment to examine the girl's arm, his fingers feeling for any lingering pain or sensitivity in the bone. Lena doubted he needed to check to make sure the girl's healing had been successful. She figured he did it for the mother and the girl, to put their minds at ease. Miracles were wondrous, but they were scary, too, and a little normality—like a doctor checking a limb to make sure it was fully healed—could go a long way to keeping people's fears at bay.

Paeon finished his "examination" and smiled at the girl.

"All better," he said.

The girl grinned again, leaned forward, and gave Paeon a hug. He hugged her back, and when the girl let go, Lena saw that Paeon looked sharper somehow, his features clearer, more distinct. She'd seen this happen many times this evening. People began coming to the clinic, drawn to Paeon by instinct—or perhaps responding to some kind of silent summons that Paeon sent out—and he began healing them. Once he finished, they expressed their gratitude toward him, sometimes only verbally, but sometimes physically, as the girl just had. And each time Paeon seemed to get an infusion of power—a literal charge, as if his patients were paying him with emotional energy.

No, not paying, she thought. *Feeding*.

The more serious the condition he treated, the greater the exchange of energy. The patients didn't seem to suffer for it. They didn't appear tired or weakened afterward. She didn't understand how the process worked, didn't understand any of this, really. But she decided she didn't need to. All that mattered was these people were being healed of maladies large and small, and while it was humbling to stand by and watch a far greater healer than she could ever hope to be work, it was a privilege to be a part—even a small one—of his mission.

The mother also gave Paeon a hug, then he drew forth his caduceus and held it out. It glowed with power, and the mother and daughter each touched it, one after the other, of their own free will, and when they drew their hands away, they belonged to him. They said their goodbyes, took their coats from the hook on the back of the door, and left. Once they were gone, Paeon returned the caduceus to his coat pocket. Lena was surprised that she always felt a pang of jealousy whenever Paeon accepted a new follower, but she couldn't help it. He'd come to her first, damn it!

Lena's office manager and physician's assistants had been just as impressed with Paeon as she had, and after becoming followers themselves, they remained at the office after hours to help. They received patients and showed them to examination rooms, and Lena knew that other patients were waiting for Paeon. He knew this as well, and he walked out of the room. Lena followed. In the hall, she saw Sarah, one of her assistants, and motioned to her that the examination room they'd left was empty and ready for a new patient. Sarah nodded and headed for the reception area to get one.

Lena marveled at how fresh Paeon looked. They'd been working for hours, ever since he'd first appeared at her practice, but he seemed just as alert and full of energy as he had then. Maybe not getting tired was part of his otherworldly powers, or maybe the emotional energy he fed on staved off weariness. Whatever it was, Lena wished she had some of it. She'd started her day early, visiting patients at the hospital starting at 6 AM before getting to her office at nine and starting to see patients there. And while working with Paeon was exciting, she could feel the day beginning to catch up with her. She stifled a yawn and told herself to ask Sarah to make a pot of coffee.

Despite being relegated to a supporting position at her own practice, Lena felt good about what she was doing. By assisting Paeon, she was helping more people than she imagined possible, and thanks to the caduceus, all of them were guaranteed to be healed. A 100 per cent success rate was unheard of in medicine, especially in oncology, but that's exactly what Paeon had accomplished since setting foot in the building. It was all like something out of a dream, and Lena knew that dreams didn't come true. Not like this, and not without some kind of catch. But what was happening was so wonderful that she didn't want to question it.

She led Paeon to the next examination room, knocked, then opened the door. She stepped back so he could precede her, then she stepped inside and closed the door behind them.

A man sat on the examination table, looked to be in his early thirties, fit, black hair, black beard. His coat lay on the table next to him, and he wore a blue turtleneck, jeans, and sneakers. He looked healthy, but Lena knew that outward appearances never told the whole story, medically.

Paeon smiled at the man.

"I am Paeon. What is your name?"

"Bill. Bill Wright."

His voice sounded strong, but it held an undercurrent of fear. Lena wondered what Bill was worried about. Could he be far sicker than he looked?

"What troubles you, Bill?" Paeon asked.

Paeon's voice was warm, caring, and reassuring, and Bill visibly relaxed.

He's got a great god-side manner, Lena thought, and smiled.

"It's an honor to meet you, sir." Bill extended his hand and Paeon shook it. "Your patients have been spreading the word about you, talking about how you can heal any kind of sickness or injury."

"Good news travels fast," Lena said.

"These people speak the truth," Paeon said. "Do you have need of my services?"

"Yes. I want to follow you. Become Bound."

"I am honored," Paeon said graciously, and he gave Bill a slight nod of acknowledgement.

Bill looked uncomfortable. "There's a problem, though. I'm already Bound."

Paeon's smile faltered, but it held.

"You may switch allegiances whenever you wish. It is permitted."

During the hours they'd worked together, Paeon had told Lena much about himself, or more accurately, about his kind and what they were doing in Corinth. She didn't think he'd told her everything, but then again, it was possible he didn't know it all himself. According to Paeon, his kind were born with a certain amount of knowledge—such as language and how to use their abilities—but their knowledge was limited, and they had to learn everything else the same way humans did: through experience. One thing Paeon understood very well about his existence was that it was temporary. Beings like him were brought into existence—and she was still fuzzy on how that process worked—and they fought each other, the winner absorbing the strength of the loser until at the end, the last survivor achieved Apotheosis—elevation to true godhood and a permanent immortal existence. Lena wasn't sure why the process had to work like this, but there were numerous precedents in nature. Only the strongest cubs in a litter survived, and only the strongest salmon got to spawn. She supposed the Apotheosis was something similar.

Part of the process was to acquire followers, humans that became Bound to an individual god. This attachment fed the god, made him, her, or it stronger. But people could switch allegiances from one god to another if they wished, so along with fighting each other, gods competed for worshippers, too. And when a god was defeated by another, the winner claimed the loser's worshippers—assuming they wished to be claimed. Gods weren't thrilled about losing followers, though, which explained Bill's nervousness.

Paeon continued, "There is nothing special you need do to switch. You need only desire it."

"I don't think it's going to be that easy for me."

Bill pulled off his turtleneck and dropped it on top of his coat. Now that his shirt was off, Lena saw that his chest was covered by a greenish-gray growth that looked like some kind of fungus. She'd never seen anything like it, and despite her medical training and years of experience, the sight nauseated her.

Paeon's smile fell away and his expression became serious.

"Who did this to you?" he demanded.

"His name is Blight," Bill said. "He's like you."

"The creature who did this is *nothing* like me," Paeon said, half in anger, half in disgust.

Bill seemed to shrink at Paeon's words. "I'm sorry. I didn't mean to insult you."

Paeon's smile returned, although it seemed forced this time.

"You have nothing to apologize for. Blight is the one who should apologize, for inflicting this… *abomination* on your flesh."

"Can you do something about it?" Bill asked. "Once I decided to switch to you, I tried to, well, I guess wish it away is the best way to put it, but nothing happened. Then I tried to cut it off. I used a sharp kitchen knife, but I only managed to remove a little before I passed out. It hurt *so* much! And when I woke up, I saw that the patch I'd cut away had grown back."

"We fight to hold on to what is ours," Paeon said. "It is our nature. But fear not. I shall do what I can."

"Why do you want to switch?" Lena asked. When Paeon frowned at her, she added, "I only want to better understand how the process works."

Bill looked uncertainly at Paeon. The god nodded to give his permission, and the man turned to look at Lena as he spoke.

"Blight talks about bringing people together by marking us with… *this*." He gestured to the growth on his chest. "It's supposed to connect us somehow. But all he really cares about is spreading his influence and increasing his power." He turned back to Paeon. "But you help people in real, physical ways, and who wouldn't want to be part of that?"

Lena smiled. "I understand entirely."

Paeon gave her an impatient look. "If your curiosity is satisfied, Lena, perhaps you'll allow me to get to work?"

Her cheeks reddened. "Of course. Sorry."

Paeon looked at her for another moment before turning back to Bill. He withdrew the caduceus from his coat pocket, but he didn't extend it toward Bill right away.

"I want you to keep in mind that treating your *condition* won't be as simple as healing a human illness or injury. I will have to counter Blight's power with my own. It will not be easy, and I'm afraid it will be far from comfortable for you."

Bill looked scared, but his voice was steady when he replied.

"Do what you have to do."

"If this is going to hurt, maybe we should give him something for the pain," Lena said.

"You have nothing that will help. You told me this is not… How did you put it? 'A general practitioner's office.' Because of this, you have little medicine in supply, correct?"

"Yes."

"And even if your practice held every medicine known to humankind, none would be able to relieve this man's discomfort. His is not an earthly condition, and because of this, your remedies would have no effect." He looked at Bill. "You will just have to do your best to endure, I'm afraid."

"I understand," Bill said. "And I'm ready."

"Good. Lie down, please."

Lena stepped forward and removed Bill's coat and turtleneck from the table. She placed them on one of the chairs in the room while Bill swung his legs onto the table and lay back as Paeon had instructed.

"Let your arms rest at your side and close your eyes," Paeon said.

Bill did so.

Paeon raised his caduceus, but instead of touching it to Bill's body, he held it a foot above the man's chest. The instrument began glowing with a soft light, and Paeon moved it slowly back and forth, as if it were some kind of scanning device. He frowned as he performed this procedure, and Lena didn't know if that was because he was concentrating or because he didn't like what the caduceus was telling him. Maybe both, she decided. After several moments, he spoke to Lena while continuing his scan.

"Come over here, please. I need you to hold him down."

Lena got a pair of rubber gloves from the cabinet—no way did she want to touch Bill's infected skin without protection—and then joined Paeon at the examination table. She stood behind the man's head and reached down to place her gloved hands on his shoulders. She hoped he wouldn't move much. He looked to be strong, and she didn't think she'd be able to keep him down if he was determined to sit up.

"Ready," she said.

Paeon acknowledged her with a nod, and then—without any obvious command from him—the caduceus began to glow more brightly than Lena had ever seen it do before. So intense was the light emitting from the object that she had to avert her gaze.

Bill's eyes snapped open, but then he squinted and turned his head to the side. When he spoke, his voice shook.

"I don't think I'm ready—"

Lena could still see well enough to make out Paeon flipping the caduceus around in his grip until the end with the wings and snake heads was pointing toward Bill. Then without hesitation, Paeon slammed the magical object down into the man's chest, and Bill let out an ear-splitting shriek of agony.

"You're killing him!" Lena shouted.

"Nonsense," Paeon said through gritted teeth. "I'm attempting to free him." Lena had the impression that it was a struggle for him to keep the caduceus inside Bill, as if another force were working to push the object out. Paeon's jaw muscles tightened, and for the first time since she'd met him, she saw beads of sweat form on his brow.

Bill's body stiffened and he tried to sit up out of reflex, but Lena kept him pinned to the table. It took all of her strength to do so, and as she continued to fight to prevent him from rising, she watched with horrified fascination as Paeon slowly began to pull the caduceus out of Bill. But the caduceus didn't emerge from the man's body alone—it pulled the gray-green fungus with it. Slowly, as if he were performing the most delicate of operations, Paeon continued raising the caduceus higher, drawing more of the disgusting growth upward. Lena realized the caduceus wasn't simply peeling the fungus away from the man's skin. It was actually removing it from inside his body through a process that she didn't understand. But then, she didn't have to understand it. It was magic, and all that mattered was that it was working.

Paeon continued raising the caduceus until his arm was pointing almost straight toward the ceiling. Thick, ropey strands of green-gray muck stretched from the mystic object down to Bill's chest. Lena saw no wounds on the man's body. There was no sign of where the caduceus had plunged into his chest, and the strands of fungus created no tears in the places where they were drawn from his flesh. The strands were, however, capable of movement, and they fought Paeon, pulling away from the caduceus back toward the body that up until a few moments ago had sheltered them. *The growth is like a parasite,* Lena thought. What if Blight, Paeon, and the rest of their kind were nothing more than high-order parasites that fed off humans? But she was so caught up in what was happening that the thought flickered through her mind and was gone. Bill was convulsing now, and it took everything she had to keep his shoulders pressed down against the table.

Paeon's arm shook with the effort of holding onto the caduceus, and for a moment Lena thought that he was going to lose this battle, that the gray-green strands would yank the caduceus from his hand and slither back inside Bill, taking the mystic object with them. But then Paeon bared his teeth, released a roar that was as much animal as human, and flung the mass toward the other side of the room. The muck came free from Bill's body with a sickening *schlurp*, struck the wall with a heavy splat, then fell to the floor with a moist smacking sound. There it lay motionless in a large greenish-gray mound that was about as big as Bill himself.

Lena tore her gaze from the muck to look down at Bill. Amazingly, the man's chest was not only clear of fungus, but the skin was smooth and unbroken. He lay still, eyes closed, and Lena pressed two fingers to the side of his neck to check his pulse, fearing the worst. She couldn't help thinking of the old joke: *The operation was a success, but the patient died.* She needn't have worried, though. His pulse was weak, but steady. He'd simply slipped into unconsciousness, probably because the pain had been too much for him. She was glad. She couldn't imagine how much that must've hurt. Passing out had been a blessing.

Paeon breathed heavily and sweat trickled down the sides of his face, but he was smiling. He still held the caduceus in a stabbing grip, but the object was no longer glowing. The light had winked out the instant the muck had hit the wall.

He looked at Lena. "How is he doing?"

"I think he's going to be okay."

"Excellent. Tend to him, if you don't mind. My work isn't finished."

Before she could ask what Paeon meant, he turned and walked toward the mound lying on the floor, flipping the caduceus into its normal holding position as he went. He stopped when he was within a foot of the muck and gazed down upon it. As bad as the stuff appeared, it smelled even worse, Lena thought, like a gangrenous wound slathered in pus. Paeon made no move to go any closer to the greenish-gray mass—she didn't blame him in the slightest for that—but she was more than a little surprised when he began speaking to it.

"You might as well drop the charade. I know who you are."

For a moment, nothing happened, but then the mound began to move. It rose upward, growing and reforming itself until it had assumed a roughly humanoid shape: blocky head, no neck, broad shoulders and chest, thick arms and legs, hands large as anvils. It possessed only the most rudimentary facial features, dark depressions that were mere suggestions of eyes and a mouth. In its right hand the figure gripped a length of broken tree limb that was covered with the same fungus-like substance that formed his body.

"I am Blight." The creature's voice was a thick gurgling, the sound a clogged kitchen disposal might make if it could talk.

"I gathered as much," Paeon said drily. "Did Bill know that he was carrying you, or did you use him without his knowledge?"

"What does it matter? He is mine, and I can use him however I choose." Blight's mouth widened in a grotesque approximation of a smile.

"I don't understand," Lena said. "What's happening?"

Paeon didn't take his gaze off Blight as he explained. "Blight wishes to challenge me, but since I haven't left the building all evening—"

"I decided to come to you," Blight finished. "Surprise!"

Lena frowned. "Why reveal yourself this way? Why not attack when Paeon was distracted?"

Both gods looked at her then. Blight's face was hard to read, but Paeon's wasn't. He wore an expression of absolute disbelief.

"It's simply not the way it's done," Paeon said, sounding offended.

"Yeah," Blight agreed. "You humans can be pretty dumb sometimes."

Lena sighed. Magic might have some advantages over science, but she doubted she'd ever come to understand it.

"Very well," Paeon said. "Since you're here, we might as well get this over with. The sooner I finish you off, the sooner I can get back to work."

"Sweet racket you got going here," Blight said. "You heal humans, and every one of them is *so* grateful, they practically beg for you to let them follow you. Great way to pick up worshippers fast, I've got to give you that."

Paeon ignored the mocking compliment. "Come, let us step outside and do what we must."

Blight's suggestion of a mouth stretched wide again. "You might care about what happens to the humans in this building, but I don't. I'm challenging you here and now." He paused, and when he spoke once more his tone became formal. "I am Blight, and in the end there shall be One."

Lena had the sense that she was witnessing the beginning of a ritual, but Paeon wanted no part of it.

"You may speak the words as many times as you wish, but I refuse to—"

That's as far as Paeon got before Blight attacked.

The muck creature raised his tree branch and rushed toward Paeon. The creature moved so swiftly that Lena wasn't sure, but it looked as if his feet didn't move, that he instead *oozed* across the floor. Before Paeon could react, Blight swung the fungus-covered tree branch at his head and the wood struck his temple with a sickening *thump*. The impact knocked Paeon sideways, and sent him staggering toward the wall. He managed to press his free hand against it to steady himself and avoid falling to the floor, but Blight didn't give him time to retaliate. The creature came at him again, tree-branch club held high. Paeon was prepared this time, though. As Blight swung the club toward his head, he ducked to the side. The club smashed into the wall, knocking a large chunk out of it, but Blight was so strong and had been moving so fast that the impact caused that entire section of wall to collapse, and Blight fell into the hallway outside.

Lena had been so stunned by the swiftness of Blight's

initial attack that up to this point she hadn't been able to do more than stand and watch. But the sight of blood trickling down the side of Paeon's head snapped her out of her mental paralysis. She started toward him, intending to help, but before she could do more than take a step in his direction, the caduceus—which he still held—glowed briefly, and the blood reversed back into the wound, which then sealed itself. As if sensing Lena's intention, he gave her a quick glance.

"There's only one way you can help me." He nodded toward Bill. "Stab that man."

And then he raced to the opening in the wall and stepped into the hallway to confront Blight.

Lena was stunned. Had she heard Paeon right? Had he really told her to *stab* Bill? It made no sense—Paeon was a god of healing. Mutilation and killing should be abhorrent to him. Confused, she quickly checked on the still-unconscious Bill to make sure he was all right, then moved cautiously toward the hole in the wall. She feared that one or both of the gods might come flying through and crash into her, but that didn't happen. Instead, she heard sounds of fighting coming from farther down the hallway: bodies slamming into walls, grunts of pain and anger, screams from terrified staff and patients… She risked sticking her head out to take a look and saw Paeon and Blight facing each other. Blight kept swinging his club, trying to land another blow on Paeon, but the other god blocked each strike with his caduceus. Lena couldn't believe Paeon's mystic object, small as it was, could deflect a blow from Blight's larger weapon, but it did. *Magic has its own rules,* she reminded herself.

Each time the club and caduceus came in contact, there was a flash of energy—half gold, half greenish-gray—and Lena realized that regardless of what appearance the gods' weapons took, they weren't really fighting with physical objects, but rather concentrated energy. This was a time when size didn't matter; power did. But if that was the case, how were gods ever supposed to win battles like this? Paeon and Blight seemed too evenly matched, but from what she understood about the Apotheosis, only one god would remain standing when it was over. So there were ways for one god to triumph over another, and that meant Paeon *could* defeat Blight. Cunning and skill didn't seem like they would be enough, not with the kind of power they wielded.

She tried to think of the situation analytically, drawing on diagnostic skills honed during her years as a doctor. Maybe there was something in each god's essential nature—not exactly a weakness but a specific quality—that could be exploited. Paeon was a god of healing, Blight a god of… what? Disgusting green-gray gunk? She tried to remember what Bill had said about Blight.

Blight talks about bringing people together by marking us with… this. *It's supposed to connect us somehow. But all he really cares about is spreading his influence and increasing his power.*

When Blight had appeared in the examination room, she believed that he'd somehow gotten inside Bill and hidden there. But what if Blight's followers *were* all connected to him, and vice versa. Maybe the growth on Bill's chest had actually been part of Blight, and the god was able to transfer his consciousness to any part of his larger self and form a body to serve as an avatar. But what if the connection went both ways? If the growth on each of his followers was a part of Blight's overall substance, then not only could he reach *out* through them, maybe others could reach *in*.

Then she understood. That must have been why Paeon had told her to stab Bill. She turned and walked back to the examination table.

Bill remained unconscious, and for that Lena was grateful. It would make what she had to do easier—for him, at least. She could hear the sounds of Paeon and Blight fighting, but she tuned them out so she could concentrate. She went to the cabinet and found a pair of regular scissors and then returned to the table. The scissors weren't exactly surgical equipment, but they'd have to do. Blight had left no residue of his substance on the wall or floor after Paeon had extracted him from Bill's body, but Lena felt confident that something of Blight remained within Bill. She still wore rubber gloves, although she would've also liked to have a surgical mask, along with a pair of goggles. She didn't have either on site, though, so she'd just have to hope she didn't become contaminated.

Lena looked down at Bill's bare chest and took a deep breath. Any injury she inflicted on Bill would be only temporary, she told herself. Paeon was a god of healing, and he would never ask her to harm someone if he didn't have a good reason—and if he didn't intend to heal that person afterward. She was a medical oncologist, not a surgical one, and the last time she'd cut into a body was during med school. Still, it wasn't going to take much skill to perform this procedure. She picked a spot on Bill's chest, raised the scissors in a two-handed grip, and took aim.

"Sorry about this," she said softly, and then brought the scissors down as fast and hard as she could.

Bill's eyes flew open the instant metal pierced his flesh and he cried out in pain. Blood spurted from the fresh wound, but Lena kept a firm grip on the scissors, which were buried in his body all the way to the handles. He thrashed on the table and clawed at her hands, trying to get at the scissors so he could pull them out, but she held on tight, doing her best not to think about the fact that she had just mutilated a patient.

"Shhh. It'll be okay, Bill. I promise."

Paeon can fix this, she told herself. *He will.*

But what if Bill died before Paeon could treat him? The caduceus was a powerful magical instrument, and from what she'd seen tonight, it could cure all manner of injury and illness. But was it powerful enough to cure death? She hoped she wouldn't have to find out.

She'd purposely avoided the heart, but from the bubbling, wheezing sound of Bill's breathing, she knew she'd punctured one of his lungs. Blood ran from his wound onto the table, over the side, and splattered onto the floor, but he was also bleeding inside, and she wondered how long it would take for the injured lung to fill with blood. She had no idea, didn't have the surgical training and experience required to make an estimation.

Just hold on, she mentally urged him.

From the hallway, she heard Blight roar in what sounded like frustration. There was a loud crash, as if another section of wall had been destroyed, and then an instant later Blight came back into the room, gliding across the floor in that eerie way of his. Lena realized the sound she'd heard had been made by Paeon. Most likely Blight had knocked the other god aside when he sensed what Lena had done to his follower. He still held his club, and he brandished it at her as he approached.

"What have you done to my servant?" he demanded.

Lena released her grip on the scissors and moved away from the examination table. She'd hoped that by wounding Bill she would also hurt Blight, kind of like stabbing pins into a voodoo doll, but the god appeared to be unharmed. All she'd managed to do was draw his attention and enrage him. He came at her, club raised, clearly intending to bring it down on her head and crush her skull, and there wasn't a damn thing she could do about it except stand there and die.

Paeon rushed into the room then, hair mussed, sweat pouring off him, clothes torn and smeared with gray-green stains. He lunged forward and grabbed Blight from behind, putting the other god in a headlock and pulling him away from Lena. Blight dropped his club and reached up with both of his large hands and grabbed hold of Paeon's arm in an attempt to break Paeon's grip. But Paeon held fast, and the two gods stood in the middle of the room in temporary stalemate.

"Run, Lena!" Paeon ordered. "Quickly, before he breaks free!"

Up to this point, Lena had managed to keep her fear at bay by forcing herself to approach this situation as if it were nothing more than a medical problem to solve. But her control over her emotions was rapidly failing, and she could feel the first stirrings of panic within her. If she didn't do as Paeon commanded and get out of here, there was an excellent chance she would die, caught in the crossfire as the two gods warred. It was something of a miracle that she hadn't been killed already. But she looked at Bill then and saw that he lay motionless once more, eyes closed. She was confident that he was only unconscious, but how much longer could he live without treatment? If she ran now, Bill would die, and it would be her fault for stabbing him. The Hippocratic oath told doctors that, above all, they should do no harm. Well, she'd done plenty of harm to that man, and she couldn't bring herself to abandon him. So she remained where she was and tried to think clearly. There had to be some way for Paeon to defeat Blight, but what—

It came to her then. Blight was like a parasite and if you couldn't remove a parasite chemically or surgically, there was only one way left to kill it, the most ancient way of all.

With fire.

She had nothing to start a fire with, but even if she had, would it be enough to harm Blight?

"Paeon!" she shouted. "Fire! Use fire!"

She had no idea if Paeon's caduceus could do anything other than heal, but if it could affect the organic matter that comprised Blight's body and raise its temperature high enough…

Paeon locked gazes with her, puzzled at first, but then understanding came into his eyes, and he smiled and nodded. He maintained his headlock on Blight and with his other hand extended the caduceus. Not toward the other god, however. Toward Bill.

The caduceus glowed a bright yellow, and without warning Bill's body burst into flame. The agony brought him out of unconsciousness, and he screamed and thrashed on the table.

Paeon spun Blight toward Bill and shoved him forward. The god stumbled and fell onto the burning man, and the green-gray fungus that was his body ignited as if it had been soaked in gasoline. Blight bellowed in pain and rage, and his cries joined with Bill's. Flames rose to the ceiling, producing noxious black smoke that gave Lena a coughing fit. As she struggled to breathe, she watched as Paeon walked over to where Blight had dropped his tree-branch club, bent down, and picked it up.

Blight fell backwards, pulling Bill's body with him. They landed in a burning heap on the floor and lay there, moaning as flames consumed them. Paeon stepped over to the bodies, looked at them for a moment, and then with a single thrust stabbed the tree branch downward, piercing both their bodies. An instant later, both Bill and Blight fell silent and remained that way. Paeon stepped back and gestured with his caduceus. It glowed briefly, and the flames rising upward from man and god diminished until they were gone, leaving behind a charred, smoking mound.

Lena—still coughing, eyes watering, and throat burning—couldn't tell where Bill ended and Blight began. A moment later, part of the mound began to glow with a bright white light. The light detached itself, formed a sphere, and then shot toward Paeon, striking him in the chest. The impact caused him to sway a little, but otherwise, it appeared to do him no harm. To the contrary, he seemed invigorated, and Lena could feel power emanating from him.

She thought she understood what had happened. Paeon had defeated Blight, and Blight's power became his. *In the end, there shall be One.*

Paeon tucked the caduceus away in his coat pocket before turning to give Lena a smile. He was no longer sweating, and his clothes were clean and looked as if they'd been freshly pressed. He wasn't just re-energized; he had been renewed.

"That was a little closer than I might've liked, but I suppose I didn't do all that badly considering it was my first battle," Paeon said. "What do you think, Lena?"

Her voice came out as a raspy croak. "Why are you just standing there? Do something to help Bill!"

Paeon's smile fell away. "I'm truly sorry, but there's nothing I can do for him. He is beyond my power."

"You mean he's dead," she said bitterly.

"Yes."

"And you're not the slightest bit sorry about that? You used him to help you defeat Blight. You actually set him on *fire*!"

Paeon shrugged. "It was your idea."

"I meant for you to do it to Blight!"

She was yelling now, and Paeon's brow furrowed. When he next spoke, his voice was tight and low, as if he were holding back anger.

"My ability to affect the physiology of another of my kind is limited at the moment, but the same is not true of humans. I was able to rapidly heat the oxygen in the man's cells, which produced the desired effect."

"Bill. His name was Bill."

Paeon scowled. "I don't appreciate your tone, Lena."

"I don't appreciate that you killed one of your patients! He came to you for healing!"

"Perhaps. He also may have aided Blight willingly." He

glanced back at Bill's blackened corpse. "We will never know, unfortunately."

"How could you do that?" she demanded.

Paeon's gaze became arctic-cold. "It was a matter of survival. Would you rather I had set *you* aflame?"

Lena didn't answer.

"I thought not. Besides, what does one life matter when compared with all those I will be able to save in the future, thanks to his—to *Bill's*—sacrifice?"

"It's not a sacrifice if you can't choose it."

"I am done arguing with you. We have patients waiting for us. I do not believe any of them or any of your staff was injured during my battle with Blight, but I want to make sure. Let us go."

He started toward the door, stepping over Bill's corpse to get there, but Lena made no move to follow him. When he realized this, he stopped and turned back to her.

"I said, let us go."

"I thought you were a god," Lena said. "But you're really just a monster, aren't you?"

He looked at her for a long moment, as if trying to come to a decision. Then he brought out his caduceus once more and pointed it at her.

"Who said I cannot be both?"

A black glow surrounded the mystic object this time, and Lena felt her body explode with pain. She slumped to the floor, like a puppet whose strings had been cut, and rolled onto her side. Her breathing was ragged, her pulse erratic, and it felt like every cell of her body was bursting with agony.

"I have afflicted you with every cancer known to

humankind," Paeon said, "along with a few you have yet to discover. I would think that as an oncologist, you would find this a fascinating experience."

Lena was in so much pain that she could barely understand Paeon's words.

"Please…" she breathed, the word almost inaudible. "Make it stop."

Paeon came over, once more stepping over Bill's body to do so, and knelt by her side.

"From now on, you shall do as I say, without question and hesitation. Is that clear?" When she didn't respond, he repeated, slowly, "Is. That. Clear?"

"Y—yes."

Paeon smiled. "Good."

The caduceus's golden glow filled her vision, and just like that, the pain was gone. But not the memory of it, though. That would remain with her always, just as Paeon wished it—as a reminder.

Paeon stood and reached down to offer her his hand. After a moment's hesitation, she took it and allowed him to help her stand.

"Now, let's get back to work, shall we?"

Paeon headed for the door, and this time Lena followed obediently. He stepped over Bill once again, but Lena detoured around the man's body, unable to bring herself to look at it anymore.

Once in the hallway, Paeon wrinkled his nose.

"Have your staff remove the body. It's producing a most unpleasant odor." He paused, then added, "Tell them to open some windows, too."

SIX

Sam is sitting next to Gretchen Underwood on the side of a hill, between a pair of large elm trees—the same spot where they sat yesterday, and the day before that. They're wearing flannel shirts, jeans, and thin jackets. The weather's cool, especially with all the shade provided by the trees, and although Sam would prefer to have a heavier jacket, he doesn't mind the temperature all that much. It's a small price to pay to get to spend time alone with Gretchen.

It's closing in on noon, and Sam's getting hungry. They've got food—sandwiches wrapped in cellophane, cans of soda, some cheese crackers and packages of cookies for snacks—stored in a khaki backpack lying on the ground nearby. They've also got weapons. Sam has a .38 handgun which Julie loaned him, and Gretchen has a bolt-action rifle. The rifle has a scope, and Gretchen is lying on the ground, sighting through it. She's watching the stream at the bottom of the hill, several dozen yards from their current position. The .38 is tucked into the back of Sam's pants. He's sitting cross-legged, and the gun feels too tight against his skin, but he does his best to ignore the sensation. No way is he going to remove the gun and lay it on the ground. His dad taught him that you never put down a weapon when you're on a hunt.

The most important thing to remember about hunting is that it goes both ways. Whatever you're after is probably hunting you as well, so always keep your weapons on you, Sammy.

Sam isn't going to hold the .38, either. Another lesson John Winchester drilled into his sons was that you never put a weapon in your hand unless you plan to use it. It's a different story for Gretchen, though. She's using the rifle's scope for surveillance right now.

They have one more weapon in addition to their knives and shotguns, but that's with Stewart, inside his backpack. It's a stake fashioned from white ash, its point honed to pinpoint sharpness. The stake's wrapped in a special crimson cloth, both to protect it and keep it from touching anything else. Why it's important that nothing touches the stake, Sam doesn't know, and he hasn't asked. One of the things he's learned about the Underwoods over the last few days is that they aren't particularly fond of answering questions. They aren't rude about it, and they aren't reluctant to talk—unless the topic relates to hunting, or more specifically, about how *they* hunt. Sam thinks it's an odd habit. He's been around hunters most of his life, and while many of them don't like to talk about themselves, especially about whatever supernatural incident spurred them to become hunters in the first place, they were only too happy to share hunting techniques and lore. Sharing such information not only made them better hunters, it increased their odds of survival. But the Underwoods are exactly opposite. They talk about anything and everything, but when it comes to hunting, they only discuss the absolute basics of what they need to do to find and kill their target, and that's it. Sam doubts Dean minds the Underwoods' silence on the subject of hunting. He's more of a doer than a talker anyway, and as for Sam, he wants out of the family business, so the less he has to talk about the hunting, the better as far as he's concerned. Still, he can't help thinking that there's some reason the Underwoods don't discuss hunting, and not knowing what that reason might be troubles him.

Since arriving at the Underwoods' home, Sam and Dean have spent most of their time in the woods on stakeouts with the family, waiting for the Sheepsquatch to make an appearance, but so far they haven't had any luck. Supposedly the creature was spotted drinking at this stream by a hunter—the regular kind—and Julie Underwood thinks this is the most likely place to catch it. Sam figures the hunter was drunk and only imagined he saw the Sheepsquatch. He hasn't said anything to Gretchen, but he's beginning to wonder if the creature is real at all. Over the years, he's learned that for every type of supernatural being that exists, there are at least three more that are mere fantasy. Maybe Sheepsquatch is one of the latter. With a name like that, it *has* to be a joke, right? Sure, Gretchen told him it has another, older name—the White Thing—but that isn't much better.

According to the Underwoods, other monsters stalk these hills as well, creatures with strange names like raven mocker, behinder, bammat, flat, skim, and toller. Sam has never heard of any of these before, and he's not sure that the Underwoods aren't joking about them. But even if they are, Julie certainly believes the Sheepsquatch is real. *The damn thing's been killing dogs, pigs, and cattle for months,* she told them, *and now a man name of Braydon Albright's gone missing. Wife hasn't seen or heard from him in over a week. I don't know for certain that the Sheepsquatch took him, but I have my suspicions.* Sam doesn't care if the Sheepsquatch—or any of the other creatures the Underwoods mentioned—exists. He's sick of hunting and killing, sick of death in all its forms. When he was an infant, his mother was killed by a demon, and sometimes it seems like one way or another he's lived with death ever since. He wants to try living a normal life for a change, just to see what it's like. A life where things like demons, ghosts, and monsters only exist in stories. So if this hunt turns out to be a wild goose chase, that's fine with him. Besides, it's a great excuse for hanging out with Gretchen.

Julie decided they should split up into two groups. She, Stewart, and Dean took a position closer to the stream, less than fifty feet from it, hidden in a cluster of small pine trees. They're armed with twelve-gauge pump-action shotguns. According to Julie, bullets won't do much more than make the beast mad, but if they—along with Gretchen—can manage to put enough rounds into the thing, it might be slowed down enough for one of them to ram the white ash stake into its heart. Julie picked Stewart to administer the *coup de grace*, and Sam knows Dean resents this. After all, he's the oldest one here—not counting Julie, of course. And as for Sam…

His main task seems to be keeping Gretchen company. His .38 doesn't have the range to hit the Sheepsquatch from here, and while he's carrying a hunting knife, as are the rest of them, if the creature gets close enough for him to use it, he knows it'll probably be too late.

On the first day of the stakeout, Sam wondered if Julie wanted him to stay with Gretchen so he could guard her, but he quickly realized how foolish the idea was. Gretchen exuded total confidence, and she handled the rifle like a pro. The morning before they first set out for the woods they all practiced shooting behind the Underwoods' house, Julie included. Not only did she want everyone to warm up, she wanted to make sure Sam and Dean were familiar with the weapons she was loaning them. They fired at paper bullseyes tacked to hay bales, but Sam paid more attention to Gretchen than he did to his target, and he quickly learned she was a crack shot. Now, Sam wonders if Julie put him back here with Gretchen because she sensed his lack of enthusiasm for hunting. He hopes that's not the case. He's been trying to hide his feelings from Dean, and *especially* from their dad, but if someone who only recently met him can tell the truth, what hope does he have of fooling the two people who know him better than anyone on Earth?

As much as Dean resents not getting to wield the white ash stake himself, Sam knows he's even more resentful that he's not the one alone with Gretchen. Not that there's much the two of them can do. They can't talk, not without risking giving themselves away to the Sheepsquatch if it's near, and Gretchen spends all her time peering through her rifle scope, only interrupting her sentry duty to get up, stretch, and go behind a tree to pee. None of this makes for a particularly romantic time. He doesn't mind—well, he minds a *little*—but the woods are so beautiful, so peaceful, that just being here is enough. The trees are old, some of the oldest in the nation, and sitting here, listening to the sounds of the stream flowing, birds singing, animals making their way through the underbrush, Sam thinks it's like being back in a time before humans had first set foot in North America, the land pure and unspoiled.

Sam's thoughts are interrupted by the loud growling of his stomach. Embarrassed, he puts his hands on his belly and presses, trying to quiet his gut, but the action only makes it growl louder. Gretchen pulls away from the rifle scope, turns to look at him, and raises an eyebrow. Cheeks burning, all he can do is give an uncertain smile and shrug. Smiling back, she gets to her feet, leans the rifle against a tree trunk, then stretches. Sam admires the way her body moves and suddenly food is the furthest thing from his mind. Gretchen walks over to the backpack, crouches next to it, and slowly unzips it, trying to make as little noise as possible. She takes out a sandwich and a can of soda, hands them to Sam, and then gets the same for herself. She then walks over to sit next to Sam, her rifle within arm's reach, and they begin unwrapping their sandwiches. As they're doing this, they hear a loud sneeze, followed by Dean's whispered, "Sonofabitch!"

Sam and Gretchen lock gazes, and an instant later they're both struggling to hold in laughter. But an instant after that their laughter dies when they hear the sound of something large moving through the underbrush. Whatever it is, it's heading in their direction. They drop their food and jump to their feet. Gretchen runs to retrieve her rifle while Sam draws the .38 and flicks off the safety. They then take cover behind the elm, Gretchen kneeling, rifle up, eye at the scope, weapon braced against the trunk and ready to fire. Sam stands behind her, .38 raised, left hand bracing his shooting arm, feet spread in a firing stance. His heart's pounding, senses sharp and alert, and adrenaline surges through his body like electricity. He hates these moments before the fighting and killing begin, but even though he won't admit it, not even to himself, these are the times when he feels most alive. Gretchen remains statue-still as they wait for whatever it is to reveal itself, but he can feel anticipation rolling off her like waves of energy. She's remained patient and virtually motionless for the better part of three days, and now that the moment to act is finally here, she's more than ready.

Sam catches glimpses of the creature as it moves between the trees. It's tall—seven, maybe eight feet—and covered in thick wool-like fur. It walks on two legs, and its arms end in a pair of paw-like hands with wicked-looking sharp black claws. Its head resembles a canine's, and a pair of long tusk-like teeth protrude from its upper jaw. Large curved horns like those of a ram jut from its skull, and a long hairless tail like an opossum's whips the air as it walks. A gut-churning stench emanates from the creature's body, like sulfur, only a hundred times worse. Sam's glad he didn't have time to take a single bite of his sandwich, let alone eat the whole thing. If he did, he'd be puking it up right now. The creature snorts and grunts as it moves, almost as if it's muttering to itself, although the sounds are solely animalistic and have no discernible pattern. As it draws closer, Sam is able to make out its eyes. He expects a monster like this to have seriously creepy eyes—glowing crimson or maybe an eerie green—but they look human, and that's far worse.

The sulfurous stench makes Sam wonder if the Sheepsquatch has any connection to demons. Sulfur is their calling card, and if the creature is demonic in some way, that will make it even harder—and maybe impossible—to kill, at least with the weapons they have. And as for the white ash stake, he's never heard of anything like that killing a demon. He hopes the Underwoods know what they're doing.

Now that he's gotten a look at the creature, he can see why people around here have dubbed it Sheepsquatch. It's bipedal, as Bigfoot is supposed to be, and its matted white fur does resemble sheep's wool to an extent. The dog face, tusk-teeth, and horns don't fit the name, though, and he thinks White Thing suits the monster better.

The creature continues moving through the woods, past their position and down toward the stream, making surprisingly little noise for something so large. Neither Sam nor Gretchen take a shot at it. The plan is to wait until it's drinking at the stream and then attack, hopefully taking it by surprise. Unless of course, the creature senses them and attacks first. But so far it's shown no sign that it's aware of the presence of humans in its woods. It doesn't sniff the air, doesn't stop and turn its head from side to side, searching. It just keeps walking toward the stream. Sam and Gretchen shift position around the tree in order to keep the Sheepsquatch in sight. Sam's worried that the thing heard Dean sneeze and will head toward him, Julie, and Stewart, but it doesn't. It continues to the stream, gets down on all fours, lowers its snout to the water, and begins drinking, lapping like a dog, its tongue long and black.

He's startled when Gretchen fires. The rifle's report echoes through the woods like thunder, and the Sheepsquatch leaps to its feet and spins around, snarling as it faces their direction. Sam didn't see Gretchen's first round strike the beast, but given how good a shot she is, he assumes the bullet found its target. She reloads, fires again, and this time he sees the Sheepsquatch jerk back as the round hits its chest. Seconds later, crimson darkens the creature's white fur. The monster lets out a terrible scream then, the sound something like the cry of a mountain cat combined with a raptor's shriek, and it starts running toward them.

Gretchen reloads, fires again. Sam keeps his .38 trained on the monster, but although his instincts are shouting at him to shoot, he knows it's not in range, so he holds his fire. As the creature starts to pick up speed, Dean, Julie, and Stewart emerge from hiding and let loose with their shotguns. The blasts strike the Sheepsquatch on the left, tearing chunks out of its face, shoulder, and arm. This time its scream is one of pain, and it stumbles and goes down on one knee. Dean and Julie advance, firing again, but Stewart drops his gun. He's wearing the backpack that holds the white ash stake, and he shrugs it off, opens it, removes the stake from the crimson cloth it's wrapped in, discards the pack, and stands, the stake gripped tight in his right hand.

Dean and Julie continue blasting away at the creature, and the Sheepsquatch's screams become deafening. The entire left side of its body is covered with blood, and it falls to all fours now, apparently weakening. Sam can't believe the creature is going down so easily. Maybe it's not as tough as it looks. Stewart shouts that he's going in, and Dean and Julie stop firing. Stewart, a huge grin on his face as if he's having the time of his life, races forward, moving so fast he's almost a blur. Since the Sheepsquatch is on all fours, Stewart is going to have to try and stake it from the back, and while the stake is eighteen inches long, Sam isn't certain Stewart will be able to force it through the creature's hide and thick back muscles to reach the heart. When Stewart is within six feet of the Sheepsquatch, he releases a loud *yee-haw!* and leaps into the air, clearly intending to land on the creature's back. It's like he's a cowboy in an old-time western, preparing to mount his horse in the showiest way possible. But as Stewart descends, the Sheepsquatch spins around and lashes out with its right arm, swatting Stewart out of the air as if he's nothing more than an irritating insect. Stewart flies toward a sycamore tree and slams into it back-first. There's a horrible cracking sound of bones breaking, then Stewart bounces off the tree and falls to the ground, motionless. Sam sees blood on Stewart's clothes, and he knows that the creature managed to snag him with its claws when it struck him.

Julie lets out a wordless cry of despair and runs toward her child. Dean, face a mask of controlled anger, steps toward the Sheepsquatch, firing round after round into its body, the creature howling in pain and fury. Gretchen drops her rifle and races toward her brother, moving with the same uncanny speed as he did. Sam follows after her, running as fast as he can, but compared to her he might as well be standing still. She reaches Stewart soon after their mother, and as Julie kneels next to her son, Gretchen bends down, snatches the stake from his hand, turns, and races toward the Sheepsquatch, leaving Julie to tend to Stewart.

Dean ejects his last shell, and when he tries to fire his shotgun again, nothing happens. The Sheepsquatch rises to its feet, its white fur splashed with red all over its body, and it looks at Dean, hatred blazing from those too-human eyes. It shuffles toward him, snarling, claws raised and ready to rend flesh. Dean draws his hunting knife, fear in his gaze, but he stands his ground.

And then Gretchen is racing past him. She runs straight at the Sheepsquatch without hesitation and slams into its chest. The creature grabs hold of her and starts to claw at her back, but then it gasps, stiffens, and falls to the ground, carrying Gretchen with it.

Dean gets to her before Sam can, and he pulls her out of the Sheepsquatch's arms and helps her to her feet. The monster lies on its side, only a small portion of the white ash stake visible in its chest. Gretchen managed to almost bury the entire length of wood in the Sheepsquatch's body. He didn't know she was that strong. He's not sure even John Winchester could shove the stake in that far.

"You okay?" Dean says to Gretchen.

Sam reaches the two of them then, and even though he knows it's stupid, he's jealous that Dean got to her before he did.

"I think so," Gretchen says.

Dean takes her gently by the shoulders and turns her around to examine her back. The Sheepsquatch wasn't able to do much damage to her before she staked him, but it did manage to slash through her clothes and cut into the skin beneath. It's hard to tell without a closer examination, but from what Sam can see, the cuts look deep.

"I'll get the first-aid kit," he says. Julie brought a backpack filled with medical supplies, and Sam starts to head toward where she, Dean, and Stewart were hiding. But Gretchen steps forward and takes hold of his arm, stopping him.

"There's no need," she says. "I'll be all right."

"But you're cut," Sam insists. "And if that thing has any toxins on its claws…"

"I'm *fine*," she says. "Stewart's the one I'm worried about."

"It'll take more than that to put me down for good," Stewart says.

The three of them turn to see Julie and Stewart walking toward them. Julie has an arm around her son's waist to steady him, and he has an arm draped over her shoulders. His face and hands are scraped and bruised, and there's blood on his clothes, but Sam thinks he looks pretty damn good for a man who should by all rights be dead.

"Dude," Dean says, "how are you walking? For that matter, how are you even *breathing*? I heard your bones snap when you hit that tree."

"Guess it sounded worse than it was," Stewart says.

Dean looks at him for a moment before shooting Sam a quick glance. Sam shrugs as if to say, *Don't look at me. I don't understand it either.*

Julie and Stewart stop when they reach the others, and then all five of them turn to look at the Sheepsquatch. The creature hasn't so much as twitched since the stake entered its body, and Sam is certain—well, as certain as you can ever be when it comes to supernatural beings—that it's dead.

Julie reaches out with her free hand and squeezes Gretchen's shoulder. "I'm proud of you, honey."

Gretchen smiles. "Thanks, Mom."

Stewart scowls. "You got lucky. If we hadn't softened him up for you…"

"Shush," Julie says. "Don't spoil your sister's moment."

Stewart shushes, but he doesn't look too happy about it.

"I don't think he looks as squatchy as he used to," Dean says.

They return their attention to the monster's corpse, and Sam sees what his brother means. The body seems smaller than it was, and the fur isn't as thick. Its horns and tusk-teeth are also smaller, and as they watch, both teeth and horns continue to recede into the creature's head. Its tail retracts, too, and within moments, where a dead Sheepsquatch once lay there is a dead naked man. He's a skinny guy who looks to be in his late fifties, with short gray hair and thick stubble. His body retains all the wounds he suffered during the fight, which means he's pretty much a mess, and the end of the white-ash stake still protrudes from his chest.

"It's Braydon Albright," Julie says.

"The missing man?" Sam asks, and she nods.

"What was he?" Dean asks. "Some kind of shape-changer? A were-squatch?"

"I guess so," Julie says. "Only last time he changed, he couldn't—or didn't want to—change back."

"How'd he get like that?" Gretchen asks.

"No way to know for certain," Julie says. "Maybe he got cursed somehow. Maybe he made a deal with a demon to get the power to change. It doesn't really matter. All I care about is that the sonofabitch is dead."

Julie removes her hands from her children, steps toward Albright's body, and gives it a vicious kick to the head.

"That's for killing my husband, asshole."

"The gods of this town certainly have been busy," Dean said. Incident reports lay spread out on the table before him. "In addition to the murders—of which there are plenty—I've got at least ten suspicious 'accidents' here. One poor bastard was bitten by what witnesses said were 'several hundred venomous snakes.' Tell me that doesn't sound…" He trailed off when he realized Sam wasn't listening to him. His brother had his own stack of reports in front of him, but instead of looking at them, he was staring at the wall, his gaze unfocused. "What's wrong? A town full of warring gods not interesting enough to hold your attention?"

"Hmmm?" Sam frowned at first, but then his expression became apologetic. "Sorry. I was just thinking."

"Whatever it was, it wasn't about this case."

"I was thinking about the time Dad left us with the

Underwoods in West Virginia."

Dean frowned. "Why would you be—" He broke off as he realized why Sam would be recalling that incident now. "I get it. Was it any help?"

Sam shook his head.

"Too bad." Dean closed the report he'd been looking at and began stacking the others on top of it. "I didn't find anything useful. No patterns to the killings, no similarities in location, no family names that keep cropping up."

"Same here." Sam slid his half of the reports to the middle of the table, and Dean placed his stack on top of it.

The brothers sat on opposite sides of a round table in a small room. Despite the sign on the door that said CONFERENCE ROOM and the official-looking framed map of Illinois hanging on the wall, the coffee maker on the counter, the mini-fridge in the corner, and the vending machine stocked with snack cakes and candy bars told Dean this place was used primarily as a break room by the sheriff and his deputies. If Sam hadn't been there, Dean would've put some money into the vending machines and snagged himself a couple packages of sweet, sweet junk food, but it wouldn't be worth listening to Sam nag him about his diet, so he made do with a Styrofoam cup of black coffee that tasted like lukewarm ink-colored water. Sam had a cup, too, his doctored with creamer and sugar substitute, but after one sip, he'd given up on it. Smart man.

The door opened and a boyish-faced man with red hair cut close to his scalp poked his head in.

"Anything else I can do for you, agents?" the deputy asked.

At least this guy was young enough not to remark on their fake identities. He hadn't so much as blinked when they'd introduced themselves.

"We're good," Sam said. "Thanks."

"You've been a big help," Dean added.

The deputy grinned. "Happy to be of service," he said, and then closed the door.

Sam gave Dean a look. "'You've been a big help?' Really?"

"Everyone needs a pat on the head now and then." Dean took another sip of his coffee and grimaced. "So what's our next move?"

"We could talk with some of the victims' family and friends. Ask a few questions, see what they have to say."

The cheap office clock on the wall said it was after midnight.

"Little late for that," Dean said. "Besides, who would we start with?" He gestured toward the stack of reports. "Lot of names in those files."

"Yeah."

"I suppose we could hit a motel, catch some Zs, get started bright and early tomorrow," Dean said.

As far as Dean was concerned, one of the most difficult things about being a hunter was getting enough sleep. You never knew what kind of hours you'd be working when you were on a case. A number of supernatural predators hunted at night, but there were just as many who hunted by day or even around the clock. Plus, when you knew there was something nasty out there killing people, it was hard to justify taking a break to rest. What if someone was killed while you were sleeping? Sure, you weren't the one sinking fangs into a victim's flesh, but it felt as if you were responsible, at least partially. If you'd been stronger and more dedicated, you wouldn't have *needed* to sleep, and that poor bastard who'd died while you were snoozing might very well still be alive. But hunters were only human, and like anyone else, if they didn't get enough rest, they weren't sharp enough to do their job efficiently. And when it came to hunting, if you screwed up, you didn't get a reprimand from your supervisor or a bad performance review that would go in your permanent file. You lost your life—*and* the lives of anyone you were trying to help. It helped Dean to think of sleep as another tool in the hunter's arsenal. Like lore and regular weapons' practice, sleep prepared you to do your best on a hunt.

But although he was the one to suggest sleep, Dean wasn't sure it was the best course of action right now. The situation in Corinth was like nothing they had ever encountered before. It was an infestation of gods, gods who were fighting in the streets and killing each other, with humans as collateral damage. If they slept tonight, even if only for a few hours, how many people would have died by the time they woke?

"I don't know," Sam said. "I'm thinking we may have to put in an all-nighter on this one."

"I think you're right."

Sam gathered up the files, and the brothers left the conference room and headed for the main reception area. Deputy Big Help—the only person on duty since everyone else had been called out to the latest crime scene—sat behind the front desk. Sam and Dean returned the files, thanked him, and told him to make sure the sheriff knew they appreciated his cooperation. They started toward the double glass doors of the entrance, but just as Dean was about to push them open, he stopped and turned back around to face the deputy.

"One last thing: You know where we can get some coffee around here this time of night?"

The deputy opened his mouth to answer, but Dean cut him off.

"Not the stuff in your conference room. I'm talking *real* coffee."

The deputy looked crestfallen, and Dean realized he'd made the last pot.

"Not that yours was bad," Dean said quickly. "It's just that the Bureau has a policy of agents not accepting more than one free cup of coffee from local law enforcement. We don't want to, uh, be a drain on your budget."

The deputy cocked his head to the side, as if he were trying to decide if Dean was putting him on or not. Finally, he said, "There's a twenty-four-hour donut shop a couple blocks west of here. They have pretty decent coffee. Great chocolate-covered crullers, too."

"*Chocolate*?" Dean said.

"That guy was right," Dean said, his words muffled by a mouthful of donut. "These crullers are amazing!"

"I'll take your word for it," Sam said.

The brothers sat in a booth inside a twenty-four-hour restaurant named Doughnutz. Slogan: *You'll go nuts for Doughnutz!* They'd changed in the car, and now they were back in civvies. Comfortable clothes, awesome-tasting donuts—as far as Dean was concerned, the night was finally starting to look up. Now if they could just find a scuzzy dive bar with some extremely hot women in it… Dean sighed. Too bad they had to work all night.

Dean had ordered a half-dozen chocolate crullers, and he'd already downed two and was working on his third. He'd planned on saving the other three for later, but as good as they were, he wasn't sure he was going to have the willpower. Sam had passed on the donuts, but they both had large cups of coffee. They were going to need the caffeine.

Dean took a sip of his coffee, considered for a moment, and then shrugged. "It's all right, I guess. At least it's hot."

The place wasn't very large: a half-dozen booths, donut display case, register on the counter, kitchen in the back. A short man with a *huge* bushy black mustache worked the counter, and Dean tried not to think about the guy shedding mustache hairs all over the donuts. The man stood behind the register, wide-eyed and alert, as if he were anticipating a sudden rush of customers. Dean had a feeling Mr. Mustache would be waiting for a while. Right now, the brothers were the only customers in the place, and it seemed likely they'd remain so for some time to come.

The donut shop had free Wi-Fi, and Sam had brought his laptop in with him. He surfed the Net, searching for any lore that might apply to Corinth's god problem, while Dean enjoyed the hell out of his crullers. He'd learned long ago to take pleasure in the little things in life, because when you were a hunter, you had no idea when it was going to be your time to move on to that great donut shop in the sky.

Sam didn't take his eyes off the screen as he spoke. "How are you doing?"

Dean didn't have to ask what he meant. He was talking about the Mark. "Fine."

Sam glanced up at him quickly, but then he returned his attention to the laptop. *Wonder of wonders,* Dean thought. His brother had actually accepted his word at face value. No skeptical looks, no follow-up questions, no arguing. But the truth was he *did* feel fine. Of course, the power of chocolate-covered crullers made anything possible.

Dean polished off his last donut and washed the final bite down with a large drink of coffee.

"How about you?" he asked. "Anything?"

"I've found a few things," Sam said, "but I don't know how useful they are. In ancient myth, the Greek gods battled their forebears who were called the Titans. Remember them? The gods defeated the Titans and imprisoned them, taking their place as the rulers of creation. The Norse gods fought the giants of Jötunheimr, but in the end the gods and the giants died in a battle called Ragnarök, after which a rebirth took place, giving rise to a new group of gods. And of course there are lots of stories about individual gods fighting each other. It's a common theme among the world's ancient religions: gods battling to see who's stronger and decide who gets to rule…"

"Couldn't some of those stories have been based on real events, though? I mean, like one human warrior fights another, people exaggerate over the years as they tell the story, and *bam*! A few centuries later, you got yourself a myth about a couple gods duking it out."

"I'm sure that's how some of the stories started," Sam said. "But given what appears to be going on in this town, I'd say that at least a few of the myths got it right. Maybe not the specific details, but the basic idea."

"All right, let's go with that for a minute. If what's happening here *is* the same kind of thing that took place in the ancient world, why is it happening again? And why now, after so many thousands of years?"

"Maybe it's part of some kind of natural—or in this case, unnatural—cycle," Sam ventured.

"You mean like how cicadas only come back every seventeen years?"

"Yeah."

Dean shuddered. "Man, I *hate* cicadas. They look like flies that OD'd on steroids."

"So if it is a cycle, and we can figure out why it started up again—"

"Maybe we can figure out a way to stop it," Dean finished. "I don't suppose you ran across a set of instructions on how to wipe out a god infestation during your last search."

"Afraid not."

"Damn Internet. It's only good for porn and cute cat pictures." When he realized that Sam was giving him a Look, he hastily added, "Uh, not that I've ever *seen* any of those cats. I mean, c'mon—this is *me* we're talking about here."

Dean took another sip of his coffee and waited to see if Sam was going to make a comment, but all he did was smile, which was worse.

"So what do we do next?" he asked.

"Talk to some worshippers," Sam said. "They must know something about how these new gods operate."

Eventually, they were going to have to confront one of these gods. Dean knew it, and he knew Sam did, too. But they needed to learn as much as possible about the gods before they approached any of them, and the best way to do that was to talk to the poor schmucks who'd been dumb enough to follow these divine poseurs.

"Let's get to it."

The brothers stood, took hold of their coffee cups, and headed for the door. Dean tossed the empty bag that had held his crullers into a trash can, and they stepped out into the cold December night.

SEVEN

Geoffrey made sure to walk at least three steps behind Adamantine at all times. He'd gotten too close once, and she'd spun around to glower at him, literal sparks shooting from her eyes in anger. He'd stammered an apology, certain that he was going to be the next to feel the wrath of her lightning, but she'd merely glared at him before turning back around and continuing onward. Of course, he couldn't remain too far behind either, or she'd chastise him for that as well. He was learning that being a follower of Adamantine—a *surviving* follower—was all about maintaining the perfect balance. The problem was, you had to find that balance by trial and error. And where Adamantine was concerned, errors could be deadly.

Adamantine gripped the spear she'd taken from Wyld in her gauntleted hand and held it vertically at her side as she walked. She led a small procession along the sidewalk consisting of Geoffrey, the three followers of Wyld's she'd claimed, and three other people, all of them witnesses to her victory over the cat god. They'd been so impressed by her display of power that they abandoned whoever they were with and whatever they were doing, and rushed to join her followers. Not that she seemed any more interested in them—Geoffrey included—than a farmer trailed by a line of cheeping baby chicks.

It was cold tonight, and he wasn't the only one shivering. The others had winter coats, but most of them didn't have hats or gloves. They hadn't expected to be spending so much time outside, and they hadn't prepared. As a homeless person, Geoffrey was used to living with the weather, but even he was getting tired of the cold. Adamantine had said she wanted to build her temple—whatever *that* meant—but so far all she'd done was wander the streets of Corinth, seemingly at random. Far be it from him to question his god, but he was beginning to think that she was crazy.

Knowing that he was taking his own life in his hands, he stepped closer to her and said, "Mistress?" He had no idea if this was the proper form of address. Trial again, and if it turned out to be an error this time, he hoped it wasn't a fatal one.

She stopped, forcing everyone in the procession to come to a halt. She remained facing forward as she answered Geoffrey.

"What is it?"

She sounded irritated, but she hadn't electrocuted him yet, and he took that as an encouraging sign.

"Your people are cold. How much longer must we keep walking?"

Adamantine didn't respond right away, and Geoffrey feared that he'd somehow offended her deeply. When she finally turned around, he couldn't help taking a cringing step backward, certain that she was going to kill him for his insolence. But instead she looked at him quizzically.

"You choose to speak to me about the others," she said.

It took all Geoffrey had to make himself answer. "Yes."

"You attempt to intercede with me on their behalf."

"Yes."

She smiled slowly, as if an idea was forming in her mind.

"Then that means you are my priest."

Geoffrey tried to say something, but words failed him. After all, wasn't that what a priest or priestess did? Serve as an intermediary between a god and its worshippers?

"I… suppose I am."

"Good. Then tell the others it shall not be long now." With that, she turned back around and continued walking.

Geoffrey turned to Adamantine's other followers. "You all hear that?"

They nodded.

"Then let's keep moving."

Everyone continued walking, and although he was just as cold as before, Geoffrey was surprised to find that he felt warmer inside. When he'd woken this morning, he'd been homeless, but now here he was—priest to an actual, living, flesh-and-blood *god*. He shook his head in amazement. This had been a day of miracles for him, and it wasn't over yet. Who knew what wonders the rest of the night might hold?

"There."

Adamantine pointed to a large building with a glowing sign above the entrance that said TECHEDGE. Fluorescent lights illuminated an empty parking lot, the asphalt plowed clear of snow. New snow had begun to fall while they walked, just light flurries, but the slowly descending flakes looked beautiful in the blue-white wash of the parking lot lights. There wasn't much homeless folk liked about winter, but Geoffrey had to admit that it sure could be pretty sometimes.

"Is this where we're going to build your temple?" he asked, then belatedly added, "My lady."

She gazed upon the building, silver eyes shining, a broad smile on her face. She looked to Geoffrey like someone looking to buy a house who'd just discovered their dream home was for sale.

"When I said *build*, I was speaking metaphorically. I believe the word you would use is *repurpose*."

Without waiting for Geoffrey's response, she started walking toward the building with a brisk stride. Geoffrey turned to address the other followers. "We'll be inside and warm soon." *I hope*, he added mentally. Then he turned back around and hurried to catch up to his mistress, the other followers close behind him.

Adamantine had led them out of downtown and to a section of Corinth where a number of retail stores were located. The town was too small to have its own mall, but it had the usual fast-food joints, chain restaurants, and shopping centers. Geoffrey had never been inside TechEdge, but from what he gathered, they sold all kinds of technology there—TVs, phones, game systems, computers... *You Need It, We Have It* was their slogan. He wasn't sure why the place appealed to Adamantine. Maybe it was because with her silvery body, she kind of resembled a robot. Or maybe she was obeying some inner instinct that told her this was where she belonged. From what he'd seen since becoming one of her followers—and now her priest—it seemed she acted on instinct more often than not. Well, if it wasn't broke, why fix it?

A trio of compact cars sat in the store's side parking lot. They were all the same make and model, painted ugly green and white, with the words *TechEdge Geek Fleet* emblazoned on the sides. The store's interior lights remained on as an extra security measure, and as they drew closer, Geoffrey could see that everything inside—walls, floor, ceiling, display shelves—was white. Signs hung from the ceiling, indicating the store's different sections, and the registers and shopping carts were located up front. He knew the glass doors of the entrance would be locked since it was well after the store's 9 PM closing time, but Adamantine didn't slow as she approached the doors. For a moment, he thought she would use Wyld's spear to break the glass, but instead she placed her gauntleted hand over the metal lock. There was a brief flash of light, a soft crackle of electricity, and then the doors slid open. The followers, Geoffrey included, applauded their mistress. Adamantine acknowledged their appreciation with a slight nod, and then she walked into the store, Geoffrey and the others trailing after her.

The instant that Geoffrey stepped inside, he was struck by a wave of dizziness and his vision went gray. He feared he was losing consciousness for some unknown reason, but then his vision cleared, the dizziness abated, and he felt more or less normal once more. But now that he could see again, he realized he wasn't inside TechEdge. Instead, he stood in the midst of what appeared to be a vast, featureless desert that stretched in all directions as far as the eye could see. A blazing sun hung high above, set in a cloudless blue sky, wind blew rivulets of sand across dunes, and the heat was so oppressive it felt as if he were standing directly in front of an open blast furnace. Sweat began trickling down his face and neck, and he squinted his eyes against the glare and the wind. Adamantine and the others were here, too, and from the way they were looking around in confusion, and—in the case of the humans—protecting their eyes, he knew everyone else was experiencing the same reality as him.

Geoffrey stepped to Adamantine's side. "What happened? Where are we?"

"I... do not know."

For the first time since he'd met her, Adamantine sounded uncertain, and this frightened Geoffrey more than the sudden transition from night to day, cold to hot, and town to wasteland. Normally Adamantine was strong and sure of herself, and Geoffrey had come to rely on those qualities— qualities he himself didn't possess. She was a god, and if *she* didn't know what was happening, if she didn't know what to do about it, what did that mean for the rest of them, mere humans that they were?

One of the followers gave a cry of alarm and pointed. "Look! Something's coming!"

Everyone, Adamantine included, turned to see a mound of sand moving toward them at rapid speed. At first, Geoffrey didn't understand what he was seeing. Was it some kind of storm? But the longer he watched the mound approach, the more it seemed to him that what they were seeing was something moving *under* the sand, like a shark moving through water. When the mound had first been spotted, it was far enough away that judging its size was difficult. But as it drew closer, Geoffrey saw that it was larger than he'd first thought. Much larger.

Several of the other followers screamed, and all seven of them rushed forward to huddle behind Adamantine, begging her to protect them from whatever was coming. Adamantine ignored them, her attention completely focused on the advancing mound. Geoffrey saw no fear on her face—which reassured him somewhat—but she still seemed unsure what was happening, and he found no comfort in that at all. Now that the mound was closer—*too close,* he thought—he judged that it was the size of a city bus, and he could make out the sound of its passage beneath the sand, a soft *shhhhhhhhhhh* that was almost, but not quite, like rain. Some of the followers wailed in fear while others beseeched their god to save them, reaching for her, touching her silver body, almost as if they were trying to push her forward and make her confront the thing beneath the sand. Irritated, Adamantine sent a small burst of electricity crackling across her back to repel those who dared desecrate her physical form, and those followers cried out in pain and yanked their hands away from her.

The mound showed no sign of slowing as it bore down on them, and Geoffrey feared that it would hit them full force, sending them flying—bones broken, internal organs ruptured—as it continued on its blind, mindless journey. But when the mound was within twenty feet of Adamantine, sand exploded into the air, and Geoffrey threw his hands up in front of his face to protect his eyes. He heard the creature before he saw it—a loud *clack-clack-clacking* noise like a gigantic insect might make. As the sand began to settle, Geoffrey was able to make out the basic features of the thing. Not all of it was visible; the majority of its body still lay beneath the desert surface. But a third of it was above the sand, and what they could see resembled a gigantic worm or snake, but its body was covered with thick flexible plates of glossy black that looked like they were made from the same substance as a beetle's shell. It had no eyes or ears—at least none that could be seen—but it did have a mouth flanked by a pair of wicked-looking pincers that opened and closed rapidly, making that staccato *clack-clack-clack.* But those pincers weren't the only weapons the thing possessed. Six black tentacles—three on either side of the head—whipped the air, each terminating in a bulbous tip with a spine on the end, like a scorpion's stinger. The stingers glistened in the harsh sunlight, as if they were wet with venom.

Adamantine said something then, speaking so softly that it was difficult for Geoffrey to make out her words over the clacking noises the creature produced, but he thought she said, "Something is not right here."

He almost laughed hysterically at that. *Damn straight something's not right,* he thought.

The sand beast's body remained where it was, but all six of its tentacles shot toward Adamantine. At the last instant before the stingers struck her, she threw herself onto the sand, and the tentacles passed overhead, missing her entirely.

They did not, however, miss the followers who'd been standing behind her. Stingers pierced flesh, and screams of agony filled the air. A tentacle slammed against Geoffrey's shoulder as it buried its stinger in the person standing to his left, and the impact knocked him to the sand. His shoulder hurt like hell, but he was unharmed otherwise. The only other follower of Adamantine's to avoid being stung was one of the newer members, a twenty-something woman with red-dyed hair and multiple piercings in each ear. Like Geoffrey, she'd received a glancing blow from a tentacle as it sought another victim, only she'd been struck on the head. She now lay on the sand, eyes closed, body motionless. He hoped she was only unconscious, but as hard as the tentacle had struck her, he feared the worst. He tried to remember the woman's name, but it wouldn't come to him. Some priest he was. A good priest should know the names of everyone in his flock. He vowed to do better—assuming he survived.

The men and women with stingers embedded in their bodies shrieked in agony as the tentacles flexed, lifting them off their feet. Some grabbed hold of the tentacles and wrestled with them, attempting to free themselves, while others thrashed and flailed, in too much pain to do anything else. Their skin began to turn black as the venom coursing through their bloodstreams did its work, and one by one the victims began to convulse. Geoffrey stared in horrified fascination as their conditions swiftly worsened, knowing that there was nothing he could do to save them.

He turned his head and saw Adamantine had risen to her feet. She still held Wyld's spear, and of course her gauntlet remained on her hand, but she made no move to employ either weapon against the monstrous thing that was killing her followers, men and women who had pledged themselves to her, who had chosen her as their god. And what was she doing? Nothing—just standing and watching as her followers died. The despair he'd been feeling was wiped away by a burning anger, and he rose to his feet and ran over to Adamantine.

"What the hell is wrong with you?" he shouted. "You're a *god*! Save them!"

Adamantine whirled on him, eyes glowing a baleful blue-white, arcs of electricity wreathing her head like a deadly crown. Geoffrey didn't shrink back from her display of fury, though. He didn't care what she might do to him, he was too angry to care.

"Foolish man," she said, nearly spitting the words. "You do not understand what is happening."

"And you do?" he demanded.

"I think so, yes." She grew calm once more and returned her attention to her followers. Their skins had become as black as the sand beast's hide, and their convulsions had begun to lessen. Geoffrey knew it was only a matter of time now before they were dead, and not much time at that.

Adamantine continued watching her followers' agony for several more moments, and then—without warning—she spun around in the opposite direction and thrust her spear forward into empty air. There was a cry of pain, and then a new wave of vertigo struck Geoffrey and a gray curtain descended over his vision once more. When it lifted, the desert was gone, taking with it the blazing sun, the stifling heat, and most importantly, the sand beast. Geoffrey stood inside the

TechEdge store, not far from where the registers were located, and he was not alone. The five men and women who'd been poisoned by the sand beast lay on the tiled floor, their skins a normal color, with no sign that they'd been impaled by large, curved stingers. Strangers—six in all—stood or crouched next to them, each wielding TechEdge products as makeshift weapons. Laptops were the most common, but one man held a tower speaker like a club. He stood close to Geoffrey, the speaker raised as if he'd been preparing to bring it crashing down on Geoffrey's head. But something had interrupted him, and he looked surprised, confused, and more than a little guilty. The laptops the others held were cracked and broken, and Geoffrey realized they'd used the devices to hit Adamantine's followers over the head and knock them out. He doubted a single blow would've been enough to do the job. They'd probably had to strike their targets several times to put them down. Why hadn't he seen or heard it, though? And what had happened to the sand beast and the desert?

Adamantine stood in the same thrusting stance she had a second ago, only now her spear was buried in the belly of a man wearing a white mask with small rectangular slits for the eyes and mouth. He was dressed entirely in black—jacket, shirt, pants, socks, shoes, even gloves—and a stream of blood ran from the spear wound and pattered onto the floor. He gripped the spear with both gloved hands, muscles straining as he tried to pull it out of his body, but despite his obvious strength, he couldn't. Of the two, Adamantine was the stronger.

Geoffrey saw other people standing farther back in the store's aisles, maybe two dozen of them, and he knew if they decided to attack, there would be nothing he could do to defend himself. But the men and women—along with several children—appeared to be unarmed, and they made no move to come closer, simply hung back and watched, expressions unreadable. That was fine with Geoffrey.

He saw a small object lying on the floor next to where the masked man stood, and he realized the man must have dropped it when Adamantine had thrust the spear into his body. He walked over, picked it up, and examined it. It was a DVD case for a movie called *Sand Quake*, and on the cover was a picture of a handful of people firing shotguns at the sand beast, which had burst forth from a desert floor to attack them.

The masked man turned to Geoffrey. "Have you… seen that one? It's a great deal of… fun." His words came out as pained gasps so soft that Geoffrey almost couldn't make them out.

Adamantine sneered. "You want fun? *This* is fun!"

With a vicious yank she pulled the spear free of the man's body, spun it around in her hands, and then struck him on the side of the head with the butt-end. The blow knocked his mask off and sent it flying, and he fell to the ground and rolled on his back, hands cradling his wounded belly. His mask hit the floor, bounced once, twice, then slid to a stop. Geoffrey stared at the man's face, or rather, lack thereof. The skin was smooth and featureless—no eyes, nose, or mouth, not even a suggestion of them. Geoffrey didn't know who the man was, but he knew *what* he was. Given everything that had occurred since they'd entered the store—not to mention his unsettling appearance, and the fact Adamantine had attacked him—he had to be another god.

Several of the faceless man's worshippers moaned in despair at seeing their god brought low, but the guy with the speaker tower—the one who'd failed to bash in Geoffrey's skull with it—shouted, "My lord Masque!" He started forward, as if intending to go to his god's aid, but when he got to Geoffrey, Geoffrey stuck out his foot and tripped the man. He went down hard, his chin slamming to the floor. He groaned once and fell still. He'd dropped the tower speaker when he fell, and it had broken into several pieces upon impact with the floor. A shame, Geoffrey thought. It was probably expensive.

Adamantine straddled Masque and folded the sharp fingers of her gauntlet around his throat. Electricity crackled across the silver surface of the glove, and Masque writhed in pain.

"Geoffrey—fetch his mask for me like a good boy," she ordered, not taking her eyes off Masque.

Geoffrey hurried to do as she asked. He ran over to the mask, picked it up, and carried it to her. The mask looked like it was made of white plastic, but it was warm and gave slightly beneath the pressure of his fingers, as if it were covered with a thin layer of flesh. He found the sensation most unpleasant, and he was happy when Adamantine took the mask from him.

She looked at the smooth surface of the god's face. "You didn't say the words."

"Yes, I did." Despite not having a mouth, his words were somehow still audible. "You just… couldn't hear them."

"Because of the illusion."

"Yes."

Geoffrey tried to make sense of what had happened.

Masque was another god, that was for sure, and he had claimed TechEdge before Adamantine and her followers had arrived. When they'd entered the store, he'd somehow created the illusion of the desert and the sand beast—evidently inspired by the movie he'd been holding—to distract them while he and his people attacked. There had been no sand beast with stinger-tentacles, but there *had* been men and women using electronic devices as weapons in order to stop the invaders. And Masque had hidden behind the illusion to make himself invisible to Adamantine so he could attack her. Only it hadn't worked. After several moments, Adamantine had seen through his illusory scenario, and she'd gotten the upper hand. Maybe Masque's power didn't work as well on other gods, or maybe the illusion he'd created had been too big and complicated to maintain for very long. Whichever the case, he'd lost, and Adamantine had won.

A thought occurred to Geoffrey then. "Uh, if he doesn't have a mouth…"

"What we hear is an illusion of his voice," Adamantine said, "but since we *can* hear it, it's no different than the real thing."

Geoffrey didn't understand this part, but he decided it didn't matter. It wasn't as if Masque was going to get the opportunity to say much more.

"In the end there shall be One," she said, grinning in triumph.

Up to this point Masque's voice had been weak and breathy, but now he spoke with surprising strength and bitterness.

"Why don't you go take a flying—"

That was all he managed to get out before Adamantine

swung the bottom edge of his mask across his throat in a single swift motion. The flesh parted as if it were tissue paper and blood gushed from the wound. His body stiffened, and then relaxed. Almost tenderly, Adamantine replaced the mask on his face, and then stood. Within seconds, his body became suffused by a white light which then contracted into a sphere, flew toward Adamantine and merged with her. When it was over, there was nothing left of Masque—even the blood that had spilled onto the floor was gone.

Adamantine threw her arms out wide and tilted her head back. Twin showers of sparks shot upward from her eyes, and her laughter echoed throughout the store. Every device on the shelves activated at once, screens large and small flickering to life. Adamantine turned toward the screens closest to her, as did Geoffrey. The same image was displayed on every one: a young woman standing before an easel, painting. The woman worked furiously, applying colors so quickly that the picture seemed to emerge on its own from the canvas instead of being created one brushstroke at a time. The figure on the canvas was quite familiar to Geoffrey—it was Adamantine.

He looked toward his mistress and saw her gazing at the image displayed on the screen of a computer tablet. She walked close to it, reached out and—after a moment's hesitation—touched her fingers to the screen. And then, as if the physical contact was a trigger, the image winked out, not just on that screen, but on every screen throughout the store.

"What was that?" Geoffrey asked.

"I am not certain," Adamantine said, still gazing at the blank tablet. "But I think we may have just witnessed my birth."

* * *

Adamantine gave Masque's followers the same choice she'd given Wyld's: follow her or die. After seeing how easily she'd defeated their master, they all wisely agreed to become hers, and she spent some time having each of them kneel before her, just as Geoffrey had earlier that day, and Binding them to her. When that task was completed, she commanded several of her new followers to tend to those that had been wounded during the battle for possession of TechEdge. Of the seven followers she'd entered the store with, three—including Geoffrey—were relatively uninjured, one remained unconscious, and three were dead. She ordered that the dead ones should be taken outside and thrown into a dumpster. Geoffrey found this cruel, but he didn't say anything to Adamantine about it, mostly because he didn't want to end up in the dumpster himself. But also because he recognized that since she'd been alive for less than twenty-four hours, she hadn't had time to develop any funereal rites for her followers. Since he was her priest, attending to such details could well fall under his job description, and he decided he'd take care of it. Eventually. For now, the dumpster would have to do.

The unconscious follower was the redheaded woman with the multiply pierced ears. She was taken back to the employee break room where there was a couch she could lie on. One other follower was assigned to sit with her and see to her needs. Geoffrey had no idea if she would recover or if she'd join her dead companions in the dumpster before the sun rose. He considered praying to Adamantine for the woman to be healed, but he decided against it. Adamantine wasn't really that kind of god. She was more of a "vengeance is mine" type.

Once that was taken care of, she commanded her remaining followers—all of them—to go out into the streets, tell everyone they met how wonderful she was, and bring back new recruits to join the flock. She could've gone out herself to tend to this task, of course, but this method was more efficient, allowing new followers to be recruited more swiftly. And when competing with other gods in the Apotheosis, building one's power as fast as possible was the key to victory.

"I'm stronger now, and I've given each of you a spark of my power," she told them. "The people you speak to will respond to that spark. It will compel them to accompany you back here—provided you are also persuasive enough with your words. See that you are. There are three vehicles parked outside. You may take two of them. Fit as many as you can within them, and the rest of you shall walk. Now go."

Geoffrey was afraid that someone—especially one of the new followers—would question her, complain about going out into the cold, ask where they were supposed to find people to talk to at this hour of the night, whine about not being permitted to take all three cars. But no one said anything, and he was relieved. The keys for the Geek Fleet cars were in the manager's office; the followers took two, and headed for the front of the store, discussing who was going to get to ride in a car with a heater and who was going to be stuck hoofing it in the cold. Geoffrey didn't go with the others. Adamantine hadn't ordered him to stay behind, but he was her priest. His place was at her side unless specially instructed otherwise.

After the others left, Adamantine began walking through the store's empty aisles, and Geoffrey followed, maintaining the now customary three steps between them. The screens were blank now, the store quiet. Adamantine had deactivated them before giving instructions to her followers, perhaps because she hadn't wanted to speak over their din, or perhaps because she wished to conserve her power. She walked past displays for cell phones, laptops, desktops, keyboards, printers, DVD and Blu-ray players, sound equipment, video game systems, and flat-screen televisions, occasionally reaching out and brushing the silver fingers of her free hand across a plastic casing or a row of keys. She was silent as she did this, and Geoffrey wisely kept his mouth shut as she surveyed her new "temple." After a time, she spoke without turning to look at him.

"My kind mature rapidly, and as we grow in power so too do we grow in knowledge. I have defeated two gods since you Bound yourself to me, and I now know much more about myself and about the Apotheosis. For instance, I know that as we speak, other gods are battling out there— dozens of them—some dying, some living, only to die the next time they face an opponent. I can *feel* it happening, Geoffrey. I can sense the exchange of power that's taking place in this town, can feel others growing stronger, just as I have. Eventually, one of them will seek me out here. Or perhaps I will go out in search of them." She shrugged. "I will know what to do when the time comes. And I have learned something else—something of the utmost importance." Now she stopped and turned around to face Geoffrey. "I know who created me, who created *all* of my kind."

Geoffrey was taken aback by this statement. He understood that Adamantine and the other gods that had appeared in Corinth weren't omnipotent, but it hadn't occurred to him that they might have been *made*. He'd imagined them as some kind of natural phenomenon that had, for whatever unknown reason, simply sprung into existence one day. But of course they had an origin. Didn't everything?

"You're talking about the woman we saw on the screens, the one who was painting a picture of you," he said.

Adamantine nodded. "My power increased after I defeated Masque, causing me to have a vision—one you and my other followers shared."

"The woman we saw on the screens… she created you and the other gods? Is she a god herself?"

Adamantine frowned. "I do not believe so. I sense that she's a human, but one endowed with special ability to make myths into reality."

"A Mythmaker," Geoffrey said.

Adamantine smiled. "Yes! And I want you to find her and bring her to me."

Geoffrey was so surprised by Adamantine's words that he spoke without thinking. "Why? More to the point, why *me*?"

Adamantine's eyes flashed with anger at being questioned by her priest, and for an instant, Geoffrey thought she might kill him, but then the fire in her eyes dimmed, and when she spoke, she sounded almost apologetic.

"Instinct, I suppose. I *feel* that it's important to have her by my side. Perhaps she will be able to tell me more about my origins and how the Apotheosis works. Such knowledge could well prove to be the difference between victory and defeat. As for why *you*..." Her features hardened then. "Because you are my servant and I have commanded you to do this for me. That is all you need to know, is it not?"

Adamantine tried to hide it, but Geoffrey understood that she was afraid. Any being powerful enough to create Adamantine and the other gods could be powerful enough to destroy her as well. Better to send an expendable servant to fetch this woman than to place Adamantine's own existence at risk.

Geoffrey bowed his head. "Of course, my lady. How am I to find this woman? Do you *sense* where she lives?"

Adamantine's eyes narrowed, as if she suspected he was mocking her, but then she thrust Wyld's spear toward him.

"Take this."

Startled, he took hold of the spear, surprised to discover how light it was. Adamantine then removed the gauntlet from her hand and held it out to him.

"Take hold of the index finger," she said.

Geoffrey was afraid to do so. He'd seen electricity course through the gauntlet, enough power to kill him a hundred times over. But he reached out with a trembling hand and gripped the finger. The metal was much colder than he expected, and a shudder ran through his body.

"Break it off."

Geoffrey doubted he had the strength to do as she said, but he tried and the finger snapped off as easily as if he had broken a matchstick in two. Adamantine then slipped the gauntlet back onto her hand, her index finger now sticking through the hole he had made.

"Put it on."

His hand trembled even more this time, and he had to concentrate mightily to keep from dropping the metal finger. He managed to slip it over his own index finger, and he felt the metal contract slightly until the fit was snug. Now that it was on him, it didn't feel quite so cold, and if it wasn't exactly comfortable, he thought he could live with the feel of it on his flesh.

"I am connected to my creator, and after my vision I can sense her, and through *that*—" she nodded toward the silver-clad finger on his hand "—which is as much a part of me as my own heart, you shall be able to sense her as well. Use it to guide you to the Mythmaker, capture her, and bring her back to me."

Geoffrey flexed his fingers, fascinated by the way the gauntlet-finger followed the movement of his joints, even though it had no apparent joints of its own. "Can it zap people?"

"No. It will only lead you to my creator. I have made it so."

He nodded. He closed his eyes and tried to sense this person who was so powerful that she could wish up gods out of thin air. At first, he sensed nothing, but then—off in the distance—he felt more than saw a small pinpoint of light. He felt it calling to him, pulling him toward it. He opened his eyes, and the light was still there in his mind, a guiding beacon, ready to help him fulfill his god's desire.

"That's why you had them leave the third car, wasn't it?" he asked. "So I could use it."

Adamantine reached out and took the spear from his other hand. She smiled.

"I can't very well let my priest walk, can I?"

EIGHT

"After this, let's look for a case in California," Dean said. "Or maybe Florida. Someplace warm."

"Sounds good."

Sam guessed the temperature was in the lower thirties. Not all that bad, really, but it was dark and the wind was blowing, which made it feel colder. They'd been walking in downtown Corinth for the last half hour, and they were surprised at the number of people who were still out at this hour. Given the amount of both pedestrians and street traffic, if Sam hadn't known that Corinth was a small town, he would've thought he was in a city with a thriving nightlife. There was an almost electric hum in the air, a mounting tension that translated into nervous energy in Corinth's citizens. They moved fast and spoke even faster, as if they had a great deal to do and not a lot of time to do it in. It felt to Sam as if something was coming—something *big*—and whatever it was, he knew it wasn't good. Dean sensed it, too, and that awareness made both brothers anxious to understand more about what was happening here. If the god infestation was building toward an event of some kind, they had to stop it before it could take place. If they failed, Sam feared that people—dozens, hundreds, maybe even thousands—were going to die. They couldn't let that happen.

The brothers had no trouble finding people willing to talk to them about the new gods that had appeared in town. The problem was these people were all *too* willing. Each of them was thrilled to tell the Winchesters how *wonderful* and *life-changing* their god was. Unfortunately, their sales pitches were short on specifics and they mostly ignored whatever questions Sam and Dean asked. They'd spoken with eleven different people in the last thirty minutes but had learned little. Sam was frustrated, and he knew Dean was, too.

"These people seem almost desperate to find converts for their gods," Sam said.

"It makes sense that the gods are recruiting," Dean said. "After all, what's a war without soldiers?"

"*That's* a disturbing thought."

"Let me know if you want another. I've got a million of them."

The one thing they hadn't seen so far was an actual god. Their followers were only too happy to spread the good news about their gods—tales of miracles performed, battles fought and won—but if they knew where their chosen deities were located, they weren't saying. Sam guessed the followers were reluctant to tell potential recruits where their chosen deities could be found until they'd made a commitment to becoming a follower. Once that occurred, the recruits would be taken before the god and some sort of Binding ceremony would take place. Sam doubted it was merely a ritual, though. His guess was that the gods used their powers to literally bind their worshippers to them on a spiritual level, but whatever the nature of the bond was, it wasn't permanent. That explained why there were so many people out trying to convince others to worship their god—because it *was* possible to switch allegiances. At least for now. As this process came closer to completion, he suspected that a time would come when changing from one god to another was no longer an option. The game of spiritual musical chairs would be over, and when the music stopped, whatever god you were Bound to would be the one you'd stay Bound to. But until then, it was like a smorgasbord of deities—you could try a little of this, a little of that, and some of the other. Sam wondered what would happen to the worshippers when this process—whatever it was—finally reached its climax. Whatever happened, he doubted it would be good for the worshippers. The monsters who called themselves gods *were* predators, after all.

"Excuse me!" a woman called to them.

She looked to be in her eighties and stood in a doorway with a gray blanket wrapped around her for warmth. Sam thought they probably would've walked past without registering her presence if she hadn't spoken to them. The brothers stopped and turned to face the woman. The business whose doorway she occupied was a twenty-four-hour laundromat called Wash-o-Rama. From what Sam could see through the window, the place was empty, probably because no one had time to do laundry when spreading the gospel of whichever deity they served at the moment.

"Yes, ma'am?" Dean said.

She smiled, and Sam saw that she shivered beneath her blanket. The cold wasn't that bad—it was still above freezing, and the doorway protected her somewhat from the wind— but he figured the temperature was probably more difficult for older folks to take. She shouldn't be out here; she should be inside where it was warm.

"I was wondering if you boys wouldn't mind my talking to you for a bit."

Her voice was pleasant and soothing, and Sam found himself wanting to hear what she had to say. He'd experienced this same effect when speaking with the other worshippers, and he theorized that they'd all been imbued by their gods with a touch of magic, just enough to catch and hold people's attention while they delivered their sales pitch. The brothers' long experience with magic of various kinds helped them recognize what was happening, which in turn allowed them to resist it, but they still felt the effect when it took place. So not only did Sam want to hear what the woman had to say because he hoped he and Dean might learn something that would help them defeat the gods of Corinth, he also listened because he *wanted* to.

But before she could launch into her spiel, Dean said, "Let me guess: You want to tell us about someone very special who's changed your life completely and can do the same for us, if we'll just let him-slash-her-slash-it into our hearts. Sound about right?"

The woman looked momentarily confused, but then she grinned in delight. "Yes! That's it precisely!"

Dean clapped his hands together and spoke with exaggerated enthusiasm. "Well, that sounds exactly like what my brother and I have been searching for." He turned to Sam. "Isn't that right?"

Sam wasn't sure where Dean was going with this, but he decided to back his play. "Absolutely!" he said, doing his best to sound excited.

Dean turned back to the woman. "It's kind of chilly tonight, so what's say we skip the preliminaries? My brother and I are looking to be Bound, and if you can help make that happen for us, we'd sure be grateful."

"That's right," Sam added. He thought he understood what Dean was doing. The sooner they encountered one of the new gods—however dangerous that might be—the sooner they could start to more fully understand what was happening in this town and hopefully do something about it. Dean had gotten tired of waiting and was looking to speed things up. Sam wasn't sure it was going to work, though. Sure, there was a kind of feeding frenzy going on when it came to recruiting new worshippers, but wouldn't the woman expect them to want to hear *something* about her god before they made a commitment? But if their eagerness to get Bound right away bothered her, she didn't show it.

"I'm happy to help," the woman said. "Overjoyed, in fact! My god's temple is nearby. If you'll just follow me?"

Without waiting for a response, she stepped out of the doorway, and Sam and Dean moved aside to make room for her to pass. She started walking down the sidewalk, moving easily enough for someone of her age, and she drew the blanket around her more tightly as the wind kicked up. Sam and Dean followed close behind.

"Ma'am, you said you're taking us to your god's… temple?" Sam asked.

"Yes. They all seem to need a place where they can gather their worshippers together and keep them close. These places don't even have to be *real* temples, just someplace they can call their own. I'm not sure why they need these places, to be honest, but then, we're only mortals, and as such, we shouldn't question their ways, should we?"

"No, ma'am," Sam said. He knew the *they* she referred to were the gods, and in this case, *temples* sounded a lot more like *lairs* to him. Monsters often had places where they hid from the world until it was time to go out and hunt again, and many times these lairs were also places where their power was concentrated. If the gods fed off their worshippers' emotional energy, they would need to keep them nearby, and to do that, they'd need a central gathering place. And *temple* sounded so much nicer than *larder*.

The woman led them to the mouth of an alley, stopped, and with a half-bow gestured for them to go in ahead of her.

"The temple's in there?" Dean asked.

"No," the woman said. "The alley *is* the temple."

Sam exchanged a look with his brother. The woman might've said *temple*, but the two of them heard *trap*. In other circumstances, they would've drawn both their guns and knives before entering the alley, but they couldn't go in armed and still pass themselves off as new worshippers eager to be Bound. They were going to have to walk in with empty hands, keep their eyes open, and be ready for anything.

The alley was a large one, wide enough for a car to pass through, and Sam and Dean were able to enter it walking side by side. Some snow remained near the walls, but most of it had either been shoveled away or removed by cars passing through the alley. The woman followed after them and called out, "It's Molly! I've brought a couple new recruits, and they're fine-looking specimens, if you ask me!" She chortled at this.

Sam and Dean exchanged another look. Being referred to as *specimens* was never good.

The alley was dimly lit, but Sam could make out a pair of dumpsters, along with a number of small mounds that he assumed were plastic garbage bags. He couldn't figure out why the trash had been left in the alley like that when there were two dumpsters, neither of which appeared to be full. He also didn't understand why the bags had been spread throughout the alley instead of being piled up near the dumpsters. But as they moved farther into the alley, what he thought were trash bags stood up, and he had his answer. They were people, presumably Molly's fellow worshippers, who'd been sitting with their backs against the alley walls, arms wrapped around their knees, heads bowed. Sam hadn't recognized them at first due to the alley's lack of lighting. Which, he assumed, was exactly how they had wanted it.

He glanced over his shoulder and saw several men and women standing in the mouth of the alley, blocking the exit.

Another group shuffled together until they stood shoulder to shoulder at the alley's other end. *Trap,* Sam thought. No doubt about it.

Dean gave Sam a questioning look that said, *Time to cut the act and start shooting?* Sam replied with an almost imperceptible shake of his head. *Not yet.* They'd come here to meet a god, and until one showed up, they'd keep playing it cool.

Sam turned to Molly. "So what do we do now?"

Molly grinned, a hint of madness glimmering in her eyes. "All you have to do is stand here and wait. Karrion will be here soon."

"That's the name of your god?" Sam asked. "Karrion?"

Molly nodded.

"I'm not trying to criticize," Dean said, "but that sounds kind of dark, don't you think? Like, Darth Vader dark."

"Oh, no!" Molly said. "Karrion's wonderful! Just ask anyone here."

The crowd of worshippers chanted their agreement in unison.

"Great Karrion is merciful. He harvests others so that we might be spared."

"Like *that* isn't creepy," Dean muttered.

By this time, Sam's eyes had adjusted to the alley's dimness, and he was able to make out the worshippers' features. They were all old, their ages ranging from seventies to nineties, he estimated. Some wore hospital gowns and slippers, blankets serving in place of coats, as if they'd escaped from a medical facility of some kind. As near as Sam could tell, none of them were armed, but their gazes shone with cruel anticipation, and he knew whatever was going to happen next, it wasn't going to be good.

One of the dumpster lids began to creak open, and Sam saw hands, one pushing the lid upward, the other gripping onto the dumpster's edge. The hands were covered by leather gloves and were almost twice the size of normal human hands. With a hard push, the dumpster lid was thrown all the way back, and a figure climbed up and over the container's edge. It landed on the ground with a solid thump, and stood there for a moment, regarding the Winchesters. The man was massive, close to seven feet tall with broad shoulders, a barrel chest, and arms and legs thick as tree trunks. He wore a pair of long-sleeved coveralls with heavy work boots, and in his right hand he gripped a huge machete, its gleaming blade dotted with suspicious-looking stains. His face was like something out of a nightmare. Half of it was covered with scar tissue, as if he'd been horribly burned at one point, and the other half had no flesh at all, was nothing but white bone—empty eye socket, grinning teeth... He was mostly bald, with patches of wiry black hair that stuck out from his head like weeds. He gazed at the brothers impassively with his one eye, and Sam saw nothing remotely human there. No thought, no emotion, only emptiness as cold and endless as space itself.

Molly still stood close to them, and she leaned forward now and spoke in a soft, reverent voice.

"Karrion keeps death at bay for his followers, and in return for this wondrous gift, we bring him sacrifices.

Young sacrifices that are full of life." She chuckled. "I'd say you two fit the bill quite nicely, eh?"

Before either brother could respond, she backed away from them to join her fellow worshippers.

Sam looked at Dean.

"Well, we *did* want to meet a god," he said.

Karrion raised his machete and came stalking toward them.

Julie is in the kitchen making dinner: roast beef, baked potatoes, honey-glazed carrots, and apple pie with ice cream for dessert. Dean, Sam, Stewart, and Gretchen all offered to help, but she shooed them out, saying, *I like working alone in the kitchen. It's relaxing.* So the four teenagers are hanging out in the living room while Julie bustles about, singing softly to herself. Dean loves the domesticity of it all. Sam was only a baby when their mother died, but Dean remembers her—a little, anyway—and he finds Julie's simple enjoyment in preparing a meal comforting. Plus, the food smells *fantastic.* Because the Winchesters spend so much time on the road, they eat at fast-food joints and greasy-spoon diners a lot. A home-cooked meal like the kind Julie is preparing is quite a luxury, and Dean intends to enjoy every single bite.

The TV is on and tuned to an old western movie called *The Searchers.* Dean has seen it a half-dozen times before, but it's so good, he doesn't mind seeing it again. The sound's turned down low, so it's hard to hear the actors, but that's okay. He remembers almost all the dialogue. He's sitting on the couch next to Stewart and Gretchen is sitting on the other side of her brother, leaving Sam the armchair next to Dean. Dean would rather sit next to Gretchen, but at least Sam isn't, so that's something. He feels a momentary pang of guilt for competing with his brother like this—although so far neither one of them has gotten into the ball park with Gretchen, let alone reached first base—but he can't help it. They meet so few girls their age on the road. Besides, he *is* the older brother, so that should give him dibs, right?

"Your mom's really happy," Sam says. It's unclear whether he's speaking to Gretchen, Stewart, or both, but Stewart answers.

"We lost our dad to the Sheepsquatch a year-and-a-half ago. Since then all mom could think about was bringing the bastard down, you know?"

Dean thinks about their father's pursuit of the yellow-eyed demon that killed their mother.

"Yeah, we do," he says.

Stewart continues, "She tried everything she could think of to get him, but nothing worked. Not until—" Gretchen elbows him in the ribs, cutting him off. He glares at her, but says, "Until we got lucky."

Gretchen ignores her brother's glare and smiles at Sam. "That's why tonight's so special. It's like Christmas, New Year's, Thanksgiving, Fourth of July, and all our birthdays rolled into one! And I'm so glad you're both here to share it with us." Dean grinds his teeth in jealousy.

"Yeah, it's awesome!" Stewart says. "After all, we couldn't have done it without you!"

Stewart punches Dean on the arm as a show of enthusiasm, but the blow lands hard, and Dean winces. He's tempted to rub the spot where Stewart's fist connected with his body, but he doesn't want to look like a wimp, so he restrains himself.

"We were happy to help," Sam says, "but we really didn't do that much."

Sammy's right. Dean managed to put some rounds into the Sheepsquatch, and Sammy might have too, although given his distance from the target, there's a good chance he missed. But their contributions to the fight were minimal at best, and he's certain the Underwoods would've defeated the beast without them. Still, if they want to thank him and Sam, Dean isn't going to turn away their gratitude—especially when it takes the form of a mouth-watering home-cooked feast.

Julie calls from the kitchen then. "All right, everyone! Come help me set the table!"

Dean's the first to his feet, and he practically runs to the dining room.

It's dark. Pitch-black, actually. Dean can't see a thing. He has a headache and his mouth is so dry it feels like it's caked with sand. He's lying on what feels like cold concrete, and his hands are bound behind his back with what he thinks is a zip tie. His ankles are bound as well. Where is he? A garage? A shed? A basement?

He opens his mouth—dry lips peeling apart like two strips of sticky tape—and tries to call out for Sam, but his voice doesn't work at first. He swallows, breathes out, then in, and tries again.

"Sammy?" The word comes out as a rasping croak.

"I'm here." Sam doesn't sound much better.

Dean's not sure exactly how close Sam is, but his voice came from nearby. Without saying anything, both brothers start to squirm around on the floor until they bump into each other.

"Do you think the others are here, too?" Sam asks.

"I don't know."

They spend several minutes calling for Julie, Gretchen, and Stewart, but none of them answer.

"Maybe they're still unconscious," Sam says.

"Maybe they're not here."

Dean hears Sam thrash around on the floor. "Too bad we've got zip ties on us," Sam says. "Otherwise we could try to untie each other."

"And if the Underwoods used duct tape, we could try to tear it off with our teeth," Dean adds.

"You think they did this to us?"

"Maybe. The last thing I remember was washing down a mouthful of roast beef with a glass of milk, and after that, lights out. I figure we were drugged."

"It had to be in the milk," Sam says. "That way they could make sure they didn't accidently drug themselves."

A door above them opens, and fluorescent lights hum to life above them. Dean and Sam squint their eyes, and listen to shoes thumping on wood as people descend the stairs. *This is definitely a basement,* Dean thinks, and a second later his vision adjusts and he sees that he's right. The basement is unfinished, with bare concrete walls that match the floor. Metal storage shelves line the walls, filled with the tools of the hunter's craft: weapons, of course, but also spell ingredients kept in neatly labeled jars, and volumes of books, some new but most very old, likely handed down from generation to generation. There are notebooks, too, along with loose pages that have been bound with twine. Much hunter lore is recorded by hunters themselves and never published, like his father's journal.

"Sorry about that, boys. I hope your headaches aren't *too* bad," Julie says.

Any hope that it wasn't the Underwoods who drugged them vanishes upon hearing Julie's words. Dean shifts around until he's facing the stairs, as does Sam, and they watch as the Underwood family steps onto the basement floor, Julie first, Stewart next, Gretchen last. Stewart steps to his mother's right, Gretchen to her left. All three of them carry handguns, but they're holding them down at their sides—for now, at least. Dean sees sadness in Gretchen's eyes, but her brother is smirking, almost as if he thinks what's happening here is a joke. Julie's face is unreadable to teenage Dean, but if he were older, he would recognize her expression as one of resignation.

He's not surprised to find that he's scared—his father once told him that only a fool, a madman, or a dead man doesn't feel fear at one time or another—but he is surprised by how *much* he's afraid. He's hunted with his father lots of times, even gone a couple times by himself when his father thought the situation wasn't too dangerous and would make a good training session for him. And while he was scared on those hunts, he also felt prepared. He wasn't bound like he is now, he was armed, and his father told him whatever lore he needed to know to get the job done. One of the things that

Dean likes about hunting is that supernatural creatures have rules that govern their behavior. Rules that explain why they do the things they do, and rules that tell hunters how to kill them. For example, ghosts want vengeance for some wrong that was done to them in life, and to get rid of them, you need to find and burn their bones. As long as you know the lore, you know what to expect from a supernatural creature. But Dean knows there are no easy answers when it comes to humans. They're unpredictable, and that's what frightens him the most. Sometimes they can do truly awful things for what they believe are good reasons. There's nothing simple about them, and that's why, in a very real sense, Dean prefers monsters to humans. At least with monsters, you know where you stand.

"I'm sorry we have to do this," Gretchen says. "We wouldn't if it wasn't absolutely necessary."

"Speak for yourself," Stewart says. "I'm enjoying this."

Gretchen shoots her brother a dark look, and Julie says, "Hush." She doesn't look at her son as she says this, though. She keeps her gaze fastened on Sam and Dean.

"The three of us had some help taking out the Sheepsquatch," she says, "and now it's time for us to pay our bill." She raises her hand—it's an effort for her to do so—and points toward the far end of the basement.

Dean knows better than to turn his back on anyone who's holding a weapon on him, but he shifts around until he can look in the direction Julie indicates. Sam does, too.

Against the far wall, resting in a pool of shadow, is a high-backed wooden chair. An emaciated naked man sits there, bound to the chair by strips of white cloth wrapped around his stick-like arms, bony legs, and sunken chest. A huge set of deer antlers protrude from his hairless head, which lolls to the side as if he's unable to keep it upright, and his eyes are moist and black like an animal's. Parchment-thin flesh is drawn tight to his skull, and his mouth—which appears to have no lips—opens and closes rhythmically, as if he's trying to speak, but no sounds emerges. His skin is leathery and colored a mottled yellow-gray, making his race impossible to determine.

"Sam, Dean," Julie begins, "allow me to introduce you to the Lord of the Hunt."

Dean doubted it would stop the reject from an 80s slasher film, but he drew his .45 and fired at Karrion, hoping that bullets might at least slow him down. He fired three rounds into the god's chest, and while Karrion's body jerked with each impact, he kept coming.

"Keep him busy, Sam!"

"You got it!"

Sam started firing his 9mm at Karrion, and the god turned to face him. He took lurching steps toward Sam, the 9mm's rounds having no more effect on him than the .45's had. As Karrion drew close to Sam, he swung his machete. The razor-sharp blade hissed through the air, and Sam jumped back just in time to avoid having his throat sliced open. At the same time, Dean tucked his .45 back into his pants and drew his knife. He ran behind Karrion, crouched down, and with a vicious swipe to the god's left leg, midway between the hip and knee, cut his hamstring muscles. Blood gushed from the wound and

Karrion's leg, no longer able to support weight, buckled, and the god fell to the ground. Dean moved away just as Karrion swung the machete toward him, and the god's formerly impassive expression twisted into a mask of frustrated fury.

Dean switched his blood-slick knife to his left hand, drew his .45 once more, and aimed it at Karrion, who was furiously swiping his machete back and forth through the air, striking nothing.

"Good thing slashers like this never run," Dean said. "Otherwise, he'd have sliced and diced us by now."

Sam had his 9mm trained on the downed god as well.

"We'd better question him while we can," Sam said.

"Okay, but he doesn't seem like much of a talker."

Karrion tried to get up onto his uninjured leg, but Sam put a round into his right kneecap, and the god went down once more.

"Hey, you!" Dean said. "Bone-Face! What the hell are you doing in this town? You shouldn't exist anywhere outside of an old VHS movie. By the way, here's a tip: You might think about covering up that ugly mug of yours with a mask. It worked for Michael and Jason—all the greats."

Karrion fixed his one baleful eye on Dean and snarled.

"At least we know he can make sounds," Dean said.

"Can't say much for his vocabulary, though," Sam said.

Dean wasn't sure what to do next. He had no illusions that they'd defeated Karrion. No way a god would go down and stay down this easy. But it looked like they weren't going to get any information out of him. Most of the gods he and Sam had run into over the years were only too happy to talk your ear off. Sam theorized the reason for this was that some gods needed a connection with humans in order to feed off them, and one way to establish that connection was through communication. Dean figured it was because gods were jerks with big egos who liked to show off how superior they were. Either way, it usually wasn't hard to get a god talking, and once you did, they'd tell you more than they realized, often giving you the one tidbit of information you needed to defeat them. But not this guy. If Karrion *could* talk, he didn't seem inclined to.

Murmured chanting filled the alley then, and Dean realized that he and Sam had forgotten about Karrion's worshippers. That was a rookie mistake, one that could still get them killed. There were enough worshippers that if they were armed—or even if they weren't—and they attacked as a group, they might well prove a threat, even if they *were* older. Dean and Sam could try to fight their way free, but in order to succeed, they'd have to kill a number of the worshippers, maybe most of them, and Dean didn't want to do that. These poor suckers had been manipulated by Karrion, and they weren't responsible for their actions—at least, not entirely.

Dean turned to look at the worshippers, half-expecting to see them coming at him and Sam with whatever makeshift weapons they could get hold of—broken bottles, lengths of pipe, pieces of wood sharpened to deadly points... But instead they stood motionless, heads bowed, hands clasped, lips moving in unison, and he realized they were praying.

"Karrion, our lord, arise and kill... Karrion, our lord, arise and kill..."

"Crap," Dean muttered.

Several of the older worshippers moaned and went limp.
They would've fallen to the ground if those closest to them
didn't reach out and help them remain upright. Dean heard
a scuffing noise, boots sliding across the ground. He turned
back to Karrion in time to see the god rise awkwardly to his
feet. The left leg of his coveralls was smeared with blood, but
while the leg itself appeared stiff, it held his weight.

"He's healing," Sam said. "The worshippers are praying to
him, literally giving him their strength."

Dean sighed. "Of course they are." He'd known they
couldn't easily defeat a god, but this situation was looking
worse with every passing second. He hated going into battle
without any reliable lore. Humans were already at a big
enough disadvantage when going up against supernatural
creatures, but if you didn't have at least an idea of what your
opponent's weaknesses might be, you really were up the
brown creek without a paddle. He gripped his knife tighter
and aimed his .45 at Karrion's head. He had no intention of
running, and he knew Sam didn't either. They'd stand their
ground, fight, and hope that luck broke their way before—

A sound like a cannon blast erupted in the alley, and an
instant later half of Karrion's head disintegrated into bone
fragments, red mist, and gobbets of flesh. The god went
down on one knee, blood pouring from his ravaged head
to patter on the ground like crimson rain, but he didn't fall.

A rough, gravelly voice followed the cannon blast. "If you
boys know what's good for you, you'll stay out of my way."

Dean and Sam turned in the direction of the voice. A man

stood in the mouth of the alley, big and tall like Karrion, and Dean knew at once that they were looking at another god. His head had been shaved almost all the way down to the scalp, leaving only a covering of black fuzz. His face was clean-shaven, with a broad nose, a prominent, square jawline, and an aggressively jutting chin. He wore a tight black muscle shirt which displayed arms so exaggeratedly swollen that Dean didn't see how he could move them, along with green fatigue pants and black military-style boots. He held an oversized weapon in a two-handed grip, its quadruple barrels smoking. It looked something like a cross between a double-barreled shotgun—with an extra pair of barrels—and an elephant gun, and even though the lighting was dim in the alley, the gunmetal gleamed as if it produced its own light. As the god moved into the alley, a number of followers entered behind him, maintaining a distance, probably as much from wishing to remain out of the line of fire as respect for their god. These worshippers were mixed in terms of age, gender, and race, although there weren't many old people in this group. All of them had guns—pistols, rifles, shotguns—but they carried their weapons down and at their sides. Dean had no doubt they would quickly raise them and begin firing if their god commanded it.

The brothers were even farther up the brown creek now, Dean thought.

NINE

Paeon stopped in front of the examination room door, but he made no move to open it.

"This isn't working," he said.

Lena nearly bumped into him when he stopped. For an instant, she swayed on her feet, a mild wave of dizziness briefly taking hold of her. She'd been drinking coffee to keep awake, and she'd reached a point where she was equally exhausted *and* wired. It was a strange state to be in. She felt disconnected from what was happening around her, and everything seemed more than a little unreal. Then again, she was working as an assistant to a god of healing who—as she'd discovered—was also a god of illness when he so wished. She should be more surprised that anything felt even close to real now.

"What's wrong?" she asked.

"This is going too slow." Frustration was evident in Paeon's voice.

"You've helped many people tonight. Even you can only work so fast. Perhaps you need a rest?"

She wasn't certain that beings like Paeon required rest. Aside from his frustration, he seemed as full of energy as he had when he'd walked into her practice. He hadn't eaten or drank, not so much as a nibble on a snack cracker or a sip of water, but it was possible that even if his body didn't tire, his mind might.

He turned to face her, scowling. "I do not need rest."

His voice was low and angry, and Lena tensed, expecting to be punished once more. She was relieved when Paeon made no move to reach for his caduceus.

"Then what's wrong, my lord?" She hoped her use of the honorific would keep him from becoming angrier with her. "You've helped dozens of people tonight, and in return, each has pledged him or herself to you. And you've fended off challenges by three other gods."

Blight had been the first god to attack Paeon, and after him had come Silence and then The Degrader. The latter two gods gave Paeon just as much trouble as Blight had, but in the end he had triumphed over them and claimed most of their worshippers as his own. As far as she could tell, the Apotheosis was working exactly the way it was supposed to, but obviously Paeon didn't think so.

"So far, all I have been doing is *reacting*," Paeon said. "Someone comes to me ill or injured, and I heal them. Gods appear to challenge me, and I fight them. One cannot achieve true Apotheosis through passivity. One must be *aggressive*."

As an oncologist, Lena understood the difference between passive and aggressive treatment. "How does one heal aggressively, my lord?"

Instead of answering, Paeon opened the door to the examination room and entered. Lena followed.

An attractive woman with straight, light-brown hair, black-framed glasses, and hoop earrings sat on the examining table. She'd removed her winter coat, as well as her shirt, and she now wore only boots, jeans, and a white tank top. She had a striking tattoo on her upper arm—a highly detailed, realistic rendering of an Indian elephant head, with swirling, interlocking designs made of blue lines on top of pinkish-purple hide. As a physician, Lena wasn't a fan of tattoos. As far as she was concerned, the risk of infection was too great. But she had to admit that this one was spectacular. But as she and Paeon approached the woman, Lena thought she'd been too hasty in her appreciation of the elephant. Now that she was closer, she could see the skin around the tattoo was red and swollen.

Paeon gave the tattoo a bored glance, then looked at the woman and forced a smile.

"What's your name?" he asked, voice flat, as if he didn't care what the answer was.

"Tera," she said, her tone uncertain. She looked at Lena, and Lena gave the woman what she hoped was a reassuring smile.

"Your tattoo is bothering you," Paeon said.

Tera nodded. "I had the last work done on it a couple days ago, and everything seemed fine. I've gone to the same shop lots of times, and I never had any trouble before, but last night it started itching and…" she trailed off.

"I can relieve your discomfort," Paeon said, "but in return, you must swear allegiance to me and come when I summon you. Do you agree to this?" He spoke the words without enthusiasm, like an actor who'd grown bored with his role.

"Yes. If half the things people say about you are true—"

"Everything they say is true," Paeon interrupted. "Now please hold still." He removed the caduceus from his pocket and touched it to the woman's tattoo. The mystical object glowed with golden light, but instead of healing the woman, she drew in a sharp breath, as if the caduceus's touch hurt her. Paeon frowned and concentrated harder. The caduceus's glow grew stronger, and in response the woman screamed. She pulled away from the caduceus and slapped a hand over her tattoo as if she'd been burned.

Lena didn't understand what had happened. Had Paeon, in his irritation, accidently harmed the woman instead of healing her? She experienced a momentary urge to take hold of Paeon's arm and pull him away from the woman to prevent him from doing any more damage to her, but she hesitated, fearing how the god might react to her interference in his current mood. Paeon seemed more curious than angry, though. He gently took hold of the woman's wrist and removed her hand from her shoulder. The flesh was now healthy, but the tattoo was no longer an image of an elephant. The ink's shape was rearranging, its colors transforming. A new image appeared, that of a young woman standing in front of an easel, painting what looked like a picture of Paeon.

Tera grimaced in pain the entire time her tattoo was changing, but when it had finished, she breathed a sigh of relief, as if the pain had eased. She then stared in wonder at the new image depicted on her skin.

"Who is that?" she asked. Then she looked at Paeon. "She's painting *you*, isn't she?"

Paeon smiled as he leaned close to examine the image. "Yes, she is. How interesting."

After a moment, he leaned back and turned to face Tera. "Please accept my apologies. This is—" He looked at Lena. "What do you call an unintended consequence of medical treatment in your nomenclature?"

"A side effect," she said.

He nodded then turned back to Tera. "Yes. I shall be happy to restore the original image."

He extended the caduceus toward the woman's arm once more, but she held out a hand to stop him.

"Please don't! I'd like to keep it. It's... special." She gazed at the new image with an almost dreamy smile. "It means I belong to you now."

Paeon didn't disabuse her of this notion, and she donned her shirt and coat. Before she left, she promised to tell everyone she knew about Paeon, and then she walked out of the examining room, rubbing her upper arm through her coat as she went.

When she was gone, Paeon closed the door behind her and turned to Lena. He looked invigorated.

"What was that all about?" Lena asked.

"As I defeat others of my kind, I grow in power. The caduceus is an extension of that power, and it used that woman's tattoo to send me a message: an image of my creation."

Lena should've been surprised to learn that Paeon had a creator—and a human one, from the look of it—but she was too overwhelmed with jealousy to care about that now. *She* was his assistant, his second-in-command, his… *priest*. Yes, that's what she was. Paeon's priest. No one else could replace her. She wouldn't allow it!

As if sensing her feelings, Paeon tightened his grip on her shoulders and leaned his face closer to hers. "Calm yourself. I do not fully understand what this woman…" He paused and cocked his head, as if listening to a voice only he could hear. "This *Mythmaker* is. But I sense that she is the key to my defeating the other gods. Before we entered this room, you asked me how one heals aggressively. The answer is simple: with preventative treatment. Instead of waiting for patients to come to me, I shall go out into the streets and find them myself. And rather than simply healing what's wrong with them, I shall make them permanently strong and healthy—resistant to all disease and injury. Then, when the final battle occurs, I shall have an army of unbeatable soldiers!"

Lena understood. Up to this point, Paeon had been treating symptoms of a disease called human frailty. But by transforming people into ultimate humans—strong and super-healthy—they would no longer be weak and vulnerable. That sounded marvelous to her. What didn't sound so great was this "final battle." She intended to ask him about it, but before she could, he leaned forward slightly, his unearthly blue eyes boring into hers.

"But those soldiers won't be enough. I shall need my creator as well. I need you to find her and bring her to me, Lena. You are the only one I can trust to accomplish this."

She felt his will reaching out to her, urging her to comply, and she knew that even if she wanted to say no—and she did—she couldn't. Not anymore. He'd become too powerful.

He went on, "This is a necessary duty, Lena. I am not sure why, but I sense that if I do not have my creator with me when the final battle is finished, even if I have defeated every other god in this town, I shall fail. Is that what you want?"

"No," she whispered. She didn't care about his achieving Apotheosis and becoming a true, immortal god as much as she cared about his ability to heal people. If he continued to grow in strength, who knew what the extent of his powers might eventually be? He could conceivably make the entire human race into a stronger, healthier, long-lived species. He could fulfill the ultimate wish of every doctor—to make the practice of medicine unnecessary and obsolete. To make that happen, she'd do almost anything.

"Then you must bring the Mythmaker to me."

He released her shoulders and removed the caduceus from his pocket. He extended it toward her and gently touched the tip of one wing to her forehead. Golden light flared briefly, and then died as he pulled the object away.

"I… don't feel any different. What did you do?"

"I believe the gods who have come to life in your town—myself included—have a special link to our creator. This is why the caduceus was able to show me her image once I became strong enough. The caduceus is able to extend this link to you, enough so that you should be able to sense her location and find her."

At first she didn't believe Paeon, but then an image of a house she had never seen came to her. She wasn't certain, but she thought she'd be able to find it, as long as she concentrated on this image.

"Why send me?" she asked. But before he could answer, she said, "Wait. Let me guess. You may have become stronger, but you're not confident that you're strong enough to face the Mythmaker yet."

He didn't answer. He didn't have to.

"Now go, and go swiftly," he said. "It's possible that other gods will soon become aware of the Mythmaker's existence too—if they haven't already—and they will dispatch their servants to retrieve her. You must get there first."

Without another word, Lena turned and ran down the hallway.

Renee stood in front of a blank canvas—the same one she'd been painting on for the last couple weeks. The paint on her palette was almost dry, and the brush she held badly needed to be cleaned, its bristles clumped and matted. She stared at the white surface before her, body trembling and weak, eyes tired and burning. Her head throbbed and her pulse pounded in her ears. She desperately wanted to get some sleep, couldn't remember the last time she'd laid down in her bed and closed her eyes, but she couldn't make herself step away from the canvas. When the—she supposed the only word for it was *compulsion*—to paint strange beings had begun, it had been manageable at first. She'd felt compelled to paint two, maybe three a day, and she'd been able to work her painting around classes, eating, and sleeping. But as the days went by, the compulsion had worsened, and she'd begun skipping classes and meals, and sleeping less. It had gotten so bad the last couple days that she hadn't done anything else *but* paint; one character after another, as fast as her hand could move. But she'd started slowing down in the last few hours, and now that her latest creation—a woman wreathed in flame whom she'd dubbed Flare—had vanished from the canvas, she waited for the next image to gel in her mind so she could begin getting it down in paint but, for the first time in weeks, nothing came to her.

She was afraid at first. Was something wrong with her? But as the moments stretched on without her hand lifting the brush to the canvas, she felt herself beginning to hope. Maybe, just maybe, it was over. She let out a shaky laugh. She could put the brush down, go into the house, fix herself something to eat. She could take a shower. God, how long had it been since she'd cleaned herself up? Or better yet, she could stagger up the stairs, go into her bedroom, flop face-down onto her mattress, and sleep for a week. Better yet, a whole month.

With a trembling hand she dropped the paint brush onto the palette, not caring that it would be ruined if she didn't clean it. She had other brushes. Right now what she needed— desperately so—was sleep. When she finally woke, she hoped her mind would be clearer, and she would be able to make some sense out of all this. Why had she felt such an overwhelming need to paint all these weird people, and—strangest of all— why had their images disappeared the moment she'd finished them? A terrible thought drifted through her mind then. Maybe she hadn't painted anything. Maybe there never had been any fantasy characters, and if that was the case, then none of them had ever disappeared. Maybe she'd imagined it all. Or worse, maybe it was some kind of hallucination. If so, did that mean she was mentally ill?

She didn't know what time it was, but it felt late. She considered rushing inside, waking her parents, and telling them she was afraid she might be crazy. But as much as she longed for her parents' reassurance, she didn't want to frighten them. One thing was certain: She was so exhausted she wasn't thinking straight. Sleep first, worry about mental health later, she decided. Now that she had a plan, she felt better, and she started toward the door that led into the kitchen.

She stopped when she heard the garage door begin to rise.

Geoffrey hadn't been behind the wheel of a car for some time, but he was pleased to discover that his driving skills hadn't atrophied. The TechEdge Geek Fleet car was a tiny cracker box of a vehicle, with an engine that made a *zeeeeeem* sound as the car moved through the streets of Corinth. But even though the engine didn't sound powerful, the car was a peppy little thing, and it didn't take him long to reach the Mythmaker's house. At least, he assumed it was the right house. The magic of the gauntlet finger Adamantine had given him had led him here, guiding him as if he were in some sort of trance, and while he had no reason to doubt its power, there was nothing about this house and its neighborhood to indicate that a being who possessed the ability to bring new gods into existence lived here. The house lay at the end of a suburban cul-de-sac: two-story dwellings with small yards, a tree or two in the front, privacy fences in back. Several inches of snow blanketed lawns and covered roofs, and most of the houses were decorated for the holiday season, although some of the decorations were more atypical than others. One home had an image of a large black bird painted on the white garage door, while another had dozens of knives hanging from a small tree in the front yard. There were no streetlights in this neighborhood—the residents probably didn't want to have to deal with the glare of fluorescent lights when they were trying to sleep, Geoffrey figured. But most of the houses had their front porch lights on, and that provided Geoffrey enough illumination to work.

He parked the Geek Fleet car in front of the Mythmaker's house, turned off the headlights and the ignition, but instead of getting out right away, he sat there for a moment and looked at the house. He'd had a home like this once. His had been a one-story ranch in a different neighborhood, but being here now and seeing these houses brought back memories: of a time when he hadn't been homeless, when he'd had a job and a wife. Good memories, but sad ones, too. God, how he missed Ellen.

You're not homeless any longer, he thought, *and you're not alone, either.* He was Adamantine's priest, and she had sent him on a vital mission, one that she trusted only him to accomplish. For the first time since he'd been laid off from the machine shop, he had a job, and he was determined to do it to the best of his ability. No matter what, he would not let down his god.

He got out of the car and started toward the Mythmaker's house.

The piece of Adamantine's gauntlet that he wore on his index finger had caused him to see the Mythmaker's location as a pinpoint of light in his mind. But now that he was close to the Mythmaker, the light shone so bright that he had difficulty seeing. He squinted in reflex, but it didn't do any good. The light was within his mind, and it would remain visible to him even if he shut his eyes tight. He wasn't certain whether he should attempt to enter through the front door or the back, but the blazing light in his mind pulled him toward the garage door instead. He walked up the driveway and stood before the garage door, wondering how he was going to get in. There was no outside keypad to operate the opener, and even if there had been, he had no idea what code to input. Should he try to lift it on his own? Would it even open that way? He didn't think so, but the light was so intense now that he was blinded. The Mythmaker was on the other side of this door—he could *feel* it! If only he could… His right hand reached out of its own accord and touched the gauntlet's fingertip to the door's surface. A tiny spark flared, and then the door began to retract.

He remembered what Adamantine had told him about the finger. It wouldn't grant him any of her electrical powers, but it would lead him to the Mythmaker. Evidently, *leading* meant it would deal with any barriers that might stand between him and his goal. Good to know.

The instant the door began to rise, the light in his mind winked out, and he could see normally again. When the door rose high enough, he crouched down, passed beneath it, and entered the garage. Once inside, he straightened and looked around. There were two cars parked inside, along with some lawn equipment and other junk stored there. But what drew his attention was the corner where a small painting space had been set up—easel, canvas, worktable with tubes of paints and jars of brushes on the surface. Even though the gauntlet's light no longer blazed within his mind, he could sense the power emanating from the area, and he knew at once that he'd found the place where the Mythmaker worked the magic that brought gods to life. The Mythmaker herself—he was surprised to see it was a young woman who looked like she was barely out of high school—stood near the inside door, staring at him with tired, bleary eyes, as if she wasn't certain he was really there. He knew he had to grab her fast before she could make noise and wake whoever she lived with, but now that he was here, he wasn't sure how to go about it. It wasn't as if he'd ever abducted anyone before.

"Who are you?" the woman said, her voice sleepy. It sounded as if she could barely keep herself awake.

Geoffrey was surprised by her question. He'd expected her to scream for him to get out of her garage, not to ask his name.

"I'm Geoffrey," he said.

"Hi, Geoffrey. I'm Renee Mendez." She gave him a faint smile, but it fell away quickly, as if holding the expression took too much effort. "Are you real or am I dreaming?"

Geoffrey wasn't sure how to answer. "Uh, as far as I know, I'm real." This was not going at all how he'd anticipated. He'd thought he would have to run in, grab hold of her, and carry her to the car, all the while trying to keep a hand over her mouth to prevent her from alerting anyone to what was happening. But she was so tired, she seemed only partially aware of his presence, and she certainly wasn't disturbed by it. Since she appeared to be in a talking mood, he decided to go that route. "I've been sent by one of your… creations. She's a silver-skinned woman who calls herself Adamantine."

Renee thought for a moment, her eyelids almost closing and then opening again several times. He wouldn't have been surprised if she'd laid down on the garage floor, curled up, and went straight to sleep.

"I remember her now. It seems like a long time since I painted her." She frowned. "Wait a minute. She *sent* you? You mean she's *real*?" The thought seemed to wake her up a bit, although she still sounded groggy.

Geoffrey nodded. "Yes, and she would very much like to meet you. She sent me to bring you to her."

Renee stared at him for a moment, as if she were struggling to process what he'd told her. "Real," she said again, and Geoffrey nodded once more. Her brow crinkled in thought. "But if *she's* real—"

Geoffrey could guess what her next thought would be. If Adamantine was real, then her other creations might be, too. He didn't want her thinking about any of the other gods she'd made, though. Adamantine had said that some of them would become aware of the Mythmaker just as she had, and they would also send servants to get the girl. He needed to take Renee away from here as fast as he could, before any of the other servants arrived.

"Adamantine is grateful that you gave her life, and she wants to thank you in person. She's *so* excited to meet you."

Geoffrey hated lying to Renee. As near as he could tell, she had no idea that she possessed the power to bring gods to life and wasn't aware that she had done so through her paintings. She knew nothing about the Apotheosis and her part in it, and while Adamantine had said she only wanted the woman for whatever insight she could provide, Geoffrey feared it was more than that. Could any of the gods become the One while their creator still lived? He was tempted to turn around and leave right now, get in the Geek Fleet car, head out of town, and keep on driving. But he knew that even if he could bring himself to disobey Adamantine's commands—something he wasn't sure he could do anymore—some other god would get hold of Renee. Regardless of what he did, the young woman was doomed. And if that was the case, then she might as well die for Adamantine as for any other god.

He stepped between the two cars until he reached her, and when he did, he took hold of her hand.

"Come with me," he said. "It's not every day that an artist gets a chance to meet one of her creations in the flesh."

She looked at him with a trancelike expression for a moment, eyes bloodshot and red-rimmed. At last she gave him another faint smile. "Very true," she said. "Okay, let's go."

She didn't make a move so Geoffrey continued holding onto her hand and led her out of the garage without bothering to close the door behind them. Renee wasn't wearing a coat, but the cold night air didn't seem to bother her as they stepped onto the sidewalk and continued toward the Geek Fleet car. When she saw the car, she said, "Do you work on computers, Geoffrey?"

He ignored her question and helped her into the passenger's seat. He buckled her in tight, and before he could close the car door, her eyes were shut and she was snoring lightly. He closed the door as gently as he could, then walked around the front of the car, got behind the driver's seat, closed the door, and started the vehicle. She stirred a little when the engine started making its *zeeeem*ing sound, but she didn't waken. Geoffrey put the car in gear and pulled away from the curb, a huge smile on his face.

He'd done it! And best of all, he'd managed to do it without having to get rough with the girl or hurt her. He knew he was being a hypocrite since Adamantine—assuming she managed to be the last god standing in the end—would most likely kill Renee anyway. Considering the girl's probable fate, not to mention his part in it, his relief that he'd been able to treat her kindly was laughable. In a very real sense, he would be just as much her killer as Adamantine would. Still, he'd been able to spare her some pain, and that had to count for something.

He couldn't bring himself to believe this, though, and as he drove out of the cul-de-sac, the Mythmaker belted into the passenger seat and sleeping, his smile fell away.

As Lena approached the house, she passed a motorcycle parked on the street outside, but she was too focused on following the mystic compass in her head to pay much attention to the bike. She pulled her Honda Accord into the driveway, parked, and turned off the engine. The garage door was up, and the lights inside were on. She took this as a less than encouraging sign, especially this late at night.

She got out, closed the car door as quietly as she could, then stood there for a moment, uncertain. She had no reason to doubt Paeon's power, but now that she was here, what if this wasn't the right house. It *felt* like it was, but how could she be sure?

"Who are you?"

She realized then that someone was in the garage, but it couldn't be the Mythmaker. The voice belonged to a male. A moment later, he stepped out onto the driveway, and she got a good look at him: probably early twenties, lean-bodied, with long greasy black hair and pale acne-scarred skin. He wore a jean jacket over a black T-shirt, blue jeans, and sneakers. He carried a length of metal pipe in his right hand, and around his neck he wore a small animal bone on a thin strip of leather. The bone seemed to glimmer with internal light, and Lena guessed it was a token from his god, probably an item he'd been given to help lead him to the Mythmaker.

Although he'd demanded to know who she was, he didn't wait for her answer. He continued coming toward her, eyes shining with an almost feral gleam, teeth bared in a snarl, hand clasping his makeshift weapon tight. The boy was thin, but he was significantly younger than she was—not to mention taller. Lena had no training in self-defense, had never been in a physical fight before in her life, and she was afraid.

"Ravage sent me to claim the woman. You can't have her."

The boy's voice was quiet, low, and dangerous. He kept his gaze fixed on hers as he approached, not running, simply walking with a brisk, confident stride that she found intimidating. As he drew near, he raised the pipe as if it were a club and bared his teeth like an animal.

For a second Lena stood frozen, but then her survival instincts kicked in. She might be shorter than this boy and have a couple decades on him, but she was also a doctor, and that meant she was an expert on human anatomy. She knew the body's strengths, and she knew its weaknesses. Instead of waiting for the boy to strike, she stepped forward and punched him in the center of his chest, where his xiphoid process was. She was careful not to hit too hard; too much pressure, and it was possible to drive the bone into the heart. She only wanted to cause the boy pain and knock the wind out of him, and she succeeded on both counts. The boy's breath gusted from his mouth, his eyes widened in surprise, and he took a step backward. Lena didn't intend to give him a chance to recover. She stepped forward once more, and this time she brought her hand down in a chopping blow to his right clavicle. It was a free joint, and it didn't take much force to break it. She felt it snap beneath the power of her strike, and the boy cried out in pain and released his grip on the pipe. The weapon hit the driveway with a clank and rolled away.

"Damn bitch!" the boy growled, and took a swing at her with his left hand. The punch was wild and she stepped back, avoiding it easily. He stumbled, off balance, and she stepped in and kicked the side of his right knee—hard. The knees are weak joints, and they only flex forward and back. They aren't meant to flex to the side, and the force of Lena's kick ruptured the tendons on the other side of the boy's knee, and he went down, howling in agony. She feared his cries would not only alert the Mythmaker to their presence but wake the entire neighborhood, and without thinking, she kicked him behind the right ear. He immediately fell silent and lay still.

Lena stood there for several seconds, gazing down at him, breathing hard, adrenaline coursing through her body, ready to attack him again if he showed any sign of movement. But an instant later the reality of what she'd done sunk in, and she felt sick to her stomach. She was a doctor! She'd taken a vow to help people, not hurt them. She quickly knelt next to the boy and checked his vitals. His pulse was strong, and he was breathing regularly. She didn't think she'd kicked him hard enough to cause serious brain damage, but there was no way to be certain without a thorough examination. She stood and reached for her phone, intending to call 911, but then she remembered why she was here. Or perhaps the part of her that belonged to Paeon reminded her. She stood there a moment longer, indecisive, and then she walked toward the garage. The boy should be out long enough for her to do what she'd come here for, and she could get medical attention for him later.

The garage looked like fairly typical—not much different from hers, actually—with the exception of a small area that had been set aside for painting. Looking at the easel and the blank canvas on it gave her a strange feeling, but she couldn't say why this was.

The Mythmaker obviously wasn't here, so Lena headed for the inner garage door, took hold of the knob, twisted it gently, and found it unlocked. She opened the door, stepped into the kitchen, and closed it quietly behind her.

The kitchen was dark, but a light was on over the stove, and she was able to see well enough to get around. As a doctor, she routinely made life-and-death decisions, and although she never took them lightly, she wasn't afraid to make them. But here she was, standing inside a strange family's kitchen in the middle of the night, and her heart pounded in her chest like it was desperate to find a way to break free.

Stay calm, she told herself. *You're in. Just go slow and quiet.*

The first thing she did was check to see if there were food and water bowls for pets. She was relieved to find none. The last thing she needed was to trip over a cat in the dark or alert a dog that would start barking furiously at the intruder in its home. She moved through the house like a ghost, checking the dining room, living room, family room, downstairs bathroom, and finding them all empty. She crept upstairs next and found three bedrooms and another bathroom on the second floor. The first bedroom she checked was set up as a home office, with bookshelves, a desk, tabletop computer, printer, and filing cabinet. The second bedroom held a queen-sized bed and while it was too dark to tell for certain, she thought two people were sleeping in it. She thought she could make out two human-shaped lumps under the covers, accompanied by two sets of soft breathing. Could one of these be the Mythmaker? How was she supposed to tell? Paeon's magic had led her to the Mythmaker's house, but she didn't know what the woman looked like. The tattoo had only shown her from the back. She watched the sleeping couple for several minutes, hoping that she would get some indication—an awareness born of instinct, if nothing else— of which might be the Mythmaker. But she felt nothing. She closed the door quietly and checked the last bedroom.

The door was already partially cracked, and she gently pushed it open the rest of the way. The hinges creaked a little, and she gritted her teeth at the sound, hoping it wouldn't wake whoever might be sleeping inside. But when she had the door open far enough, she saw that she didn't have to worry about waking anyone. The bed was empty. As she stood in the doorway, she felt something urging her to step inside, so she did so, reaching out to flick on the light without thinking about it. The light revealed that almost every inch of the walls was covered with sketches and drawings produced with different media—pencil, charcoal, ink, colored pencil—as well as paintings done with watercolors, acrylics, and oils. The most common images depicted were animals, plants, and trees, and although Lena saw no renderings of godlike beings, she had no doubt that she was looking at the work of the Mythmaker. The room was more than a little messy—unmade bed, clothes strewn on the floor—and the latter told Lena that this room belonged to a young woman. There were a handful of stuffed animals positioned around the room. A couple atop a dresser, one on a study desk, a couple on a bookcase. They were the sort of toys a young girl might have—kitties, doggies, jungle animals—all cute and cuddly, but the fact that there weren't many of them, and that they were set up as decorations instead of something to play with, told Lena they were probably keepsakes, and the girl was older, maybe even college age. But none of that really mattered now. What mattered was that the girl wasn't here.

Lena turned off the light and left the room without

bothering to close the door. She walked past the other bedroom—which she now assumed belonged to the girl's parents—went back downstairs, headed for the kitchen, and stepped into the garage. She thought she understood what had happened: The Mythmaker had been working at her easel when a servant from some other god arrived and took her without closing the garage door behind them. Whoever it was, she was certain it hadn't been the boy who'd attacked her. They had both arrived too late.

She was disappointed, of course—she hated to let Paeon down—but she was also relieved. She was a doctor, and she'd taken an oath to do no harm. She'd broken that oath when she'd stabbed Bill in the chest, but because the Mythmaker had been captured by someone else, she wasn't going to have to betray it again, at least not yet. But if Paeon was going to win the war of gods that had come to Corinth, he would probably have to kill the Mythmaker in the end—how could he be the most powerful one left if she still lived?—and as his priest, she would have to help him. She decided not to think about that now. She needed to return to him and report her failure, and she'd have to be careful not to look relieved when she did so.

She looked for the boy she'd rendered unconscious, but he was gone, as was his motorcycle. She hadn't heard its engine, so she assumed he'd walked the bike away from the house before starting it. She wondered if he would return to his god and report his failure, as she intended to. Considering that his god was named Ravage, Lena didn't think he or she would take the news well.

Lena walked to her car, and as she was about to climb

inside, a short, heavyset man in a ski mask and thick winter coat came jogging up the driveway. He stopped next to Lena, breathing hard, his breath misting on the cold night air.

"Stand aside!" he said between breaths. "I have come to claim the Mythmaker... for my god Icythus, and... no one else will—"

"You can cut the speech," Lena said. "She's gone."

And without waiting for the man to reply, she got in her car, closed the door, and began backing out of the driveway.

Sam and Dean pulled up next to one of the dumpsters as the new god approached Karrion. They both maintained grips on their guns and knives, although Sam didn't know why they bothered. Conventional weapons didn't appear to have more than a temporary effect on these gods.

As the military-style god approached Karrion, one of his worshippers called out, "Kill him, Armament!" and several others picked up the refrain.

Dean looked at him. "Not a bad name," he said.

Sam shrugged. He supposed it was as good as any.

Karrion, his head little more than a mass of ragged, bloody meat, rose unsteadily and turned to face his new opponent. Despite his horrific injuries, his one eye glared balefully out of his ruin of a face, and his grip on his machete was solid. Sam wasn't sure, but he thought Karrion was already starting to heal, but even with his worshippers praying as hard as they could, the process was taking longer than when he and Dean had wounded him. It appeared that an injury from a fellow god was harder to shake off.

Armament fired his quadruple-barreled shotgun again, but this time Karrion moved far more swiftly than Sam had thought him capable of, and he managed to dodge the blast. Two of Karrion's worshippers moaned and went limp, one slumping against the alley wall, the other falling to the ground. At first Sam thought they'd been hit by the rounds from Armament's weapon, but there were no bloodstains on their clothes and their bodies remained intact. Armament's ammo could probably reduce a human body to little more than a blood-smear, so the fact these two hadn't immediately disintegrated was a clear indication something else had happened to them. But what?

Karrion continued moving swiftly, becoming a blur as he ran toward Armament. The other god was in the process of trying to track Karrion with his weapon when Karrion rushed past, slicing his machete into Armament's right bicep. Blood sprayed the air, and the wounded god roared, more in fury than in pain—although there was plenty of the latter in his voice as well. His overlarge muscles might've looked as if they were made of rock, but his bicep parted easily beneath Karrion's razor-sharp machete blade, and Armament could no longer hold onto his weapon with that hand. His fingers slipped off the gunstock and his arm fell to his side, useless.

Speaking of falling, another of Karrion's worshippers slumped to the ground, and Sam thought he understood what was happening. That these gods possessed their own power was clear, but when they wished to, they could also draw energy from their worshippers to augment their power,

which was what Karrion was doing now. Normally he moved
like the stereotypical movie slasher that he resembled—
slow and determined. But when he needed to kick things
up a couple notches, such as in a duel with another god,
he drained energy from his worshippers to make himself
stronger and, in this case, faster. But his worshippers paid the
price, weakening and falling unconscious, maybe even dying,
all to help their god survive.

Karrion ran behind Armament, and while the other god
was momentarily distracted, he slashed his machete across
Armament's back, cutting deep. Armament howled in pain,
sounding more like an animal than a man, but when Karrion
made to strike once more, Armament spun around, swinging
his shotgun like a club. The four barrels hit Karrion in the
side, snapping his ribs like kindling.

Dean sucked in a breath. "Man, that had to hurt!"

The gun's impact caused Karrion to stagger-step to the side
in order to remain on his feet, but in the process he lost hold
of his machete and the blade fell to the ground. Karrion's
worshippers gasped and wailed at the sight of their master
losing his weapon, and for a moment, Sam felt as if he were
watching a professional wrestling match, the kind where all
the moves are carefully choreographed, all the blood is fake,
and the audience loves to boo and hiss their favorite villains.

Armament's gaze fixed on the machete, and a wide grin
spread across his face. He ran over to the weapon, and
since his right arm was still out of commission, he bent
down, dropped his shotgun, grabbed hold of the machete,
and stood. He turned to face Karrion just as the other god

recovered and came running at him, hands outstretched, fingers hooked into claws. The loss of his blade didn't seem to deter the slasher god in the slightest, and it looked like he intended to tear Armament apart with his bare hands.

"Why'd he drop the gun for that thing?" Dean said. "The gun's the better weapon."

Sam was thinking the same thing when Armament stepped forward to meet Karrion's charge and rammed the machete into the slasher god's chest. Karrion shrieked and grabbed hold of Armament's wrist, attempting to pull the blade from his body, but even though he only had use of one hand, Armament was too strong. The blade remained up to the hilt inside Karrion's body, and blood poured from the wound. Karrion's body began jerking, as if all his nerves were firing at once, and then with a sudden final spasm, his hands fell away from Armament's wrist and his body ceased moving. Armament let go of the machete with a shove, and Karrion fell to the ground with a meaty thud. Karrion's worshippers wept and cried out in despair, but Armament's cheered and hooted, celebrating their god's victory.

Dean looked at Sam. "You have to admit, that was pretty bad-ass."

Sam didn't reply. He was too busy watching Karrion's body. A soft white light enveloped the dead god, covering him from head to toe. The light grew brighter and more intense, and then it contracted until it had formed a basketball-sized sphere. Karrion's corpse was gone, replaced by the light sphere. *No,* Sam thought. *It* became *the sphere.* The sphere rose in the air several feet, hovered there for a moment, and then streaked toward Armament. Sam expected the ball of light to smash into the god, but instead it passed into his body and was gone.

Armament let out a booming laugh of triumph, curled his hands into fists and he raised them—*both* of them—to the sky. The wound he'd sustained in the battle with Karrion had been healed. More than that, he looked stronger and more vital than he had when he'd entered the alley, as if he'd fed on the energy of his fallen opponent. It made sense. If gods could drain human energy, why not each other's?

Grinning, Armament turned in a slow circle, fists still held high. Sam wouldn't have been surprised if the sonofabitch took a victory lap next.

"We have to get that gun, Sammy," Dean said, his voice low.

Dean wanted to ask his brother why Armament's four-barreled shotgun was so important all of a sudden, but then he thought he understood. Even though the shotgun seemed far superior to the machete, Armament had discarded his own weapon in favor of Karrion's. Sam could think of only one reason why Armament might have done that: because while the shotgun could hurt Karrion, the only weapon that could kill him was his own. And that meant the only thing that could kill Armament...

Sam nodded and together the brothers dropped their own weapons and ran toward the four-barreled shotgun. Armament's back was to them as they made their move, but some of his worshippers saw what the brothers were doing and called out warnings to their god. Armament spun around, but not before Sam and Dean had reached the weapon. The damn thing was big and heavy, and Sam knew there was no way a single person could hope to hold and fire it, let alone handle the recoil's kick.

"We have to do it together!" Sam said.

Working swiftly, the two of them managed to brace the butt of the gun on the ground and raise the barrel up at an angle.

"I don't know about this," Dean said. "If Armament used all four barrels on Jason Junior—and it sure as hell sounded like he did—there won't be any shells in it. And we don't have any extra-grande ammo."

"It's a magic weapon," Sam said. "It only *looks* like a gun. What it fires is pure power. It shouldn't need reloading."

"You know that for a fact?"

"When do we ever know anything for a fact?"

"Fair enough."

Instead of attacking them right away, Armament put his hands on his hips and watched the brothers struggle to get the gun into a firing position that they could handle. His eyes twinkled with merriment.

"Dinner *and* a show!" the god said, and his worshippers laughed.

The brothers ignored him. "You work the trigger," Dean said. "Okay."

Sam pressed one of his hands against the side of the barrels and put the index finger of his other hand on the trigger. Dean used both of his hands to brace the barrels, and Sam hoped that when this was over, they both wouldn't end up with broken arms.

Smiling in amusement, Armament started walking slowly toward them.

"You're mere humans," he said. "There is no way you can hope to operate my weapon without injuring yourselves. But I admire your bravery, however misplaced it is. Stop this foolishness now, and I'll allow you both to become Bound to me."

"What if we politely decline your oh-so-generous offer?" Dean asked.

Armament's smile faded and he scowled. "Then I'll kill you both with my bare hands."

Because of the angle they held the gun at, the brothers had to wait until Armament was close enough to be in range before they could fire. *Just another couple steps,* Sam thought.

"It's a shame you won't be around to see me triumph over my brothers and sisters and claim my rightful place as the One. But in these last few remaining moments of your lives, you can console yourselves with the knowledge that at least for a short time you were able to experience my magnificence before death claimed you."

"Dude, you are laying it on *thick*," Dean said. "I'm used to bad guys that think they're hot stuff and love to hear the sound of their own voices, but you—well, you're something special."

By this point Armament had come within ten feet of them.

"Now?" Sam said softly.

"Let 'er rip," Dean said.

Sam tried to squeeze the trigger, but it wouldn't move. It was large enough to get three fingers on it, so he did so and tried again. It took an effort, but in the end, the trigger moved, and the world disappeared in a blast of thunder, fire, and smoke.

TEN

Dean sat up. His ears were ringing and his head throbbed. He looked over to see Sam lying on the ground, his eyes closed.

"You all right, Sammy?" He could barely hear his own words, so he repeated them more loudly, not caring if he was shouting. This time Sam opened his eyes. He groaned—or at least, he looked like he groaned since Dean couldn't hear him—and sat up. He winced and put a hand to his head.

"What happened?" he said. He frowned then reached up with a hand to touch one of his ears.

Dean heard his brother's voice, but it sounded muffled, like he was hearing it through a dozen feet of cotton. He wasn't exactly sure what had happened, so he took a second to look around. They were still in the alley, and both groups of worshippers remained. Karrion's—those who hadn't collapsed during the battle, that is—stood lined up against the alley walls, while Armament's crowded at the mouth of the alley. Dean was less than thrilled to see that Armament's group still had their guns drawn, although as yet no one was aiming at them, which he took as a hopeful sign. Armament's weapon lay on the ground nearly twenty feet from where the brothers sat. Dean guessed it had skidded backward when they'd fired it, but as far as he could tell, it appeared undamaged. He couldn't say the same for his hands, though. The skin on his palms and fingers was torn and blistered, and the bones ached like hell. He gritted his teeth as he flexed his hands and wiggled his fingers. They hurt, but he didn't think anything was broken. He was about to ask Sam if his hands were okay, when Sam pointed.

"Look."

Dean looked where his brother indicated and saw Armament lying on the ground. Well, three-quarters of him, anyway. The blast from his quadruple-barreled mega-shotgun had taken off his head and shoulders, along with the upper half of his chest. His arms were no longer attached to his body, and they lay on the ground nearby. Blood had sprayed both alley walls, along with several of Karrion's worshippers, who'd had the misfortune of standing in the wrong place when a significant portion of their god's killer had disintegrated.

"Nice shot, if I do say so myself," Dean said. He rose to his feet and reached an aching hand toward his brother. Sam took it and grimaced, but he let Dean help him up.

"Your hand okay?" Dean said.

Sam massaged the fingers of his right hand with his left. "Yeah. I don't think anything's broken, but it might be sprained."

Dean nodded to where Armament's gun had ended up. "With a kick like that, we're lucky our hands are still attached."

Sam nodded.

The brothers stepped over to what was left of Armament. The damage his shotgun had done was even more impressive close up.

"Damn," Dean said. "Maybe we should look into getting one of those four-barreled jobs for ourselves. It'd make hunting a lot easier. We roll into town, find a monster, aim, fire, and *pow!* No more monster, and it's Miller time."

Armament's ravaged body started to glow then, just as Karrion's had when he'd died. The brothers had no reason to think the white light was dangerous, but then again they had no reason to think it wasn't, so they stepped back several feet. They—along with all the worshippers in the alley—watched as the glowing light enveloped Armament's corpse. The same thing happened to the blood on the ground, the walls, and even on the worshippers. It began to glow, too. Just as had happened with Karrion, the light contracted into a sphere and rose several feet into the air until it was chest-level with the Winchesters. The blood became small flecks of light that drifted over to join the main mass. For a second, Dean was afraid the sphere would come flying toward them. After all, they *had* been the ones to kill Armament. But it hung in the air for several moments before simply fading away to nothing.

"I guess only other gods get to feed on a god's energy," Dean said, "which—when you think about it—means these guys are cannibals. Which is just plain wrong, even for monsters."

Sam looked thoughtful. "They're like sand tiger shark embryos that devour their littermates in the womb until only the strongest survive to be born."

Dean looked at his brother. "You've been watching Animal Planet again, haven't you? I guess it makes sense. So what's the womb? The whole town?"

"I guess so," Sam said. He glanced around, frowning. "The gun's gone."

Dean looked around then. "So is Karrion's machete. Looks like their weapons are made of the same stuff they are, and when their owners take the last train to Purgatory, they do, too. Too bad. That machete would've made a hell of a souvenir."

Sam nudged his brother. "Check it out."

Dean looked and saw that both sets of worshippers were leaving the alley, shuffling along silently, heads bowed, as if they were depressed or drained of energy. Maybe both. That was fine with him. He'd rather not fight a bunch of pissed-off cultists if he didn't have to. He wondered if they would go home, or—more likely—if they'd return to the streets in search of a new god to Bind themselves to. The thought depressed him.

"I don't know about you, Sammy, but I'm cold and tired, and I could use another cup of piping hot coffee to get me going again."

Sam smiled. "Along with a donut or two?"

Dean grinned. "Or three."

Renee was still asleep by the time Geoffrey made it back to TechEdge. He parked the Geek Fleet car at the side of the building and turned off the engine. For several moments he sat behind the wheel and considered what to do with Renee. He was reluctant to wake her, not only because she obviously needed to sleep, but because he feared that finding herself in strange surroundings might jolt her into full awareness. And if that happened, she might get scared, start screaming, maybe try to escape. If she bolted from the car before he could get hold of her, there was no way he'd be able to catch her. She was young, her body still strong, while he was older, and a couple years of living on the street had taken their toll on his health. If she got outside, she'd take off like a jackrabbit, and all he'd be able to do was stand there and watch her disappear into the night. He wished he'd thought to look for some rope in the Mendezes' garage to tie her wrists and ankles so she couldn't run. But he'd never done anything like this before, and he was basically making it up as he went along. He'd been lucky to find her almost asleep on her feet and so groggy that she'd accompanied him without his having to do much to convince her. But now that he was back at TechEdge, he knew he couldn't count on his luck to keep holding. He needed to find a way to prevent her from escaping.

He checked the glove compartment and the backseat, but he found nothing that would be of any help. He popped the trunk, got out of the car—careful to close the driver's side door gently so as not to wake Renee—and walked round to the open trunk. There wasn't much inside: a spare tire, a jack, and a roadside emergency kit. The latter contained a pair of jumper cables, and he wondered if he could use them to bind her wrists, but he quickly dismissed the idea. The cables were sheathed in thick black plastic, and he doubted he could tie them tightly enough to keep her from pulling free. Besides, the plastic was hard and cold, and the moment it touched her flesh, it might wake her. He was still standing there, trying to decide what to do, when he heard Adamantine's voice.

"What is taking you so long?"

Despite her disapproving tone, he was happy to see her. She stood next to the Geek Fleet car, her silvery skin and clothing gleaming in the fluorescence of the parking lot lights. In that moment, she looked as if she were made of starlight, and Geoffrey thought he'd never seen anything so beautiful.

"She's sleeping, my lady, and I… I don't have anything to prevent her from escaping if she wakes."

He was afraid that she would chastise him, or worse, punish him, but she did neither. Instead, she walked up to him, removed the piece of her gauntlet that she loaned him from his hand, and returned it to her own finger. Metal flowed together, and the gauntlet was whole once more. She then walked around the vehicle to the passenger side and bent down to look through the window.

"That's her," she said. She spoke these words softly, almost reverently, as if she were in awe.

And why wouldn't she be? Geoffrey thought. *It's not every day that a god gets to meet her creator.*

He walked over to stand near Adamantine and watched the god's face as she gazed upon the woman from whose mind she'd been born.

"She looks like any other human, doesn't she?" Adamantine said, not taking her eyes off Renee. "If you were to encounter her on the street, you would see nothing to hint at the vast power that lies within her. But *I* can sense it, roiling beneath her unassuming veneer like the waters of a rushing river, and now that she is so close, I can practically *taste* it." She placed a palm against the glass of the passenger-side window, as if by doing so she hoped to draw some small measure of Renee's power into herself.

Looking at Adamantine now, Geoffrey was struck by a sudden realization.

"You resemble her," he said. "A little, anyway. Mostly your eyes and mouth."

Adamantine answered without turning to look at Geoffrey.

"Naturally. You humans are fond of saying the gods made you in their image, but in truth you make us in yours." She continued gazing upon Renee for several more moments until the cold began getting to Geoffrey and he started shivering. As if aware of his discomfort, she said, "Go into the store and find some power cables to use in lieu of rope. I shall remain out here and watch her."

"Her name is Renee Mendez," Geoffrey said.

Adamantine's silver eyes glowed a hungry blue-white.

"As if that matters," she said.

Lena didn't drive back to the office building where her practice was located. Paeon had said he intended to go forth into the streets and begin transforming people into "ultimate humans," but she had no idea exactly where he'd gone. He might've used his magic to implant the location of the Mythmaker's house into her brain, but he hadn't bothered to give her a homing signal that would allow her to find him. So when she reached the general neighborhood of her practice, she removed her phone from the inside pocket of her coat and called one of her physician's assistants. Sarah answered on the second ring.

"Hey, Sarah. This is Lena. Can you tell me where Paeon is?"

"He's at the corner of Marshall and McAllister. He's been leading us up and down the streets, stopping everyone he can find and touching them with that magic wand of his. When he's finished enhancing them, he asks if they want to become Bound to him. Of course they all say yes!" She laughed then.

Enhancing, Lena thought. *Is that what he's calling it?*

Marshall and McAllister was only a couple blocks west. She could be there in a few minutes.

"Thanks, Sarah. You must be so tired and cold by now."

"Not at all. Paeon enhanced the staff before we left the office. I barely notice the cold, and I have more energy than ever before. I feel like I could run a marathon if I wanted!"

Sarah laughed again, and Lena thought she sounded a bit like she was drunk. Lena wondered if an "enhanced" human's body produced massive quantities of dopamine, oxytocin, serotonin, and endorphins, the so-called neurochemicals of happiness. If so, it was no surprise that the people Paeon enhanced were so eager to Bind themselves to him. He was basically drugging them. She supposed it could be a natural effect of the enhancement process, and maybe it was, but that didn't mean it wasn't also a damn effective recruiting tool.

"Okay. I'm on my way there. See you in a few."

"Sure thing, Lena! And when you get here, you need to have Paeon enhance you right away. You won't believe how good you'll feel afterward!"

Lena disconnected and tossed her phone onto the passenger seat. She had mixed feelings about the idea of becoming enhanced herself. On the one hand, who wouldn't want to possess ultimate health? But on the other, if the process radically altered her body's neurochemistry, her personality—her very *self*—would change. She would, in a sense, become a different person, and that was a frightening prospect. She wasn't sure she had any choice in the matter, though. If Paeon insisted on enhancing her, would he accept her refusal? If she was his second-in-command—his priest—he couldn't allow her to spurn the greatest gift he had to offer. How would it look to his other followers? No, Paeon would force her to accept enhancement, and he had the power to ensure her compliance. She'd learned that first-hand when he'd used the caduceus to temporarily inflict her with cancer. The pain had been beyond anything she'd ever imagined, and she wasn't eager to experience it again. So if Paeon wanted to enhance her, and he would, there was nothing she could do to prevent it.

That's not true, she realized. There was one thing she could do. She could keep driving, head out of town, hit the highway, and never look back. Yes, she was Bound to Paeon, but he himself had said that humans could switch their allegiances from one god to another merely by willing it. Following that logic, one could be able to *unbind* themselves from a god without choosing another. Of course, Paeon could've been lying, or at least simplifying the truth. She had a hard time believing gods would let go of their followers that easily. But even if Paeon didn't want to release her, she didn't think he had the power to force her to return to him, and even if he did, the more distance she put between them, the weaker his summons would be. He was, for all intents and purposes, a child god, one who was maturing rapidly but had yet to come into his full power. And if another god managed to defeat him in battle, he never would. *In the end there shall be One.* So there was a good chance she could escape him, one way or another. All she had to do was press her foot down on the accelerator and drive like hell.

She almost did it.

But she had helped Paeon Bind dozens of people, and she felt responsible for what might happen to them. And although she was beginning to have doubts about her role in the Apotheosis, she still believed in the potential of Paeon's incredible healing powers to do great good in the world. That, more than anything else, was what made her continue driving toward the corner of Marshall and McAllister.

Geoffrey needn't have worried about the specifics of getting Renee into TechEdge. The woman barely stirred from her sleep as he wrapped computer power cords around her wrists and ankles, and then carried her inside the store. How long had she been awake, painting one god after another, and how much of her own life energy had gone into the creation of each new image? It was a wonder that she hadn't slipped into a coma when she finally finished.

There were quite a few more people inside the store than when he'd left—a sign that Adamantine's recruitment drive was proving successful—and they gathered around to gaze upon the Mythmaker with wonder and curiosity. Geoffrey doubted they knew who and what Renee was, but as they were all Bound to Adamantine, he supposed they recognized the Mythmaker on an instinctive level. More than a few tried to reach out and touch Renee as he carried her toward the back of the store, but in each case, they withdrew their hands before making contact, almost as if they were afraid of what might happen if they did.

Adamantine was waiting for him in the employee break room. The redheaded woman who had been wounded in the battle with Masque no longer rested on the couch, and since Geoffrey hadn't seen her as he carried Renee through the store, he feared that she had died in his absence. He wanted to ask Adamantine what had happened to the woman, but he decided he'd rather not know right now. He didn't want to think about her body lying in the dumpster out back with the others. He gently deposited Renee onto the couch, and other than turning onto her left side and shifting her weight a bit to get comfortable, she didn't move. A moment later, her breathing deepened, and she was sleeping soundly again.

Adamantine looked at her for a few moments, and then she motioned for Geoffrey to come with her. She walked out of the room, and Geoffrey followed, closing the door softly behind him. She started toward the center of the store, and Geoffrey accompanied her.

"How long do you think she will sleep?" he asked.

"She shall awaken before the end," Adamantine said.

"Sounds ominous," Geoffrey responded.

Adamantine ignored the remark. "I want you to select

two people to guard her. Make sure they both have…" She hesitated, as if the word she wanted eluded her. "Those small devices that allow you to speak to one another at a distance. There are some in this store, are there not?"

"Cell phones," he supplied. "Yes, there are many here."

"Good. Make sure you have one as well. I want them to be able to contact you when the Mythmaker wakes."

"You make it sound as if we're going somewhere," Geoffrey said.

"We are. Now that I have increased the number of my followers and the Mythmaker is in my possession, it is time to go out into the city and engage more of my fellow gods in battle. Defeating them is the fastest way to increase my strength, and I shall need all the power I can acquire if I am to be the One."

"Please excuse me for saying this, but is it wise for you to leave Renee here? The others will do their best to take care of her, but most of them aren't fighters. Hell, they aren't even armed. What if some other god gets wind that she's here and tries to steal her?"

"Your concerns are understandable, but you have no need to worry. Now that she is within the walls of my temple—the center of my power—she is hidden from the senses of my fellow gods." She smiled. "She will be perfectly safe here."

Geoffrey didn't feel as confident about that as Adamantine obviously did, but he decided not to push the matter any further. He'd just end up making her angry, and that was something he preferred to avoid.

"I also want you to select a half dozen people to accompany

us," Adamantine said. "They should be young and strong. I may need them for… support."

Geoffrey had a pretty good idea what sort of *support* she was talking about.

"I'll take care of it."

At that moment, a group of around twenty people entered TechEdge. Geoffrey recognized some of them as Adamantine's followers, and he assumed the remainder were more new recruits.

"Make the arrangements we discussed," Adamantine said. "Meanwhile, I shall welcome the new members to our family."

Geoffrey did his best to overlook the undisguised hunger in her voice as she started toward the entrance. He turned away rather than watch her Bind the newcomers and then headed off to do his god's bidding.

"What *is* that thing?" Dean looks at Julie as he asks this, hoping she won't notice him pulling against the zip ties binding his wrists and ankles. They're too tight and there's no give. He assumes Sam's are the same.

"Honestly, I'm not really sure," Julie says. "The Lord of the Hunt is just a nickname I gave him. Seems to fit, though, doesn't it?"

"He's some kind of wood spirit," Stewart says. "We found him a couple weeks after the Sheepsquatch killed Dad."

"He's old," Gretchen says. "I mean, *really* old. We're talking like thousands of years."

"Maybe *tens* of thousands," Julie says. "I managed to find some Native American lore that describes a creature like him, but according to those stories, he was here long before humans of any kind set foot on this continent, so who knows how old he is? He could be as old as the world itself."

"From the way he looks, I can believe it," Dean says.

"Why are you holding him prisoner?" Sam asks.

Julie laughs at this, and Gretchen and Stewart smile.

"He's not a prisoner," Julie says. "He's so weak, he can barely move. We tied him to the chair to keep him from falling over."

Dean looks around the basement, seeking something, anything that he can use to get him and Sam out of this situation. He remembers what his father once told him: *If you find yourself without a weapon, there's always something you can use. Keep a cool head and you'll find it.* His gaze locks on one of the storage shelves. It holds a number of weapons, including several knives, and the set of shelves next to it holds jars filled with powders and chemicals. A plan begins forming in Dean's mind, but he needs Sam to keep the Underwoods' attention off him while he gets in position. He looks at Sam, but Sam's looking at the Lord of the Hunt, and Dean can practically see the wheels turning in his brother's head.

Dean lets out a soft *ssst*. Sam's eyes flick to him, and Dean flicks his own eyes toward the Underwoods, hoping that Sam gets the message. Sam hasn't hunted as often as Dean has. He's younger, and their father has been careful about exposing him to the dangers of hunting. *More careful than he was with me,* Dean thinks, and suppresses a wave of resentment that accompanies the thought. So Sam doesn't have the same amount of experience at thinking on his feet as Dean has. But they're brothers, and given how often John Winchester has left the two of them alone over the years, they've become much closer than most siblings. They're highly attuned—maybe at times too much so—to each other's thoughts, feelings, and moods. But Dean's relying on this closeness now, and when he sees Sam give him a slight nod, he's relieved.

It's game on.

"Why did you bring him here at all?" Sam asks. "Why not leave him where you found him? Weak as he is, he doesn't look like he's a threat to anyone."

As Sam speaks, Dean begins to scoot his body closer to the shelves containing the chemicals. He keeps his movements to a minimum and makes sure to look at Sam the entire time, hoping to keep the Underwoods' attention on his brother and away from him.

"He's not a threat, dumbass," Stewart says. "He's like a genie in a lamp."

"You mean he grants wishes?" Sam asks.

That's it, Sammy. Keep them talking… Dean scoots a fraction of an inch closer to the shelves. He only needs to hook a foot around one of the metal rods, and he's already halfway there.

"He gives life," Gretchen says. "Strength, speed, endurance…"

Stewart grins. "For a price."

"That's why the three of you are so high-energy," Sam says. "The Lord of the Hunt gave it to you."

"When we first found him in the woods, we let him be," Julie says. "He appeared harmless enough, and there are a lot of strange things living in these hills, not all of which are dangerous. When we can in these parts, we tend to live and let live."

"But then you checked the lore," Sam says, "and when you learned what he could do, you realized you could use him."

Another inch…

Julie's expression turns grim. "I was determined to take down the sonofabitch that killed my husband, and I intended to do whatever it took to make that happen. The Lord of the Hunt grants strength to those who sacrifice to him, and I realized that if he could make the three of us stronger, we'd have a better chance of finding and killing the goddamn Sheepsquatch. So we began bringing him sacrifices. Nothing big at first. Small animals like squirrels and rabbits. Alive, of course. He won't accept anything dead. He… I guess you can say he *absorbs* them."

"It's really disgusting," Stewart says. "He takes hold of the animals, hugs them to his chest, and then his body just kind of sucks them in. I almost puked the first time I saw it happen." He turns to Gretchen. "She did."

Gretchen blushes in embarrassment but doesn't say anything.

"I bet you didn't get much energy in return for such small sacrifices," Sam says. "Especially not when it was spread between the three of you."

Almost there, Dean thinks.

"True," Julie admits. "We started trying larger sacrifices— cats, dogs, pigs—as well as more than one at a time. That helped, but it was never enough. We came close to catching the Sheepsquatch a couple times, but he always managed to get away."

"That's when we realized that the Lord needed bigger and better sacrifices," Stewart says. "Something much higher up on the food chain than kitties and doggies."

"You mean people," Sam says.

"Yes," Julie says, "but who could we use? One of us? Gretchen volunteered—" she pauses and gives her daughter a loving smile "—but I'd already lost my husband, and I couldn't bear the thought of losing one of my children, too. I considered sacrificing myself…"

"But we wouldn't let her," Gretchen says. "We were already one parent down, and we didn't want to become orphans."

"*I* thought we should pick someone from around here," Stewart says, "but Mom said there was too good a chance we might get caught."

"There aren't that many people living in this area," Julie says. "If someone went missing, it would be noticed."

The tip of Dean's boot now touches one of the shelves' metal supports. He's almost ready…

"So you decided to wait for us to show up?" Sam says.

"We didn't know you were coming, idiot," Stewart snaps.

Julie scowls at him. "Be nice. These are good boys, and they've helped us out a great deal. And remember, their father is an old friend of mine."

Stewart purses his lips in irritation, but he doesn't reply.

"When your father called me to come get you, I realized we'd been given an opportunity," Julie says. "John knows how dangerous hunting can be. If we told him that the two of you were killed helping us go after the Sheepsquatch, he'd believe it."

"And since the Lord leaves nothing behind when he feeds, there'd be no evidence that anything different happened," Stewart says, grinning again.

"I don't understand," Sam says. "I thought the Lord needed to be fed *before* you hunted. If that's true, why didn't you sacrifice us to him as soon as we got here?"

"You *are* John Winchester's sons," Julie says. "If you boys were even half the hunter he is, I knew we'd have to catch you off guard. Plus, I figured we could use your help on the hunt. So I made a deal with the Lord. We'd give him *two* human sacrifices—a pair of strong young men—in return for granting us the energy we would need to kill the Sheepsquatch. It had been a long time since he'd fed that well, and he agreed. He gave us the energy we needed, we got the Sheepsquatch, and now it's time for us to hold up our end of the bargain. It's nothing personal. If it helps, think about how many people will be spared because the Sheepsquatch is gone. That could never have happened without your sacrifices. When you look at it that way, what you're doing is very heroic. I think if your father knew about this and could look at it unemotionally, he'd be proud of you boys for what you're about to do."

Dean slowly slides his foot around one of the shelves' support rods.

Sam looks at Gretchen. "Are you okay with this?"

A tear runs down her cheek. "I'm sorry," she says, her voice barely above a whisper.

"Enough talk," Stewart says. "It's feeding time."

Julie sighs, and she gives the brothers an apologetic look, as if to say she wishes her son had better manners. "I suppose you're right. The Lord is hungry, and I don't know how much longer he can wait." She turns to her children. "Keep them covered, but don't shoot unless you have to, and if you *do* shoot, shoot to wound. They're no good to us dead." She clears her throat and then speaks in a louder voice. "Lord of the Hunt! We thank you for giving us strength in our time of need. Please accept these two offerings as tokens of our gratitude. May their lives sustain you and—"

Dean yanks the storage shelves over with his foot. Both he and Sam roll out of the way as jars of glass and clay tumble to the basement floor and shatter, releasing their contents. The shelves hit the floor an instant later. Dean has no idea what chemicals the Underwoods kept stored here, but he knows that hunters often have need of some pretty volatile stuff— not all of it natural—and he's gratified to see several small-scale explosions happen, followed by a cloud of foul-smelling smoke that rises into the air. The cloud is large and thick enough to hide them from the Underwoods, which is exactly what he'd been hoping for.

"Get them!" Julie yells, but then there's the sound of snapping wood, and she shouts, "Wait! The Lord is moving! Stay back!"

Dean doesn't like the sound of that. He sits up and scoots across the floor on his butt, ignoring pieces of broken glass and clay. He holds his breath, hoping that Sam's doing the same, and he squints his eyes shut. It's not like he can see much anyway. The cloud stings his flesh, and it hurts like hell. He wonders if he's going to end up looking like Freddy Krueger when this is all over. Assuming he survives, of course.

Eyes closed, he heads for the shelves where the knives are stored. When he reaches it, he shoulders it over, and it falls to the ground with the sound of clanging metal. He reaches blindly, searching for a knife, and he finds one when he slices his index finger on its edge. He grabs the handle and starts to call for Sam, but then he sees his brother has scooted over to him. The cloud is already beginning to dissipate, and Dean sees a shape coming toward them—a human shape, with large antlers protruding from the head. Evidently, Julie ringing the dinner bell was enough to get the ancient monster off his wrinkly butt and moving. Dean knows he and Sam have to work fast.

They position themselves back to back, and Dean quickly slices through the zip tie around Sam's wrists. Sam then takes the knife and does the same for his brother. Dean grabs a second knife while Sam cuts the tie binding his ankles, and Dean follows suit. As soon as they're free, the brothers rise to their feet, only to see all three of the Underwoods pointing their guns at them.

"Please don't move," Julie says. "You'll only make it worse for yourselves."

Dean doesn't want to, but he turns around and sees the Lord of the Hunt coming toward them, moving with awkward, jerking motions, as if the creature has forgotten how to operate its body. The chair the Lord was tied to lies in pieces on the floor, and the cloth strips that held it in place are torn and discarded. Its head lolls to one side as it comes, and a thin rope of drool stretches from its lipless mouth. Its moist black eyes shine with unmistakable hunger, and it reaches skeletal hands toward them, bony fingers eager to grab hold of warm flesh. All of this is bad enough, but to Dean, the worst thing is the way the creature walks, sliding the leathery soles of its feet across the basement floor— *whsssk, whsssk, whsssk…*

"Uh, Dean…" Sam says, staring at the Lord of the Hunt with wide, frightened eyes.

Dean's pretty damn scared himself, but he won't allow himself to show it, not in front of his brother.

"Let's take him out," Dean says, doing his best to sound like their dad.

The brothers grip their knives tight and move forward.

ELEVEN

Sam's eyes water and his exposed skin stings. The chemical cloud that resulted from Dean knocking over the shelves is little more than a haze now, but it feels like he's sucking in steel wool every time he breathes. He doesn't have time to worry about that, though, not with an antler-headed mummy coming at them—a *hungry* antler-headed mummy.

Dean reaches the creature first. The Lord grabs for him, but the monster is slow, and Dean easily evades his grasp. He slams his knife into the Lord's side, the blade sliding between the ribs and entering the creature's heart. It's a good move, Sam thinks. The heart is a weak point for many supernatural beings. Unfortunately, it appears that the Lord isn't one of them. His arm lurches outward and strikes Dean, knocking him away and sending him stumbling into another set of shelves, this one full of books and papers. Dean hits the shelves hard, knocking them against the wall. They rebound and fall forward, hitting Dean in the back, their contents spilling all around them. Dean fights to keep his balance and manages to do so, but he's momentarily distracted. Worse, he no longer has hold of his knife. His hand's bleeding—Sam guesses he cut himself when he was first trying to get hold of the blade—and he wasn't able to maintain his grip when the Lord hit him. The knife is still stuck in the monster's rib cage, leaving Dean unarmed.

Sam glances at the Underwoods. Instead of coming to their Lord's aid, they merely hang back and watch. Has the Lord forbidden them to interfere or are they afraid to get too close to him, in case he might try to feed on one of them? Sam supposes it doesn't matter. He's simply grateful he and Dean don't have to contend with the Underwoods as well as the Lord right now.

Sam attacks just as the Lord turns toward Dean. He has to go in low to avoid skewering himself on the monster's antlers—the points of which look sharp as hell—so he doesn't have his choice of targets. Since stabbing the heart didn't work, he'd rather go for the head, as decapitation is another time-honored monster-killing technique. But the antlers make this impossible right now, so he's forced to try the heart, too. Maybe Dean's blade didn't actually strike the Lord's heart, or if it did, maybe it didn't penetrate deeply enough to kill the creature. He knows it's a long shot, but at this precise instant, it's the only shot he has. He too has little trouble keeping away from the Lord's grasping hands, and he's glad he and Dean don't have to fight the creature in its prime. If the Lord was at full strength, Sam knows they wouldn't stand a chance.

He thrusts his knife into the creature's chest from the right side, giving the strike a little extra *oomph* to force the blade in as deep as possible. Unfortunately, he has no more luck than his brother did, and the strike has no effect on the Lord. This time, though, the creature doesn't lash out and knock Sam aside. Instead, one of his claw-hands shoots forward, moving far faster than Sam would have expected, and bony fingers wrap around his throat and squeeze, instantly closing off his airway.

Sam withdraws the knife and thrusts it into the Lord's midsection several more times in rapid succession, but the creature doesn't react. No blood comes from the wounds, only small puffs of dust. Lungs burning, vision starting to go gray around the edges, Sam panics. He tries to stab the Lord in the eye, hoping to reach the monster's brain, but his swing is wild, his aim off, and the knife connects with the antler on the left side of the creature's head. The impact sends a jolt up through Sam's arm, and he hears a loud *crack*. He barely registers the antler detaching from the Lord's head and falling to the floor. His attention is caught by the sight of a vertical seam opening in the middle of the monster's chest. It yawns wide like a toothless mouth, and all Sam can see inside is darkness. He remembers Stewart's description of how the Lord feeds—*He takes hold of the animals, hugs them to his chest, and then his body just kind of sucks them in*—and then he feels the creature pulling him toward the fissure of blackness. Sam can feel cold wafting forth from the opening, and he wonders what waits for him on the other side. He prays that he'll lose consciousness before he finds out.

But then the Lord of the Hunt stiffens, throws back its

head, and lets out a scream that is in no way remotely human. Its hand springs open, and Sam—freed from the monster's grasp—staggers backward, gasping for breath. Dean stands behind the Lord, teeth gritted, face a mask of fury as he shoves the creature's broken-off antler deeper into its back. In this moment, Sam thinks that Dean has never looked so much like their dad before.

The Lord of the Hunt might shrug off knife attacks, but he isn't immune to his own antler. Several of the sharp points have penetrated the creature's leathery skin, and Dean keeps up the pressure, pushing them in even deeper. The Lord continues to scream, hands waving uselessly, as if trying to grab hold of its attacker, but they only succeed in slashing through empty air. And then—so fast Sam almost doesn't register it happening—the Lord of the Hunt collapses into dust. One instant it's standing there, the next it's gone, leaving nothing behind but a small mound of grayish-yellow powder in its place, and the knife that Dean had left stuck in its side. Dean—the antler he was holding gone, turned to dust like the rest of the creature—looks at his hands with awed puzzlement, as if he's just witnessed a particularly baffling magic trick. Sam figures he's wearing the same expression as his brother right now. And then he remembers...

"The Underwoods!" he says.

He spins around to face them, knowing the knife in his hand is no match for their guns, but also knowing that he won't go down without a fight. He expects to hear triple blasts, to feel the impact of bullets slamming into his body. But he hears and feels nothing. The Underwoods are no longer standing.

They lie on the floor, arms and legs bent at odd angles, and while they still hold onto their guns, they make no move to raise them. Their bodies are emaciated, their skin leathery and mottled, just as the Lord's was. Their eyes are wide and staring, and at first Sam thinks the three of them are dead, but then he hears a soft breath escape Gretchen's mouth. He rushes over to her, ignoring Dean's call for him to stop, that she could still be dangerous. He kneels beside her, leans down, and places his ear close to her mouth so he can hear her.

"So... sorry." She breathes more than speaks these words. "We shouldn't have... have..." Then she lets out a final wisp of breath and is gone.

Sam checks her for a pulse with a trembling hand, and then he does the same for Julie and Stewart. All three of them are dead.

Sam stands, and Dean walks over to join him. For a time they gaze upon the Underwoods' remains, and then together they head up the stairs.

"Seriously, Sam—you have *got* to try one of these crullers." Dean fished one out of the bag and held it out to his brother. "Come on, at least smell it. You know you want to..."

Sam didn't respond right away. He was gazing through Doughnutz's front window, lost in thought.

Dean raised his voice slightly. "Sam, you okay?"

"Hmmm?" Sam turned to look at Dean, and then his gaze fell on the cruller. "No thanks. Coffee's all I want right now." As if to illustrate his point, he picked up his extra-large cup and took a sip.

"Too much coffee on an empty stomach's not good," Dean said. "Let Mr. Cruller help."

Sam just smiled and took another sip of coffee.

Dean shook his head in disappointment. "You'd think by now you'd know to listen to your big brother. So, what were you thinking about?"

Sam looked around before answering. Doughnutz had significantly more customers than the last time the brothers had been in, and the drive-thru had a steady stream of traffic. Dean figured they were all worshippers of one god or another, or maybe they were between gods, trying to figure out who would be a good candidate to try their luck with next. Most were in pairs or small groups, and their conversations were lively, good-spirited, and most of all, loud. *It's like they're celebrating a damn holiday,* he thought. *God's Day.*

Satisfied that no one was paying them any attention, Sam turned back to Dean.

"I was thinking about the time Dad was in the hospital in West Virginia, when he left us with the Underwoods."

Dean frowned. "Why? No—wait. I get it. You figure old Antler-Head was a god."

Sam nodded. "We'd never encountered one before, so we weren't sure what it was, but yeah, I think it was a god."

"Me, too. But not like the ones in this town. That guy was seriously old school."

"He was ancient. If he'd been in his prime, we never would've beaten him."

"What do you mean *we*? As I recall, *I* was the one who took him out and saved your butt."

"You had no idea you could kill him by stabbing him with his own antler. You got lucky."

"And what's wrong with that?" Dean asked.

Sam smiled. "Not a damn thing."

Dean smiled back and the two sipped coffee for a bit. Then Dean asked, "You think the Lord of the Hunt got started the same way as these new gods?"

Sam shrugged. "Maybe. Then again, different gods might be born different ways. Who knows? The thing I keep thinking about is, why the antler? How come he was vulnerable to that and nothing else?"

"These new gods can be killed by their own weapons. Maybe it's the same kind of thing. Antlers can be used as weapons, right?"

"But they were attached to his head. He didn't carry them like these gods do—they were part of him."

"How do you know what these gods do?" Dean challenged. "We've only encountered a couple so far. Maybe some of them are antler-compatible."

"I suppose."

Dean could tell by Sam's tone that there was something about the Lord of the Hunt's antlers that still bothered him. Dean had no idea what it was, though.

"I've been thinking about something else too," Sam said. "What if *we're* the reason this is all happening?"

"I know we both have a thing when it comes to taking responsibility for bad stuff that happens, but in this case, Sammy, I just don't see it."

"Hear me out. As near as we can tell from the lore, this

process is cyclical, right? It only happens every few thousand years. So what triggers it? What would make a species feel compelled to reproduce?"

Dean shrugged. "If they were humans, I'd say a little soft music, some good booze…" He trailed off and then became serious. "No. It would be when their numbers get low, wouldn't it? When they're on the verge of extinction."

"Exactly. There aren't many ancient gods left around anymore, and the reason for that is—"

"Hunters," Dean finished. "More specifically, us."

Sam and Dean had come up against all manner of supernatural creatures during their careers—monsters, demons, witches, angels… and gods. They'd killed a number of so-called deities over the years, some of them pretty big names in the mythology department.

Sam nodded. "I'm not saying we did it all by ourselves. I'm sure lots of gods were killed over the centuries by hunters and Men of Letters all around the world. But what if we pushed the species past the tipping point and kicked off a new reproductive cycle?" Sam paused, and when he continued, his voice was softer. "It's not like we haven't caused bad things to happen before. Some of them *really* bad."

One of the hardest parts of hunting—at least as far as Dean was concerned—was trying to figure out what the right thing to do was in any given situation. It wasn't always as easy as "find monster, kill monster, go home." In fact, it rarely was. The brothers did their best to protect people from the dark forces that sought to prey upon them, but their best wasn't always enough—which was hard to deal with—and sometimes their actions made things worse. A few times, a *lot* worse, as in threat-to-the-entire-world's-survival worse. So far, they'd managed to clean up the messes they'd made and keep the globe spinning, but what if one day they failed, and everyone and everything on the planet died, and it was all their fault? It was thoughts like these that kept Dean up at night.

"I hate to say this," Dean began, "but if we manage to stop this from happening here, won't it just start up again somewhere else?"

"Are you saying we should let things run their course? Do you know how many people will die if we do?"

"And if we stop it, how many more will die when it starts all over somewhere else?" Dean countered. "It could happen anywhere in the world, right? So all the people who've already died here will have died for nothing—"

"And even more people will die when it begins again," Sam said.

"Yeah."

The brothers were silent for several moments, and then Sam said, "'Do I dare to eat a peach?'"

"Huh? I thought you weren't hungry?"

"It's a line from a poem by T.S. Eliot," Sam explained, "called 'The Love Song of J. Alfred Prufrock.' It's about a man who desperately wants to do something, but he can't bring himself to because he's afraid of the consequences. What if doing something ends up being worse than doing nothing?"

"Sounds like this Prufrock was a hunter." Dean sighed. "I've never been too good at hanging back and waiting to see how a situation plays out. I guess we'll just have to do what we always do: keep moving forward, do our best, and hope it all works out."

"I guess so," Sam said. "It sucks sometimes, though."

"It sure as hell does," Dean agreed.

They talked for a little while about what their next move should be. With the number of gods in town, Sam suggested they put a call out to other hunters to come help them but Dean thought it would take too long for them to arrive. He suggested they try to contact Castiel since angels were capable of killing gods, and Sam agreed.

"Cass," Dean said, keeping his voice low, just in case anyone might be able to hear him over the din of conversation. "You got your ears on?" Seconds ticked by, and when after a full minute Castiel didn't appear, Dean said, "I guess not."

"He's probably busy doing… something," Sam said.

"Sure. IAS."

Sam arched a questioning eyebrow.

"Important Angel Stuff," Dean said. "But I'm only using the word *stuff* because we're in public."

Too bad Cass didn't answer, Dean thought. *We could really use his help on this one.* From what they'd seen so far, it looked like the only way to kill the gods was with their own weapons. But getting those weapons away from them wouldn't be easy. In fact, it was almost guaranteed suicide.

"So now that we've gotten up close and personal with a couple of the New Gods on the Block, what do you think of them?" Dean asked.

"They certainly seem modern, at least on the surface. Karrion resembled a killer from an 80s slasher film, while

Armament was like Rambo on steroids."

"But you don't think they're actually modern?"

"Not really. They strike me as being newer versions of ancient archetypes. Karrion would be a god of death—"

"And Armament would be a god of war," Dean said. "I get it. So these gods are what? Copycats who aren't imaginative enough to come up with original archetypes?"

"I think what's happening in this town is a natural process, and these gods—despite their names and appearances—are fulfilling the basic roles of their species."

Dean frowned. "Are you talking about… I don't know. Supernatural genetics?"

"Something like that. Think about it. There are different pantheons in mythology, but the same sort of gods show up in all of them: storm gods, sun gods, sea gods, gods of speed, gods of strength…"

"I wouldn't mind meeting a goddess of love. You think there's one of those out there?"

"I hate to say it, but given the way Karrion and Armament went after each other, if there had been a love goddess in this town, she's probably dead by now."

"If that's true, Valentine's Day is really going to stink around here."

Before either of them could say anything else, the door opened and Sheriff Deacon walked in. The brothers waved when they saw him, and he came straight over to their booth.

"You boys still at it, too? Least you were able to change into civvies. Wish I could get away with that. Long nights like this one would be more bearable if you could wear comfortable clothes while you worked."

"Sounds like you've been busy," Sam said.

"*Too* busy. There have been seven more deaths since we last spoke." He shook his head wearily. "If this keeps up, the county morgue is going to run out of room."

"I take it that the deaths were all due to more 'weird accidents,'" Dean said.

The sheriff frowned at Dean as if he didn't like his tone. "As a matter of fact, they were. You mind if I ask where you boys have been? I thought you came to town to investigate these kind of deaths."

Dean held up a cruller. "Donut break," he said.

The sheriff's frown deepened, but then it vanished and he grinned. "Don't blame you. Those are damned good, aren't they?"

Dean took hold of the bag and held it out to the sheriff. "Want one?"

The sheriff held up a hand. "No thanks. I don't eat stuff like that anymore. The body's a temple, you know."

Dean hadn't noticed before, but not only did the sheriff seem unaffected by the long hours, he was wide awake and full of energy. He looked better than the last time they'd seen him, too. He'd been in decent shape before, but now he looked... *better*. He was more muscular, and his skin tone was healthier, as if he'd spent the last few days in the sun. His black hair and mustache were thicker, glossier, and his teeth were so white they practically gleamed. Sam had mentioned the Underwoods a few minutes ago, and the sheriff's transformation made Dean think of how the three of them had been during the hunt for the Sheepsquatch—fast, strong, and bursting with energy that had been on loan from their god. Energy that had been taken from them, along with the remainder of their life forces, when the Lord of the Hunt died. Dean suspected the sheriff had gotten his bio-makeover from a similar source.

"I thought cops were supposed to practically live on donuts," Dean said.

"I've turned over a new leaf. I hitched my caboose to a fellow named Paeon, and I'm damn glad I did! This is the best I've felt in my entire life!" He thumped a fist on his chest to emphasize his words. "You boys should consider doing the same. I convinced my deputies to follow Paeon, and not a single one of them regrets it."

Sounds like the sheriff has gotten himself some of that new-time religion, Dean thought. "Thanks, but I don't think—"

Sam quickly interrupted him. "Paeon sounds like he's a healer of some sort."

"He sure is," Sheriff Deacon said. "Pardon the pun, but he's a genuine miracle worker!"

"In that case, I think we *would* like to meet him," Sam said. He looked at Dean. "Right?"

It took a second for Dean to figure out where Sam was going with this. They had to hope that if Paeon was a god of healing, he wouldn't be violent like Karrion and Armament. And if that was true, then maybe they would be able to question the god without getting their heads hacked off by a machete or blown off by a quadruple-barreled shotgun.

"Yep. Sounds awesome."

Dean's reply was less than enthusiastic, and Sam gave him

another look before turning once more to the sheriff.

"Can you take us to meet Paeon?" he asked.

Sheriff Deacon grinned. "Sure thing. All we have to do is step outside."

He pointed at the window, and Dean and Sam turned to look. Across the street stood what looked like a doctor straight out of a soap opera. He was too tall, too handsome, and his lab coat was white as fresh-fallen snow. Dean wouldn't have been surprised if light glinted off the man's perfect teeth when he smiled. The man wasn't wearing winter clothes—no heavy coat, no hat, scarf or gloves. But then he didn't need them, did he? Gods didn't have to worry about unimportant details like frigid temperatures. A number of men and women crowded around Paeon; worshippers or prospective worshippers, Dean assumed. One of them remained close to his side, a short but attractive woman who seemed almost dwarfed by the god.

"Who's the woman standing with him?" Dean asked.

"That's Lena Nguyen," the sheriff said. "She's a doctor, too, but the normal kind. She's Paeon's personal assistant, or something like that. All the gods have one."

"Interesting," Sam said.

Dean didn't know what was so interesting about it. The supernatural equivalent of one percenters thought they were so important that they needed a human pet constantly at their side. Big surprise.

"Let's go say howdy," Dean said. Sam nodded, and the brothers rose from the table.

"I'll join you as soon as I can," Sheriff Deacon said. "Lena sent me over to get coffee and hot chocolate for everyone, and it'll probably take a while."

Dean clapped the sheriff on the shoulder. "Get some crullers, too. Those things are delicious."

The brothers then headed for the door, leaving behind a smiling, but puzzled, sheriff.

Geoffrey followed Adamantine down the sidewalk, a handful of her other followers walking directly behind him, along with a number of new recruits. While Adamantine lacked anything even remotely resembling warmth and compassion, she exuded strength and power, and Geoffrey was always surprised how many people were attracted to that. But then, he supposed he shouldn't be, as he was one of her followers, too. Things had certainly changed for him since meeting Adamantine. For the first time in a long time, he had a purpose, a family, a sense of community, and—best of all— he had a *home*, even if it was a hijacked electronics store. But one thing hadn't changed: He was still stuck outside in the cold, just like any other night. He supposed it was a small enough price to pay for everything he had gained, but he couldn't help thinking longingly of the heater in the Geek Fleet car, and wishing he was behind the wheel right now, heat on full blast.

Adamantine walked at a fast pace, as if she were determined not to waste any time. They came to the last building before the intersection, a stately, sturdy old thing of red brick that had probably been built in the early twentieth century, Geoffrey guessed. *They don't make them like that anymore*, he thought. As Adamantine approached the corner, she slowed, then stopped. Geoffrey and the others stopped as well, but when Geoffrey started to ask her if something was wrong, she turned to him and pressed a silver finger to her lips. *Silence,* the gesture said, and Geoffrey shut his mouth. Moving slowly, Adamantine placed her hands on the side of the building and peered around the corner. She stood like that for several moments, watching, but watching what, Geoffrey couldn't say. But then she motioned for him to join her, and he did so, moving just as cautiously as she had.

"What is it, my lady?" he whispered.

"See for yourself," she whispered back, then retreated several steps to make room for him. He stepped forward and leaned his head out past the edge of the building so he could see.

A crowd of men and women stood halfway down the block, grouped around a tall man in a white coat who was obviously another god. But the man projected an aura of power that Geoffrey—after having been in Adamantine's presence for half a day—could feel even at this distance. He pulled his head back and turned toward Adamantine.

"He's as strong as you," he said, then mentally added, *Maybe stronger.*

He thought Adamantine might be angry that he'd suggested any god could possibly be her equal—let alone her superior—but she broke out into a huge grin and said, "I know."

Since leaving TechEdge, they'd encountered two different gods: a harvest maiden named Cornucopia and a hideous multi-tentacled thing called Yithuggug. Adamantine had fought and killed both of them without much trouble, and she'd acquired most of their followers. She destroyed those who'd refused to Bind themselves to her, just as she'd done with those two worshippers of Wyld. He supposed he'd been unable to keep the horror he felt at watching them die from his face, for Adamantine had told him, *I can't allow them to lend their strength to another god, not if I want to be the One.*

With each god she dispatched, Adamantine grew exponentially stronger, and she now emitted such power that Geoffrey's entire body tingled when he stood too close to her, as if an electric current coursed through him. Sometimes the sensation was so strong that his teeth ached and he felt tiny hot pinpricks of pain on his skin, as if invisible sparks were shooting off of him.

That's why she's so excited to see this new god, he thought. *She doesn't view him as a threat. To her, he's just another energy source to be drained, although a damn sight more powerful than those last two.*

Adamantine had brought Wyld's spear with her. Geoffrey was glad that she'd only felt the need to hold on to this particular trophy, the one from the first god she'd defeated. If she'd kept it up and collected the weapons from every god she fought, she'd never be able to carry them all. He'd probably have been the one forced to drag all the items around. *Be grateful for small favors,* he told himself.

"Are you thinking about challenging him?" Geoffrey asked, even though he knew it was a stupid question.

"Of course! Can't you feel the power flowing from him? If I can add his energy to mine, I'll be unstoppable!"

If *is the operative word,* Geoffrey thought.

"Go forth and announce me," she said.

He suppressed a sigh. Somewhere along the line she had decided that it was more "dignified" if he approached the god she wished to battle and announced her name and intentions. After this, she would come forward, head held high, affecting a regal bearing as if she already was the One, and having to fight her way to the title was merely a dreary formality. Geoffrey hated this new duty of his. Not only did he feel silly doing it, Yithuggug had been so annoyed that the loathsome creature wrapped several tentacles around him and nearly crushed his rib cage before Adamantine had stepped in.

"Yes, my lady," he said, trying not to let on how unenthusiastic he felt about the task. He walked around the corner and started toward the god and his group of followers—

—just as a ball of fire flew across the street to strike the god, instantly engulfing him in a blazing-hot inferno.

Sam and Dean had just stepped into the parking lot of the donut shop when they saw a tall, slender woman whose hair appeared to be on fire. She stood on the sidewalk, a group of people behind her, and she drew her right arm back like she was getting ready to throw a baseball, then flung it forward. Her hand had been empty, but as her arm curved downward, a ball of flame shot from her palm and soared through the air toward Paeon. The woman's—no, the *god's*—followers cheered, clapped, whistled, and hooted, sounding more like excited sports fans than worshippers.

Sam had time for a single thought before the flame struck

Paeon, and it was this: *I wonder if gods are fireproof.* He had his answer a second later when fire erupted across Paeon's body, and the god bellowed in pain. No human could've produced that sound. It echoed like thunder, and Sam felt the asphalt beneath his feet vibrate, as if the town was experiencing a minor earthquake. His ears—which were still ringing from when he and Dean fired Armament's quadruple-barreled shotgun—felt like someone had rammed knives into them. He clapped his hands over his ears to protect them, and he wasn't surprised to see Dean do the same.

The fire god's worshippers began to chant in unison: *Flare, Flare, Flare, Flare!*

She turned to them and bowed, as if she were a stage magician who'd just performed an especially astounding trick. The flames that rose from her head didn't seem to bother her, nor did they appear to be damaging her skin in any way. The parking lot lights revealed that her skin was red, as if she had suffered severe sunburn, and her eyes were a solid glowing orange.

"Thank you, all," she said, and as she spoke, Sam could see tiny flickering flames behind her teeth, and he thought, *She's like a furnace inside.*

She wore a black leather jacket over a rock concert T-shirt for a band Sam had never heard of called Rhapsody of Fire. Black jeans and thigh-high black boots completed her outfit.

Paeon's cries began to diminish in volume, and the ground no longer trembled beneath their feet. Sam gingerly pulled his hands away from his ears, and although they still hurt, it was nothing like before. He nodded to Dean, and his brother uncovered his ears as well.

"Man," Dean said, "that girl is—"

"Don't say it," Sam said.

"Smoking hot!"

Sam sighed while Dean grinned.

Flare blew a kiss to her followers, turned, and walked into the street, moving toward Paeon with long, purposeful strides. Paeon was still wreathed in flame, but he no longer cried out in pain. The woman who was his "assistant"—the sheriff had said her name was Lena Nguyen—stood close by, too close for safety, Sam thought. She was yelling at Paeon, but Sam couldn't hear what she was saying, partially because of the ringing in his ears and partially because of the distance between them. An instant later, the flames shrank and then were extinguished altogether. Paeon's flesh and clothes were burned to such a degree that it was impossible to tell one from the other. Sam couldn't believe that the man was still on his feet. Even for a god, the level of pain he was experiencing had to be excruciating.

Flare was halfway across the street when Paeon, moving stiffly, reached toward his chest, pried back a blackened section that could've been clothing, flesh, or a sickening combination of both, and removed a small rod-like object that had also been charred by the fire. He gripped it tight in his charred fist and a golden glow burned away the soot covering its surface. Now that Sam could see the object clearly, he recognized it as a caduceus. The glow flashed brightly, covering Paeon from head to toe, and when it faded, he looked completely normal again. Skin smooth and healthy, hair unburned, features all where they should be. Even his clothes had been restored to their undamaged state.

"Now *that's* some damn powerful magic," Dean said.

By the time Flare reached Paeon, he was as good as new, although several of his followers looked worse for wear. They leaned on each other for support, and a couple had passed out and were being tended to by fellow worshippers. Sam wondered what would happen if a battle became too intense—would the gods drain so much energy from their followers that instead of feeling ill or weak, they died? *Of course they would,* he thought. *They're monsters, aren't they?*

Flare curled her hands into fists and they burst into flame. She drew back her right arm, clearly intending to deliver a fiery punch to Paeon's jaw, but before she could strike, he lunged forward, almost as if he were fencing, and jammed his caduceus into her sternum. The artifact glowed with black light this time, and the flames rising from Flare's fists extinguished. She moaned, hunched over, and put her hands on her belly. She took several steps backward, fell to her knees, and dropped her chin to her chest. The fire that rose from her head like a deadly halo sputtered and went out, revealing her bald head. *The fire* was *her hair,* Sam realized. Around her head she wore a copper circlet. The fire had hid it before—perhaps had even come from it—but now it was plain for all to see.

"That thing on her head," Sam said. "That has to be her weapon."

"Bet you're right," Dean said. "What do you think Paeon did to her? Isn't he like a god of medicine? Shouldn't he have,

I don't know, cleared up her acne or improved her digestive health, something like that?"

"Paeon can heal, yes. But he can hurt, too, when he wants."

The brothers turned to see Sheriff Deacon standing next to them. He held three drink carriers containing coffee and hot chocolate, one stacked atop another so high that they blocked the lower half of his face.

Deacon continued, "And as long as a god has a physical body, he can affect it just like he can a human's—as long as he can touch them with that golden doodad of his."

"Please don't say 'golden doodad,'" Dean said. "It sounds wrong in *so* many ways."

Sam ignored them. His attention was focused on the scene playing out between Paeon and Flare. Paeon walked over and gazed down upon her, his expression an unsettling mixture of compassion and satisfied cruelty. When he spoke, his voice was loud, as if it were amplified. *He wants everyone in the area to hear his words,* Sam thought. He wasn't surprised. He and Dean hadn't met a god yet that wasn't a full-tilt diva in one way or another.

"It was poor form of you not to say the words. I would give you a chance to say them now, just to make sure we dot our I's and cross our T's, but considering that I have rearranged your internal organs, I doubt you're capable of speech right now."

He still held his caduceus in his right hand, so he reached down with his left, took hold of the copper circlet, and removed it from her head. He held the object up so he could examine it, turning it back and forth so he could look at it from all sides.

"Beautiful craftsmanship. The design is elegant in its simplicity." He looked at the circlet for another moment, while Flare continued to press her hands to her abdomen and whimpered.

Sam couldn't imagine the pain she must be feeling. Even for a god, having your internal organs "rearranged" had to be an agony beyond endurance. If Paeon had done the same thing to a human, he or she would've died instantly. Only Flare's divine nature had kept her alive this long.

Paeon looked away from the circlet and down at Flare once again. "Well, if you feel no need for the words, I suppose there is no need for me to speak them either."

He raised the circlet high, and with a single swift motion brought it down hard on Flare's head. A horrible crunching sound filled the air, and she slumped over onto her side, her skull shattered. She lay motionless for a moment, then—as the brothers had witnessed with the other dead gods—white light enveloped her as well as her weapon. The two lights merged into a sphere that hovered in the air for an instant, and then streaked toward Paeon and disappeared into his body. Flare and her circlet were gone.

Paeon's followers cheered and clapped for their god's victory, but not Dr. Nguyen. She looked weary, emotionally if not physically. Her reaction—or lack thereof—made sense to Sam. What sort of doctor could stand by and watch someone be murdered and not be affected? It went against everything physicians stood for.

Sheriff Deacon was just as thrilled as Paeon's other worshippers.

"I told you he was great! Come on, I'll take you over and introduce you."

Sam looked at Dean and Dean gave a slight shrug in return, as if to say, *Your call.*

Sam wasn't sure what to do. Now that they'd had a chance to see Paeon in action, it was clear he could be as ruthless as any other god. If he figured out they were hunters, he'd probably use his caduceus to turn them inside out—or worse—and without some kind of weapon of their own, the brothers would be helpless against him.

"Now might not be the best—"

Before Sam could complete the sentence, a tall woman whose body and clothing appeared to be formed entirely of silver came walking around the corner of a building at the end of the block. As soon as she was in sight, Sam felt tremendous power emanating from her, and if the way she looked hadn't marked her as a god, her regal bearing and the energy she exuded would have. An older African-American man in shabby clothes stood on the sidewalk halfway between the corner and where Paeon and his worshippers stood, and as the silver woman drew near, he glanced over his shoulder at her. But rather than run in fear, he gave her a deferential nod, faced forward, and started walking toward Paeon. The silver woman came after him, moving more slowly now, maybe to give him a chance to reach Paeon ahead of her. A moment later, a dozen people came around the corner and trailed after the silver woman. Her worshippers, Sam figured, or at least some of them.

"Paeon certainly attracts the ladies, doesn't he?" Dean said. "Then again, he *is* a doctor."

"Do you think that guy walking ahead of her is her assistant or familiar or whatever they're called?" Sam asked.

"Maybe," Dean said. "Guess she likes the grungy look."

"Guys, I'm going to head on over," the sheriff said. "I need to add my support to the group in case another fight's about to start. Besides—" he shifted the drink carriers to get a better hold on them "—these things are getting heavy."

Sheriff Deacon started walking across the street then, and he reached his fellow worshippers the same time the African-American man drew near Paeon. The man stopped ten feet from the god and began speaking, his words hesitant but clear.

"I wish to announce the advent of my lady Adamantine, strongest and fiercest of gods. Gaze upon her countenance with awe, tremble in her presence, and prepare yourself for death at her hands."

"How much you want to bet she wrote that herself?" Dean said.

"Come on," Sam said. "Let's get closer so we can hear better."

"You mean get killed more easily," Dean said, but when Sam stepped into the street, he followed.

TWELVE

The brothers took up positions on the sidewalk not far from where Sheriff Deacon was passing out hot drinks. The way people grabbed them and then hurried to find a good vantage point to watch the two gods made Sam think of spectators at a sporting event getting their refreshments and settling in before the action started.

By this point, the silver god—Adamantine—had walked up to Paeon and stood facing him. They were on the sidewalk, standing on a section of concrete blackened from Flare's fiery attack on Paeon. The humans on both sides had backed off to make room for the two gods, but not so much room that they would be safe when the gods started fighting, Sam thought. Now that Paeon and Adamantine were in close proximity, the air seemed to crackle with unseen energy. Sam felt his skin begin to tingle, and if he looked in a mirror right now, he wouldn't have been surprised to see his hair standing on end, as if he'd been exposed to a massive electrostatic charge.

Paeon was the first to speak.

"I am Paeon."

"I am Adamantine," the silver god said.

And then both at the same time: "In the end there shall be One."

It sounded to Sam like a ritual of some sort, but not one that all gods followed, he guessed. After all, Armament hadn't spoken these words to Karrion.

"Round One," Dean said. "Too bad nobody has a bell to ring."

The gods didn't immediately start fighting. Instead they stood looking at one another intently, brows furrowed, jaws clenched, hands bunched into fists, their combined power building until Sam could detect a distinct hum in the air. It was like standing close to a huge generator while someone slowly increased the power. Paeon's caduceus pulsed with black light, and tendrils of electricity curled around the gauntlet Adamantine wore and raced up and down the spear she carried.

"Looks like she's some kind of lightning god," Dean said.

Sam nodded without taking his eyes off either of them. This situation reminded him of the way wild animals sometimes faced off against one another, displaying signs of strength and aggression in an attempt to intimidate their opponent while at the same time trying to determine which was the most powerful.

The energy pouring off the gods continued to build until it became painful for the humans gathered on the sidewalk. Sam winced as the tingling sensation on his skin intensified to a point where it felt like he had been hit with one of Flare's fireballs, and from the looks on everyone else's faces—Dean's included—it was clear they were experiencing the same thing. And then, just when it felt as if all that power might be released in a single unimaginably powerful explosion, it dissipated, gone so swiftly that the suddenness made the gathered humans gasp in surprise. The burning sensation was gone, and the air was clear and still again, although Sam thought he could detect a lingering smell of ozone, like after a lightning strike.

"It appears we are too evenly matched," Paeon said with a slight smile. His caduceus no longer glowed, and electricity no longer coruscated along the length of Adamantine's spear.

"Yes, it does." Adamantine smiled as well.

"Get a room, you two," Dean said, and a number of worshippers from both sides glared at him. Neither god reacted, though.

"If we fight now, it is likely neither of us would win," Paeon said. "We would only be wasting energy we shall need for the final battle."

"Agreed," Adamantine said. Her smile broadened. "And I think it is clear now that the two of us shall be the ones to fight in that battle."

"Perhaps. You *are* the strongest of my kind that I've encountered. But there are still others who remain. I can sense them. Perhaps one of them shall meet me in the end."

"Or meet *me*," Adamantine said. "But there are only a mere handful of others. They will be gone in a few hours, and I wager that you and I will be the only survivors in the end. Can you not *feel* it? It is inevitable."

"One thing I can feel is that you have *her*," Paeon said.

"Our progenitor. She is not with you at present, of course. I would sense the Mythmaker if she were among your people here, but you *do* have her." He inhaled through his nostrils then slowly exhaled. "I can smell her on you."

Mythmaker, Sam thought. *You mean someone created them?* This could be exactly what he and Dean were looking for. If they could find out how these new gods had been born, maybe they could figure out how to kill them as well.

Adamantine bristled at this, and her eyes literally flashed with anger.

"I warn you, Paeon, do not attempt to take her from me."

Paeon held up a hand. "I have no intention of doing so. I have no doubt that you shall keep her safe until such time as she is needed."

Sam and Dean looked at each other. This sounded like another piece of the puzzle.

Paeon continued. "I assume you are holding her at your temple. Please, don't bother denying it. Where else would you keep her? To make matters simpler, perhaps we should meet there for the final battle. It will save you the trouble of having to transport her elsewhere."

Adamantine narrowed her eyes, as if she were inwardly debating the merits of Paeon's suggestion.

The assistants of both gods—Dr. Nguyen and the man in the worn clothing—stood near their respective master or mistress. They'd been watching the conversation between the gods with close attention and more than a little trepidation, but now the man stepped over to Adamantine, a worried look on his face.

"I beg your pardon, my lady, but I'm not sure this is a good idea," he said.

Adamantine didn't look at him, but she flicked her gauntleted index finger and a small arc of electricity leaped from the metal and stung the man on the cheek, instantly charring a small patch of his skin. He yelped and covered the injured area with a hand.

"Quiet, Geoffrey," she said softly, as if she were too busy thinking to yell at him.

He shut his mouth, but he didn't move away from Adamantine.

"Brave man," Sam said.

"Or maybe a glutton for punishment," Dean said.

"Meeting later *will* give both of us time to increase our power," Adamantine said. "Then we shall be able to complete the Apotheosis at last."

Dr. Nguyen stepped to Paeon's side then.

"One of you may be stronger than the other by then," she said.

Paeon gave her a grim smile. "Precisely."

"But it could be *her*," Dr. Nguyen said, concern evident in her voice.

His smile became gentle. "I appreciate you looking out for me, Lena, but you know that this is how it must be. In the end—"

"There shall be One," Lena finished wearily. "I know." She turned to Adamantine and glared at her. Given the intensity of her look, Sam thought that if the woman had been a god, Adamantine would've been dead on the spot.

Despite Adamantine's earlier admonishment for Geoffrey to remain silent, he said, "All he wants to do is kill you. Please don't make it easier for him."

Adamantine didn't bother to reprimand him for talking out of turn this time. She ignored him and continued looking at Paeon for several more moments, considering his offer. Finally, she nodded.

"I am in agreement."

Paeon grinned. "Excellent! When shall we meet?"

Adamantine considered. "As I said earlier, only a few of our brothers and sisters remain, and they will seek us out just as we seek them. Our work should be completed before dawn."

"Then we shall meet at dawn, the birth of a new day." Paeon seemed pleased by this. "How appropriate. I need know only one more detail…"

"The location of my temple," she said.

Geoffrey looked as if he were going to protest once more, but in the end he said nothing. *Not just a brave man,* Sam thought, *but a smart one, too.* He doubted anything Geoffrey said could change Adamantine's mind. He wasn't sure that Adamantine's mind *could* be changed, even by herself. What was happening here was part of an ancient mystical cycle, as inevitable and unchanging as the movement of the Earth around the Sun. Not that the Winchesters weren't going to do their damnedest to stop it, though.

"There is a place of commerce not far from here called TechEdge," Adamantine said. "Do you know it?"

Paeon looked to Lena, who reluctantly nodded. Paeon turned back to Adamantine.

"Yes," he said. "I shall see you there at dawn."

Then without another word, he turned and began walking down the sidewalk away from Adamantine. Lena hurried to catch up to him, and his followers stepped aside to let them through. When they had passed, the worshippers followed. Adamantine watched them go for several moments before turning and walking in the opposite direction. Geoffrey followed several steps behind her, and just as Paeon's followers had done, hers let the two of them pass and then trailed after them. Sam and Dean remained standing on the sidewalk, and soon they were alone.

"Fact-finding mission accomplished," Dean said. He held up his bag of donuts. "And I still have some crullers left. That's a win in my book."

They both had coffee as well, but by now it had gone cold. There was a trash can close by, and Sam tossed his cup inside. Dean did the same, but he kept the donuts.

"One good thing about this mess is that Dr. McDreamy and the Silver Diva are going to do most of our work for us," Dean said. "They'll kill the rest of the surviving gods before their grudge match begins at dawn."

"Yeah, but by that point they'll both be so powerful that we may not be able to stop them," Sam said.

Dean shrugged. "Maybe they'll take each other out and save us the trouble."

"I doubt it. Remember the words they spoke before fighting? 'In the end there shall be One.'"

"So you're saying that there's going to be a clear-cut winner, no matter what?"

"I don't know for sure, but yeah, that's what I think."

"If that's true, then at least we'll only have to deal with one god."

"One god who's absorbed the power of all the others that were born in this town," Sam pointed out.

"Yeah, that'll suck." For a moment, the brothers were silent, but then Dean continued, "What do you make of that Mythmaker talk? You really think these gods had a creator of some kind?"

"They had to come from somewhere."

"I suppose. You think this Mythmaker is another type of god?"

"I don't know," Sam admitted. "But from the way they spoke about her, she has some kind of role to play in this final battle of theirs."

"Maybe if we can find her, we can throw a hell of a big wrench into this cycle of theirs and stop them," Dean said.

"Maybe. Did you notice how their two assistants acted?"

"Yeah. They both didn't seem too thrilled about their guy or gal going up against the other. I figured they didn't want to see their god die."

Sam shook his head. "It's more than that. I'm not sure either of them is comfortable in their role. Especially Lena."

"Man, for a minute there, I thought she was going to kick Adamantine's metal ass. Good thing she didn't try, or she'd have ended up a crispy critter. Speaking of which, we now know it was Adamantine who killed those two people we saw when we first got to town."

"She seems a lot more ruthless than Paeon, doesn't

she?" Sam said. "He showed that he can use his powers offensively when he hurt Flare, but overall, his archetype is a god of healing, while Adamantine's archetype is a god of lightning, or in modern terms, electricity. Even if he increases his strength in the next couple hours, if I had to bet who would win in a fight between them, I'd put money on Adamantine." Sam thought for a moment. "Maybe we can use that. There's a good chance that Lena's already figured out that Paeon will lose. And from the way she acted toward Adamantine, my guess is she'd do just about anything to protect him. If we can get close to her and get her talking…"

"She might tell us what we need to know to stop Adamantine," Dean finished. "And we can use that knowledge against Paeon, too. That's a good idea. Devious, but good."

"Let's go then," Sam said. "They can't have gotten far. We should be able to catch up with them without too much trouble."

"You go, Sammy. I think one of us should see if he can get to this Mythmaker they talked about. Paeon said Adamantine was keeping her at TechEdge, which is evidently her 'temple.' Although personally I can think of way cooler places to use as a temple than a cheap electronics store."

"If you were a god, your temple would probably be a diner that serves the greasiest hamburgers in the world."

"Or the spiciest chili dogs," Dean said. "I'm not picky. But if we can find the Mythmaker and get her away from Adamantine, we might short circuit this process of theirs. What did Adamantine call it?"

"The Apotheosis," Sam said. "It's a word that means ascending to godhood."

"Right. If everything goes the way it's supposed to, then the winner gets to graduate from baby god to great big grown-up god. So what we need to do is give them a bad case of Apotheosis Interruptus. If we make it so things can't work they way they're supposed to—"

"Neither of them can win," Sam said. "And if that happens, then maybe they'll both die."

Dean nodded. "So you go see what you can learn from the good doctor, and I'll slide on over to TechEdge while Adamantine and Geoffrey are still out hunting down the other gods, and I'll see what I can do about the Mythmaker. With any luck, one way or the other we'll nip this Apotheosis thing in the bud."

"Sounds like a plan," Sam said.

The brothers turned away from each other and, just as Paeon and Adamantine had done, went their separate ways.

Sam caught up with Paeon's group after two blocks. The god stood in the parking lot of a twenty-four-hour pharmacy, surrounded by men, women, and—despite the cold and the lateness of the hour—children, and he spoke with each of them, smiling and touching his glowing caduceus to their chests one by one. Sam made his way to Lena's side and watched Paeon work for several moments before asking, "What's he doing?"

Lena turned to look at him. "You're Unbound?" she asked.

"At the moment. But I was impressed with the way Paeon

dealt with that fire god, and I'd like to learn more about him. You seem to be his…" Sam spread his hands. "I'm not sure what the term is."

"I'm not altogether clear on it myself, but *priest* seems to be the word most people use, including the gods themselves. Not that I feel much like a priest." She smiled. "But I'm happy to answer your questions. Paeon is Binding these people, and in so doing he's also…" She paused, searching for the right words. "Well, I suppose you could say he's upgrading them."

Sam frowned. "How so?"

"He's giving them perfect health, but more than that, he's raising them to the upper limits of what the human body is capable of. Wait a second." She reached into her coat pocket and brought out a ring of keys. She had a small multi-purpose tool attached to the ring as well. She took hold of it and unfolded a knife blade. "Watch," she said, and then she used the blade to slice open the tip of one of her index fingers. The wound sealed before a single drop of blood could emerge. She held up her finger to show him the smooth, unmarked flesh.

"That's amazing," he said.

"Isn't it?" She folded the knife into the multi-tool and put the keys back in her coat pocket. "That's the reason I follow Paeon. He has the ability to help humanity realize its full potential." She scowled. "Unlike the others."

"You mean Adamantine?" Sam asked.

"Yes. What does a god like her have to offer? Nothing. She only wants to dominate humans and use us to increase her own power. She's like a leech." Lena practically spat this last word.

"So Paeon doesn't need people to make himself stronger?" Sam asked.

Lena didn't answer right away. When she finally did, she said, "In his case, it's more a matter of symbiosis. We share our strength with him, he shares his power with us."

It sounded to Sam as if she were rationalizing her support of Paeon. She seemed more than a little doubtful, and he wondered if deep down she truly believed what she was saying.

"He can do more than heal, though. He did something to the fire god, twisted her insides around or something."

Lena paled as she looked away from him, and Sam knew he'd touched a nerve. Lena was a doctor, someone who'd dedicated herself to helping people, not harming them. Seeing Paeon use his power to hurt and potentially kill someone had to be difficult for her. More than that, from the strength of her reaction to his words, he sensed that she might well have had a taste of Paeon's wrath herself. After all, if she was his priest and she displeased him, wouldn't he punish her? And if he had, it would be hard for her to reconcile her idea of Paeon as a savior for humanity with the reality of him being a monster who happened to be wrapped in a pretty package. Those kind of monsters were the hardest to recognize.

"I can see he's using that wand of his to change people," Sam said. "Is that where his power comes from?"

She turned to look at him once more, eyes narrowing in suspicion. "You ask a lot of questions, don't you?"

Sam shrugged and did his best to appear innocent. "Binding yourself to a god is a big step. I just want to understand everything I can about **Paeon** before I make a commitment, you know?"

Her expression eased and she smiled. "I understand. After all, I expect patients to ask about my qualifications, so why wouldn't you ask about Paeon's? Honestly, I don't know how his power works. It can't all come from his caduceus, though. If it did, it would be too easy for another god to take it from him and render him powerless. And I've seen him fight gods—not just Flare—and win. When the defeated gods vanish, their weapons vanish, too. If the weapons held all the power, wouldn't they remain, and wouldn't the winning gods be able to use them to add to their overall strength? But the weapons are important. As near as I can tell, they're the only way to…"

She hesitated then, and Sam knew she was about to say: *The only way to kill them.* Instead, she said, "…channel and focus their power."

"I see. Interesting." Sam understood that Lena was Paeon's priest, and as such she had to protect her god's secrets, regardless of whatever ambivalence she might feel toward him.

Paeon had finished with the rest of the crowd and now approached them, a kindly smile on his face. "Who's this young man, Lena?"

"I didn't get his name." She turned to Sam, a questioning look on her face.

"Sam," he said. He tried to appear calm and relaxed, but inside he was nervous. If Paeon found out he was a hunter, the god would most likely kill him instantly by rearranging his internal organs, as he had done with Flare, or maybe cause him to have a fatal heart attack or devastating stroke. There were so many ways that a god who possessed the power to alter the human body could kill, and none of them were pleasant. But Paeon gave no sign that he thought Sam was anything but what he presented himself as—another potential worshipper.

Lena turned toward the god. "Sam's been asking about you. I believe he'd like to join our family."

"I hope you've only been saying positive things, my dear." Paeon's smile broadened, and he winked at Sam. There was a cold undertone to his voice, though—a very slight one—and Sam knew it was a warning to Lena. Paeon was giving her a message: *You'd* better *have been saying positive things, if you know what's good for you.*

Lena swallowed once, but then she managed a smile. "Of course."

"Excellent!" Paeon looked at Sam, his intense blue eyes seeming to glitter like chips of ice. "And have you come to a decision?"

Time to roll the dice, Sam thought. If he wanted to stay close to Lena, he was going to have to accept the god's "gift." He just hoped he'd be able to think clearly afterward. Lena still seemed able to think for herself, so with any luck, he should be able to as well.

"I'd like to join you—if you'll have me," he said.

Paeon's smile became warm and welcoming. "It would be our honor, Sam."

He held out his caduceus, and it began to glow with soft yellow light as he extended it toward Sam. When the tip of the rod touched his chest, energy exploded throughout his body. Electric fire raced along his nerve endings, his senses became heightened, and he felt stronger and more alert than he ever had before. He felt like he could take off right now and compete in a triathlon without breaking a sweat or breathing hard when he finished.

Paeon pulled the caduceus away from Sam and frowned.

"You must've led quite a dangerous life, Sam. Your body showed signs that you sustained numerous injuries over the years, many of them quite serious."

Paeon and Lena looked at him, both clearly expecting an answer.

Sam was having trouble concentrating. He felt so good it was almost like being on some kind of super stimulant, and he thought, *I bet this was how the Underwoods felt when the Lord of the Hunt granted them strength.* Then again, he had a hard time imagining the Underwoods had ever felt *this* great. Paeon and Lena were still waiting for him to answer, and he forced himself to concentrate.

"I was into extreme sports when I was younger," he said, "and I got banged up a lot." He waited to see if either Paeon or Lena would challenge his explanation, but it seemed to satisfy them both. The god put his hand on Sam's shoulder then.

"Well, you're good as new now, Sam. Better, even." Paeon grinned.

Sam couldn't help it. He grinned back.

Before any of them could say anything more, an inhuman shriek split the air. The three of them turned to see a nine-foot-tall humanoid lizard striding down the street toward them, followed by several dozen men and women. The creature had a pair of overlarge rubies in place of eyes, and they pulsed with crimson energy.

Paeon sighed. "Excuse me, Sam. I have some work to attend to."

As Paeon moved off to accept this latest challenge, Sam found himself praying that the god—*his* god—would be victorious.

Dean returned to Doughnutz, got in the Impala, and used his phone to get directions to TechEdge. It wasn't very far away, less than a five-minute drive. But it took him at least twice the time because there were so many people out walking in the streets. It was as if the entire population of Corinth had left their homes in the middle of the night to participate in the Apotheosis. Maybe they had, he thought. Whatever power was ultimately at work here could have affected the whole town by now, and as events were moving rapidly toward a climax, every man, woman, and child was being compelled to take part. Hell, it was even possible that it was happening to him and Sam, too. They thought they were working to stop the Apotheosis, but what if they really had become part of it, like everyone else in Corinth? What if their actions were actually helping to make the Apotheosis happen somehow? It was a damn scary thought, and one that Dean didn't want to examine too closely, so he continued driving and did his best to make his way through the crowds without running over anyone.

When he finally reached TechEdge, he parked in the lot of the business next door, a discount furniture store called

Cheap Seats. He figured there were a couple ways he could play this. He could go around the back of the TechEdge building and try to sneak in through a rear entrance or maybe the loading dock. Then he could make his way into the store and try to locate the Mythmaker. The problem with that was a business like TechEdge would have surveillance cameras, and if Adamantine's followers were monitoring them, they'd see him coming. That didn't mean he couldn't get in, of course. He'd gotten past more than one security system in his time, but it would make getting inside trickier. Option Number Two was to walk up to TechEdge's main entrance and present himself as a new worshipper eager to join the ranks of Adamantine's happy little minions. Both Adamantine and Paeon had kicked their god-killing-slash-recruiting drives into high gear, and it would seem natural enough that a new follower would show up on TechEdge's doorstep tonight. This option should get him inside easily enough, but it would be harder to find the Mythmaker then because everyone would be watching him. He'd have to wait until they'd gotten used to his presence so he could slip away and look for her. Still, it seemed like his best bet.

He got out of the Impala and headed across the parking lot toward TechEdge, still carrying his gun tucked against the small of his back. No way was he going in unarmed. He would just have to hope that Adamantine's followers weren't on the ball enough to search any new recruits who entered the building, and if they were—well, he'd burn that bridge when he came to it.

The lights were on inside the building, and he could see

a pair of worshippers standing by the front door, keeping watch on the parking lot. They saw him coming, so he smiled and gave what he hoped was a friendly wave. They opened the door as he approached, and waited for him. The guards—a middle-aged man and a young woman—looked like ordinary people. They were obviously cautious, but neither carried themselves as if they'd had military or police training. That was good. Civilians were easier to fool.

Dean kept the smile on his face as he drew near.

"This is Adamantine's place, right?" he said.

The guards looked at each other for a second, but neither replied. Dean went on.

"I'm here to join the flock, or whatever you call it. I caught her act in town, and I've got to say, she made quite an impression on me… the electricity, and that whole silver thing she's got going on. That's what I call a god, you know what I'm saying?"

Dean had reached the guards, and they stood shoulder to shoulder in the doorway, blocking him from entering. They looked at him for a long moment, and then the woman said, "You're not Bound."

Takes one to know one, I guess. "Adamantine was kind of busy. I guess she figured she'd get around to Binding me when she could."

The man frowned. "She would never be too busy to gather up another lost soul and make him part of our family."

A true believer, Dean thought. *Just what I need.* "I don't know what the basic procedure is around here, pal. All I can tell you is Adamantine ran into a god called Paeon, they made a date to meet here at dawn, and then they both beat feet to get ready for whatever's going to happen here. I figured if this is where the action's going to be, then this is where I should come. But if you don't want me…"

He started to turn away, but the woman grabbed his shoulder before he could take a single step.

"No, please! Come in and join us!" she said. "There is much to be done!"

Dean smiled at her. "Well, if you insist…"

Once Dean was inside TechEdge and had a chance to look over Adamantine's "army," one thing became very clear to him. No way in hell were any of these people even *close* to being soldiers. There were well over a hundred of them in the store—a mix of genders, races, ages, and physical types—but they all had one thing in common: none of them looked like they'd ever been in a fight before. Hell, most of them looked as if they'd surrender the first time someone gave them a harsh look. Still, word of the upcoming battle had spread swiftly, and Adamantine's followers were doing their best to arm themselves with whatever they could find in the store— scissors, box cutters, even pens, and when there weren't enough of those to go around, they improvised, dismantling electronic devices and pulling apart display shelves for anything that they could grip in their hands and use to hit or cut an opponent with. He admired their determination, but he knew Adamantine had never intended the poor sonsofbitches to be warriors. Their real purpose in the final battle was to serve as energy reserves for her, living batteries that she could drain whenever she needed a power boost.

He was tempted to try to explain the reality of their situation to them. If he could convince them they were being used, maybe some of them would get the hell out of here before things went straight down the toilet. Even if he only managed to save a few lives that way, it would be worth it. But if he did that, he'd reveal to the others that he wasn't a true believer like them, and they might decide to try out their makeshift weapons on him before the real fighting got started. It would be better if he could find the Mythmaker and somehow find a way to short circuit the whole Apotheosis. That way, he could save everyone here.

Everyone was so caught up in preparing for war that no one paid any attention to him. He pretended to search for a weapon, walking up and down the aisles, occasionally picking up a laptop or a game console, looking it over, then putting it back before moving on. While he did this, he thought, *If I were Adamantine, where would I hide someone as important as the Mythmaker?* There were only a few places he could think of: the warehouse, the managers' offices, and the staff break room. He made his way toward the back of the store where the stereo equipment was displayed. Tucked in one corner was an open entrance to a small hallway, and when Dean was sure no one was looking in his direction, he walked inside.

The first things he saw were doors for the men's and women's restrooms, with a water fountain located on the opposite wall. He continued on and came to an office. The door was shut, but there was a glass window which provided a view of the cramped space within. Desk, filing cabinet, a couple chairs, but no Mythmaker. The hallway ended in two branching corridors, one right, one left. Dean flipped a mental coin, headed left, and when he saw the two men standing in front of a closed door, he knew he'd found the break room.

Both of the men were in their thirties—one lean, one a bit overweight—but from the measured way they gazed at him as he approached, Dean knew they both knew how to handle themselves in a fight. He didn't think they were veterans or police officers, probably just local toughs who liked to duke it out in a bar parking lot with whoever had pissed them off that night. But that didn't mean they weren't dangerous in their own way.

"Hey, fellas. Why aren't you out there getting ready with everybody else?"

The heavier guard—whose head and lower face were covered with black stubble—scowled and said, "Who the hell are you?"

Dean wanted to punch the jackass, but instead he gave the man a smile that he hoped didn't look too strained. "My name's Dean, but you can call me New Guy. I just got here not too long ago."

"So why should we give a damn?" the leaner man said. He had greasy brown hair and a scraggly goatee.

So much for everyone being part of one big happy family, Dean thought. "No reason. But I'm surprised to find you two back here. I mean, you guys are the only ones I've seen in this place who look like they can fight. And they've got you standing guard?"

The two men exchanged glances then turned to look at Dean once more.

"It's an important job," Stubble-Head said.

"Yeah," Goatee added, sounding more than a little defensive.

Dean held up his hands in a peacemaking gesture. "Never said it wasn't. But everyone out there is preparing for some kind of big battle with another god's followers and, just between the three of us, none of them look like they know what the hell they're doing. They're only going to get themselves killed and let Adamantine down."

"Aw, they're not *that* bad," Goatee said. But then he looked at Stubble-Head and added, "Are they?"

"They could really use someone who knows what it's like to fight," Dean said. "You can't have good soldiers without good generals, am I right?"

"What, you mean us?" Stubble-Head said.

"Why not?" Dean said. "You guys look like you know how to handle yourselves a hell of a lot better than everyone out there." He hooked a thumb over his shoulder.

Stubble-Head puffed out his chest. "Damn straight." He turned to his companion. "C'mon, Earl. Let's get out there and whip those wimps into shape."

"But, Larry, we're supposed to stay on guard until Adamantine comes back," Earl said. He sounded nervous, and Dean didn't blame him. He imagined Adamantine took an extremely dim view of those followers of her who disobeyed her orders.

"I can fill in for you guys," Dean said. "It's not like I'm doing anything else right now. Besides, it'll make me feel like I'm contributing, you know?"

Earl still looked doubtful, so Dean decided to sweeten the pot.

"Look, if Adamantine gives you any grief, you can just blame it on the new guy."

Earl smiled with relief. "Well… okay. I was getting bored standing around here anyway."

Larry and Earl left then, and Dean took up a position in front of the door. The two men gave him one last glance before turning the corner, and Dean nodded and gave them an informal salute. He waited a few moments, and when he was confident they were out of earshot, he turned, took hold of the knob, found it unlocked, and opened the door.

He stepped inside and saw a young woman sitting up on a couch. She stretched, yawned, and said, "Where the hell am I?"

THIRTEEN

Dean gave the woman—whose name was Renee—a quick rundown on what was happening in Corinth. Long before he was finished, he realized how insane it all sounded. Hell, it even sounded crazy to *him*, and given the kind of life he led, he ate, breathed, and slept crazy twenty-four-seven. But to his surprise, Renee accepted his explanation without question.

"This is going to sound weird, but the whole time I was painting those pictures, I had the feeling that something more was going on—something *bigger*, you know? But bringing gods to life…?" She shook her head. "Talk about life imitating art."

"And it's not over yet," Dean said. He explained that Adamantine would soon be returning and that when dawn arrived, another god named Paeon would show up to fight her. He told her she, as the Mythmaker, was supposed to play an important role in this battle, but he had no idea what that role was.

"Mythmaker, huh? That title's a lot more impressive than

'Struggling Art Student.' But what would they need me for?
I've already brought them to life."

"Like I said, I don't know why they need you, just that they
do. Or at least *think* they do. Whatever the truth, the most
important thing is to get you out of here before sunrise. If we
can keep you away from them, there's a chance—"

"I'm glad to see you are awake, Renee."

Dean turned to see Adamantine standing in the doorway,
Geoffrey in the hall behind her.

Adamantine fixed her baleful blue-white gaze on Dean and
smiled.

"Who is your new boyfriend?"

"Getting close to dawn," Sam said.

Lena glanced up at the sky. "Yes. I should call those who
remained at my practice and tell them to start heading for
TechEdge." She took a phone from her jacket pocket and
made the call.

Paeon and his followers—who now numbered well past
a hundred—were gathered in a small park. Fires had been
started in a couple trash cans, and people stood around them,
more for the emotional comfort created by their cheery glow
than from any real need to warm themselves. Ever since
Paeon had enhanced him, Sam hadn't felt the temperature at
all, and he knew it was the same for everyone else here. Paeon
walked among his people, chatting with them, laying his
hands on their shoulders, smiling and laughing. Occasionally
a new person approached him, and he touched the caduceus
to them, transforming and Binding them. Since Sam had

joined Paeon's followers, the god had bested a half-dozen challengers, but they hadn't seen any other gods for the better part of an hour, and Sam was beginning to think that there were no other gods left—except for Adamantine, of course. The thought was exciting. It wouldn't be long now.

Lena finished her call, disconnected, then put her phone away.

"They'll meet us at TechEdge, and they'll make sure to let everyone else know, too."

"Everyone else?" Sam asked.

"Not all of Paeon's followers accompanied him tonight or remained at my practice…" She paused, then corrected herself. "I mean his *temple*. Many of them went home to tell their loved ones about Paeon and what he can do for his followers. I assume a number of Adamantine's people did the same. My people will spread the word that the Apotheosis will soon reach its culmination, and everyone will converge on TechEdge at the appointed time."

The part of Sam that belonged to Paeon felt only joy at the thought of all those people coming together to support their god as the final battle began. But the part of Sam that remained free, that was a hunter with the last name of Winchester, was appalled by the number of followers on both sides who would soon be gathering at TechEdge. There would be hundreds of them, maybe more. Hell, the whole damn town might show up.

"Aren't you a little… concerned?" Sam asked.

Lena gave him a puzzled look. "What do you mean?"

"I know that we all heal super-fast now, but just how

serious is this fight going to be? Are people going to bring weapons? Is everyone going to try to kill each other?"

Lena didn't answer right away, and Sam knew that she hadn't thought this far ahead. Maybe Paeon's influence had kept her from considering the ramifications of the final battle, but from the look on her face, she was considering them now.

"I don't know what's going to happen," she admitted. "We will just have to trust in Paeon, won't we?"

Sam wanted to shout at her, to tell her she was a doctor and that it was against her medical oath to condone the slaughter to come. But when she spoke Paeon's name a feeling of well-being washed over him, and it carried away his doubts and fears, leaving him with nothing but happiness. He was looking forward to the battle to come, and he hoped that he would serve Paeon well.

Paeon was talking with a group of children, squatting on his heels to put himself on their level, when he stopped and cocked his head, as if he were listening to something only he could hear. He looked up at the sky then, and a wide smile spread across his face.

He stood and in a loud voice announced, "It is time."

Everyone in the park cheered—Lena included—but no one cheered louder than Sam.

Adamantine didn't look any different than the last time Dean had seen her, but she now emanated such strong waves of power that it was difficult to see her clearly. The air around her rippled, like the distortion caused by heat waves rising from a road in summertime.

She raised her gauntlet, pressed it against Dean's chest, and a skein of electricity flowed outward from the metal to briefly envelop his body. His jaw clenched and his muscles contracted tight, but it was over in a second. The electricity winked out, and Adamantine pulled the gauntlet away from him. Dean couldn't see it, but both of his eyes were now a solid silver.

"I don't know what advantages the power you carry will give you, but you will take it with you into battle and use it in my name. Yes?"

Dean looked at Renee. She recoiled from his silver-eyed gaze, but the sight of her horror meant nothing to him. All that mattered was doing his god's bidding.

"Yes, my lady," he said.

Dawn pinked the eastern sky as Paeon, Lena, and Sam strode into TechEdge's lot, a hundred or more of Paeon's followers behind them. Dozens of cars, trucks, vans, and motorcycles were parked off to one side, and people stood around the vehicles, waiting for the arrival of their god. Many of them carried guns, while others held knives, baseball bats, tire irons, hammers, or various makeshift clubs. More vehicles were parked on the opposite side of the lot, but their drivers were nowhere in sight. Sam assumed the cars and trucks belonged to followers of Adamantine who had come to join the party. He presumed they were inside TechEdge, waiting for the fun to start.

Sheriff Deacon walked up next to Sam. He carried a pump-action shotgun and was grinning ear to ear.

"Is this a great day or what?" he said. "I am *so* glad I joined Team Paeon. We are going to kick some major ass today, am I right?" The sheriff raised his voice on these last few words, and the people close by let out cheers and shouts of agreement.

Sam wanted to smile, but he couldn't bring himself to. He had no doubt Paeon would be victorious this day, and that was a wonderful thing, but he couldn't help thinking about all the damage Paeon's followers could do with their weapons, and from the unhappy look on Lena's face, she was thinking the same thing. Sam found himself thinking of the Underwoods then, of how they'd justified feeding him and Dean to the ancient Lord of the Hunt as part of accomplishing some greater good. What was the good here? Lena believed—or maybe just hoped—that Paeon would use his powers to transform the human race into a stronger, healthier species. But if the god truly was a healer, would he be leading his army into battle like this, knowing full well that any number of his people might die before the fight was over? No, a true healer would refuse to fight, or at least refuse to involve anyone else in his battle. Paeon wasn't a physician; he only looked like one on the outside. Inside, he was just another monster out for all the power he could get.

And with that thought, Sam felt the last vestiges of Paeon's control fade from his mind. He still felt stronger and more energized than he ever had before in his life, but he was able to think for himself again. He wondered why no one else seemed able to throw off Paeon's control, and he chalked it up to his experience as a hunter. He'd lost count of how many times supernatural entities had attempted to mess with his mind, and he supposed that over the years he'd developed if not an immunity to mind control, at least a resistance.

He leaned closer to Lena and spoke softly in her ear. "Lena, you know what's about to happen is wrong. You're a *doctor*. You can't let this continue."

She didn't look at him as she answered, but her mouth tightened, and he could hear the tension in her voice. "It's too late. Can't you feel it? It's like we're being swept along in a tidal wave. This is going to happen no matter what we do. It *has* to."

Despite his plea to her, Sam knew she was right. This wasn't just him and Dean inside a spooky abandoned house hunting down a lone monster or trying to banish a ghost. They were dealing with two gods who were followed by hundreds of people, all of them fulfilling their roles in a cosmic cycle that could well be as old as time. You might as well try to derail an oncoming train by parking a child's tricycle on the tracks. They had to do something to stop it, but *what*?

Paeon waved to his followers who'd been waiting, and they moved forward to join the main mass of his force. United, they continued marching toward TechEdge's main entrance, Paeon leading them. Sam thought furiously, desperately trying to come up with some kind of plan—and he found himself thinking about the Underwoods again, or more precisely, about his and Dean's fight with the Lord of the Hunt.

"You ready?"

The woman who asked the question was Gayle, the paramedic he and Sam had spoken to when they'd first arrived in Corinth. Her eyes—like the eyes of everyone inside the store with the exception of Renee—were pure silver. Dean didn't ask her how she'd come to Bind herself to Adamantine. It didn't matter. All that mattered was that they followed the same god.

"You know it," he said.

He hadn't drawn his .45, and the rest of Adamantine's followers had gotten rid of the makeshift weapons they'd scavenged from the store. They no longer needed such things, not after Adamantine had shared a portion of her vast power with them. Dean flexed his fingers and tiny tendrils of electricity coiled around them. He smiled. This was going to be fun.

The aisles of TechEdge were crowded with men, women, and children, all of them silver-eyed, all of them just as eager as Dean for the battle to begin. The only two people who didn't seem excited were Geoffrey and Renee. They stood next to Adamantine by the store's entrance, but while Adamantine gazed through the glass at Paeon and his army, Geoffrey only looked at Renee. Her wrists had been bound with a length of computer cable, and Geoffrey had hold of her arm to keep her from trying to escape. The man had a sorrowful expression on his face, as if he was worried about her, and Dean supposed he couldn't blame him. Whatever role the woman was destined to play in today's events, he doubted she'd survive—and if she did, she sure as hell wouldn't be the same. But that was okay. Omelets and broken eggs. Besides, if she died, she wouldn't be the only one who did so today. War resulted in casualties, no two ways around it. The trick was to keep your side's losses to an acceptable number.

What about the kids? If any of them die, I suppose they'll be acceptable losses, too?

It was his voice that he heard in his mind, but it was as if another part of himself—a deeply buried part—spoke the words.

Dean stood at the front of the store, not far from Adamantine, Geoffrey, and Renee. He glanced back over his shoulder and noted how many children—from teenagers down to toddlers who could barely walk—numbered among Adamantine's followers. He knew it was the same situation with Paeon's people. Entire families had Bound themselves to one of the two gods, and every member had shown up today determined to do his or her best to ensure their chosen deity was victorious.

Are they here of their own free will? his other voice said. *Or is it because Adamantine and Paeon are forcing them to be here? And what about you? Since when do you let anyone lead you around by a leash?*

This last thought galled him, and he felt anger rising. He'd been controlled too many times over the years — when he'd been turned into a soldier of Hell, when the archangel Michael had attempted to use him as a vessel, when he'd become an actual black-eyed demon—and he'd be damned if he would let it happen again. He fought back against Adamantine's control with all his will. At first nothing happened, but then he felt a small jolt deep inside himself, and he knew the connection Adamantine had forged between them when she'd forcibly Bound him was gone. He'd done it. He was his own man again.

Through the glass windows in the front of the store, he saw

that Paeon and his troops were on the move. Sam was out there somewhere, and he hoped his brother had had better luck coming up with a plan to stop this madness, because he sure as hell didn't have one. Dean knew if he planned to try something from this end, he had only moments left to act before Adamantine commanded her worshippers to rush outside and engage the enemy. She'd ordered Geoffrey to keep Renee inside and safe until the battle was over, and if he could get to her, maybe he could—

"The time has come!" Adamantine shouted, her unearthly voice causing the entire store to shake. And then her followers—with the exception of Dean, Geoffrey, and Renee—shouted back, *"In the end there shall be One!"*

Time's up, Dean thought.

Adamantine threw open the front doors and stepped out into the early morning light, electricity coruscating across both her gauntlet and her spear. Her followers pushed forward, eager to be close to their god when the fighting began, and Dean found himself pressed in on all sides by shouting men and women, their silver eyes gleaming, hands sparking with electricity. He pushed, hit, and kicked, trying to force his way free so he could get to Renee, but his efforts were in vain. There were too many people, and all he could do was let them carry him through the entrance and into the parking lot. He looked back over his shoulder and saw Geoffrey and Renee had moved out of the entrance and were now looking through a window. Renee looked scared and Geoffrey—with his new silver eyes—looked sad, and then Dean was shoved forward so hard he almost lost his balance.

He knew if he went down now he'd be trampled, so he faced straight ahead and did his best to keep up with the crowd's momentum. And then, so fast he tripped and bumped into a man ahead of him, the crowd stopped.

The first rays of dawn tinged the horizon as Paeon and Adamantine stood facing each other, their respective armies massed behind them.

"I'm gratified to see you survived to reach this point," Adamantine said.

Paeon smiled and inclined his head to acknowledge her comment. "Did you have any doubt?"

"No," she said. "I knew it would come down to the two of us."

"As did I."

"Soon it will be only one," she said.

"As it should be. Are you ready?"

Adamantine smiled. "Since the day I was born."

Paeon raised his caduceus and it began to glow with dark energy. Adamantine leveled her spear at him in a two-handed grip, and the electricity coursing along its length doubled in intensity. Neither god gave a visible command, but their followers cried out in fury and ran toward one another.

The battle had begun.

Lena watched in horror as Paeon's and Adamantine's followers began fighting. Paeon's people moved with a speed born from the enhancements their god had gifted them with, and they struck with their weapons, acting so swiftly that Adamantine's people didn't have time to defend themselves.

Voices cried out in pain, blood spilled, and the first wave of wounded and dead fell to the asphalt. Adamantine's people might have been slower than Paeon's, but their god had given them something extra-special as well. They stretched out their hands toward their enemies and bolts of crackling electricity leapt from their fingertips to strike their foes. Instead of screaming when the lightning struck, the victims' bodies went rigid, and they began to shake all over as their nervous systems overloaded. The incredible healing abilities that Paeon had given to his worshippers struggled to throw off the effects of the electrical attacks and repair the damage done to their bodies. Some managed to recover, following up with counterattacks against their enemies, stabbing them, shooting them, or simply bashing them in the head. But others weren't so strong, and they fell to the ground, dead, their healing capacity overwhelmed by the sheer amount of energy that had been forced into their bodies.

Lena was so shocked by the nightmarish battle taking place around her that at first she paid no attention to Paeon and Adamantine, but this was partly because the two gods stood toe-to-toe, neither moving, both frozen in place as if they were statues. Paeon's caduceus was pressed against Adamantine's forehead, while the tip of her spear was embedded in his left shoulder. A nimbus of energy cocooned them, a blend of the caduceus's dark power and Adamantine's electricity. The effect was quite beautiful in its own way, and the energy bubble continued to grow as the gods threw more and more of their power at each other. Lena hadn't been sure what to expect when the gods started fighting, but it hadn't been this.

They weren't really doing anything, just standing there and glaring at each other. It was nothing like the other battles between gods that she'd witnessed, but then she realized that at this point, it wasn't about who could strike the swiftest or inflict the most damage. It was all about raw, naked power, pure and simple. Paeon and Adamantine were locked in a war of energies, and all the strength they'd claimed from the gods they'd killed, all the energy provided by the lives of those worshippers fighting around them, were their weapons now. The real battle was happening on a level that no human could hope to comprehend, and when it was over, there would be One. But the Apotheosis wouldn't be complete then, she realized. In order to become a true immortal, the victor would have to absorb the energy of the being with the power to create gods—the Mythmaker.

Lena couldn't let that happen. She had been wrong to help Paeon, she saw that now. He wasn't a god; he was an inhuman thing interested only in increasing his own power, and if he became the One, he would be no better than Adamantine. In the end, there really was no difference between them. They were both monsters, and all monsters knew how to do was kill.

Fine. She was a doctor, and every doctor knew that in order to help your patient, sometimes you had to perform a little surgery.

She saw Sheriff Deacon lying on the ground less than a dozen feet from where she stood. His body was blackened and smoldering from having been electrocuted by one of Adamantine's followers, and the sight sickened her. But it was too late to do anything to help him now. But she could put the shotgun that he still gripped in his charred hand to good use. She hurried over to his corpse, doing her best not to get caught in the combatants' crossfire, grabbed hold of the shotgun, and yanked it out of his dead hand. He had been so badly burned that a couple of his fingers broke off like bits of charcoal, but she forced herself not to look at them. She briefly examined the shotgun. She'd never fired one before, but she'd made it through med school and residency, and she was confident she was smart enough to figure out how to operate the weapon. It was pump action, which meant there might still be shells inside, but she figured she would need all the ammunition the gun could hold. She checked the sheriff's coat pockets for extra shells, found a couple, and loaded them into the gun. When she was finished, she looked down at the sheriff.

"I'm sorry for what happened to you. I'm going to try to make it right."

Then she turned and headed for Paeon and Adamantine.

Dean saw Lena retrieve the dead sheriff's shotgun and start toward the two gods, who at the moment were barely visible within the giant glowing ball of energy that surrounded them. Whatever the doctor had in mind, he knew it wasn't going to work, and he started toward her, hoping he could intercept her before she did anything to get herself killed. But he only managed to take a few steps before one of Paeon's people was suddenly standing in front of him. The man had moved so fast that at first Dean didn't register his image, and his hands were halfway up and ready to discharge deadly bolts of electricity before he realized it was Sam.

"What's with the silver eyes?" Sam asked, his words coming out in a rush as if his entire metabolism had been speeded up.

"Tell you later. Right now we need to stop Paeon's priest before she makes what's likely to be a fatal mistake."

Sam glanced over his shoulder at the woman, who was still advancing toward the energy bubble containing the two gods, but he quickly turned his attention back to Dean.

"You'll have to handle it. I need to find the Mythmaker."

Dean had hunted alongside his brother far too long to question him in the heat of battle. Besides, he didn't have time for talk if he was going to have any chance to help Lena.

"Geoffrey's holding her captive inside TechEdge. Be careful, though. He's been transformed into a living battery like the rest of us, so he's—"

"Got it. Thanks." Sam sped off, weaving his way between warring worshippers as he ran toward the TechEdge building.

"You're welcome, Flash," Dean muttered, and then started running—at a much slower velocity—toward the shotgun-toting doctor.

Geoffrey watched from the safety of the building as Adamantine and Paeon clashed, their respective armies fighting around them. As Adamantine's priest, he should've felt tremendous excitement upon seeing the final stages of the Apotheosis begin, but all he felt was empty inside.

"Why do you do it?" Renee asked. "Follow her, I mean."

Geoffrey turned away from the window to look at her. If he and Ellen had been lucky enough to have had a child, she would've been this girl's age. Maybe a little older. He couldn't believe that such an ordinary-looking person possessed the ability to imagine gods into existence. Oh, she was pretty, but she didn't look like someone who had the power of creation itself surging inside her. All the gods she'd willed into existence—at least those that he'd seen—*looked* like gods. They were more than human—larger than life and gifted with extraordinary power. But this average, unassuming young woman had within her a power far stronger than any of those gods wielded. She was the Mythmaker.

She looked at him expectantly. He remembered her question then, and he decided to answer it honestly.

"At first I followed her because she threatened to kill me if I didn't. I knew she'd do it because I saw her kill a friend of mine who'd rejected her. But it didn't take long before I *wanted* to follow her. Maybe that's part of their power, to make us want to follow them, to make us *need* them. But if so, that wasn't all of it. It felt good to be able to believe in something—some*one*—that was real. It made me feel important, made me feel like I mattered, for the first time in a long time."

"And now?" Renee asked.

Geoffrey looked out the window at the fighting once more. Adamantine and Paeon were surrounded by a sphere of energy, and many of their worshippers lay on the asphalt, hurt or dead. Paeon's people fought with weapons and speed, while Adamantine's fought by unleashing the electrical power that she'd lent them. Neither side looked as if it had an advantage, and Geoffrey feared that before the sun had risen very high in the sky, most—if not all—of the people he was looking at now would be dead.

"It just seems so meaningless," he said softly.

He saw a man break away from the mass of people and then come running toward the building's entrance. Given the speed with which he ran, Geoffrey knew he was one of Paeon's people. It appeared that while Paeon fought Adamantine, he had ordered one of his soldiers to abduct the Mythmaker. That was all right, though. Adamantine had anticipated this might happen.

"Stay behind me," he said to Renee, and then he raised his hands and summoned the energy that Adamantine had implanted within him. Electricity crackled and sparked between his fingers, and he prepared to fight, although at this point he didn't know why.

Sam slowed as he approached the entrance to TechEdge, marveling at his enhanced body's abilities. He'd just run faster than he ever had before and he was barely winded. *I could get used to this,* he thought.

Sam figured Geoffrey possessed the same electrical power as the rest of Adamantine's followers. Sam had managed to dodge a number of electrical bolts as he'd run through the fighting armies, but he'd seen their effect on others. The bolts inflicted so much damage so swiftly that even the healing abilities of Paeon's ultimate humans had difficulty coping with them. Because of this, he knew it would be foolish to go up against one of Adamantine's people unarmed. He might be stronger and faster than an ordinary human at the moment, but he couldn't move faster than electricity. He drew his 9mm and reached for the door handle—

—only to be hurled backward as a blast of lightning crashed through the glass and struck him in the chest. He flew twenty feet through the air and landed on his back with the sound of snapping bones. He felt sharp pain shoot through his left arm, and a heaviness pressed down on his chest. *I'm having a heart attack,* he thought. The electricity from the blast had disrupted the electrical current of his heart, like defibrillator paddles used to harm instead of help. His body bucked as muscles contracted and released, and his vision began to go dark as the pain in his chest became excruciating. Compared to it, his broken bones and the shards of glass embedded in his flesh were nothing.

I can't die, he thought. *I still have work to do.*

He watched as a man stepped through the opening where the door had been. His figure was little more than a hazy gray silhouette to Sam, but he thought he was looking at Geoffrey.

"Don't get up, boy. I'll kill you if I have to, but I'd rather not. The choice is yours."

The man's voice was firm, if not unkind, and although Sam thought he detected a certain reluctance underlying the words, he believed Geoffrey was telling the truth. Paeon's gift of healing was already doing its work, and Sam's vision began to clear. The heaviness on his chest lessened, and his bones began fusing together. It would still be a few minutes until he was in fighting shape again, but he didn't have time to wait. The more time he wasted, the more people died fighting Paeon and Adamantine's war. He'd managed to hold onto his gun when he'd fallen, and without sitting up—because he wasn't sure he could yet—he raised his hand, aimed, and fired.

Geoffrey cried out as the bullet struck him, and he spun to the side and fell to the ground.

"No!"

A young woman came out of the building, moving awkwardly because her hands were tied behind her back with a length of thin black cable. This, he assumed, was the Mythmaker.

"Don't kill him! He doesn't want to help Adamantine, not really!"

Sam had healed to the point where he could sit up. It didn't hurt as much as he feared, so he gave standing a try. He was weak and stiff, but he managed to accomplish that maneuver as well, although with more difficulty. He no longer felt any pain within his chest, although the flesh where the electricity had struck him still stung. But that too faded quickly. He felt his body push out the glass that had struck him when the door exploded, and shards tumbled to the ground around him. A moment later, he felt good as new. Better, in fact.

At that instant, he could almost understand why the Underwoods had made their deal with the Lord of the Hunt. He felt strong, confident, able to accomplish anything, and those kind of feelings could become very addictive very fast. For a second, he remembered the hot, foul taste of demon blood in his mouth, and he knew that he had no right to judge the Underwoods. Both he and Dean had made deals of their own with supernatural forces, most of which they'd lived to regret in one way or another.

He thrust those thoughts aside and gazed down at Geoffrey.

The Mythmaker knelt down next to him and quickly examined him. Sam could tell just by looking the man would likely live. The round from the 9mm had struck him in the left shoulder, and although the man's eyes were closed, his chest rose and fell regularly, so he was breathing okay.

The woman evidently came to the same conclusion, for she stood, a look of relief on her face.

"Thanks for not killing him," she said.

Sam didn't tell her that he'd been aiming for the man's heart, but his vision had been so poor and his grip so unsteady that he'd been lucky to hit the guy's shoulder.

"What's your name?" Sam asked.

"Renee Mendez," she said. The air was filled with the sounds of shouting and screaming, along with the *pop-pop-pop* of gunfire and the *crack-sizzle* of released electricity. She looked past Sam at the fighting, and an expression of horror came over her face. "Did I cause this?"

So she knows she's the Mythmaker, Sam thought. *Good, that'll make this easier.*

"It's not your fault," Sam said. "None of it is. But I think you might be able to stop it if you're willing to trust me and do what I say. I won't lie to you, though. It'll be dangerous."

Renee gazed upon the battle once more, and her expression of horror was replaced by one of determination.

"Okay. What do we have to do?"

FOURTEEN

Dean ran as fast as he could, firing off low-level blasts of electricity to force people to get out of his way. But even so, he wasn't able to reach Paeon and Adamantine before Lena did. He watched as she raised the shotgun, aimed it at the pulsating sphere of energy surrounding the warring gods, and began firing, pumping shells into the chamber one after another until she'd used them all. Dean was impressed. Not many people could stand and fire upon a pair of gods without so much as flinching. If she ever decided to give up medicine, she'd make a hell of a hunter.

He wasn't sure what Lena hoped to accomplish with her bravery, though. He'd seen Paeon heal the burns he'd suffered when Flare attacked him, so he doubted a few shotgun shells would do much more than tickle him. And as for Adamantine... well, her skin *was* made of some kind of metal, and if it wasn't impervious to damage, it had to be resistant as hell. But then, as if the energy sphere itself had been angered by the attack, a tentacle of black light combined with silver electricity emerged from the sphere and whipped through the air toward the doctor. It coiled around her with the speed of a striking snake, and she threw back her head and screamed.

Dean reached her then, and he thrust out his hands and released twin bolts of electrical energy at the tentacle. His efforts seemed to have no effect, and so he gritted his teeth and gave it everything he had, unleashing every ounce of power that Adamantine had given him. But the tentacle, being made of energy itself, appeared to absorb all the electrical power that Dean sent into it without any harm. And still Lena screamed...

Then, as abruptly as if someone somewhere threw a switch, her screaming stopped.

The tentacle released her and retreated back into the energy sphere. She fell to the ground, limp and lifeless, and Adamantine and Paeon continued to stand toe-to-toe within the sphere, locked together in motionless combat, neither showing any sign that they were aware of what had just happened.

Dean felt exhausted, as if he'd been drained of energy—figuratively *and* literally—but he went to Lena, knelt next to her, and put his fingers to her neck to check her pulse. Nothing. He wondered why she wasn't healing like the rest of Paeon's people. Maybe the combination of the two gods' power had been too much for her system to handle, even with Paeon's upgrades. Whatever the reason, she was dead, and there was nothing... He had a sudden idea then. He'd tried to pour every bit of electrical power his body possessed into his attack on the energy tentacle, but if he had some left, even if only a little…

He rubbed his hands together and placed them on Lena's chest. Energy released, her body convulsed, and then she fell back and was still once more. He was about to try again when her eyes flew open and she drew in a gasping breath.

Dean smiled. "Welcome back, Doc."

Sam and Renee had an easier time reaching the energy sphere than he'd expected, but that was because the followers of both gods—those who hadn't already fallen in battle, that is—began to collapse like falling dominoes, and there were few left to impede their progress. He saw Gayle the paramedic go down, and he wished he could stop and see if she was all right, but he knew they were running out of time, and he pushed on.

"What's happening?" Renee asked.

"I think Paeon and Adamantine are drawing on their worshippers for extra power," Sam said.

"Are they dying?"

"I don't know." One thing he *did* know: They had to hurry before the gods got around to draining him and Dean.

They found Dean kneeling next to Lena, who was sitting on the asphalt. She looked as if she were fighting to stop herself from passing out, and Dean had a hand on her back to keep her steady.

Dean looked up as they approached. "About time you two showed up."

Lena frowned as she looked at Renee. "Who's this, Sam?"

Then she looked at Dean. "And who are you?"

"Short version?" Dean said. "Sam and I are brothers who hunt and kill monsters for a living. This young lady is Renee. She dreamed up the gods that have been crawling all over your town like super-powered cockroaches lately."

"I didn't mean to!" Renee said. "I don't even know how I did it!"

"Like I told you," Sam said, "it's not your fault. It's just something you were born with. But we need you to tap into that ability now."

"What do you mean?" she asked.

"Yeah, I'm interested in hearing the answer to that one, too," Dean said.

"The process that's happening here—the Apotheosis—isn't complete yet, and I think that means we can still stop it." Sam gestured to the energy sphere. "You created the gods. Maybe you can *un*create them, too."

"Now *there's* an idea," Dean said, rising to his feet and helping Lena do the same.

"I didn't create them exactly," Renee said. "I painted them. One after the other, as if I was in some kind of trance. As soon as I finished one, it would disappear from the canvas, and I'd start another."

"I think painting was a way to help you focus your power," Sam said. "I don't think you actually have to do anything but... imagine."

A wave of weariness came over him then, so intense that the world seemed to spin and the next thing he knew he was lying on the ground.

"Sammy!" Dean started toward him, but then he stumbled and fell to his hands and knees.

Lena knelt next to Dean and put her hand on his shoulder. She looked at Sam and said, "What's wrong?"

Sam struggled to answer her; he didn't have enough strength left to speak. He watched as Dean slumped onto his side, still conscious, but no more able to move than his brother.

Lena looked back and forth between the brothers, panic in her gaze. "I don't…" She trailed off then, took a deep breath, and when she next spoke, her voice was calm. "The gods must've done something to them."

"They're draining the boys' energy to use against each other," Geoffrey said.

Sam couldn't turn his head to look at Geoffrey, but he managed to shift his eyes enough to see him. He had one hand pressed to his wounded shoulder, and while he looked barely able to stay on his feet, he managed to keep standing.

"They haven't gotten around to us yet because we're their priests," Geoffrey said. "But I imagine it'll be our turn soon."

"What can we do?" Lena said.

"You can't do anything," Renee said. "But I can. At least I can try." She closed her eyes and furrowed her brow in concentration.

At first nothing happened, and Sam feared that he'd guessed wrong, but then the energy sphere began to flicker, once, twice, and then it began to flash rapidly on and off, like a strobe light. Sam felt his strength returning; only a little, but it was enough to allow him to speak.

"You're doing it, Renee! Keep it up!"

Her brow furrowed even more, and she balled her hands

into fists as she concentrated even harder. And then, almost as if it were a bubble that simply popped out of existence, the energy sphere vanished. Paeon and Adamantine stepped back from each other, confused expressions on their faces, as if they had no idea what had just happened, or for that matter, who they were or what they had been doing. They no longer radiated power and strength, no longer seemed much like gods at all. They looked like nothing more than two humans dressed in costumes. Even Adamantine's silver skin had lost its metallic sheen and was now a dull gray.

Renee might've been able to unimagine much of the gods' power, but it seemed she wasn't able to unmake them completely. They still existed, and—depowered or not—that meant they were still dangerous.

Adamantine was the first to recover her wits, and she gave the five humans a venomous glare.

"It was a clever attempt, I grant you, but you cannot stop us that way. We have grown much since we were born and have become too strong to be dismissed so lightly."

Dean sat up and rose unsteadily to his feet. His eyes were no longer silver, and Sam knew that the enhancements that Adamantine and Paeon had given them were gone.

"You mean you both stole enough of your worshippers' life forces to keep your asses from going poof," Dean said.

Sam gave his brother a look, and Dean shrugged.

"Sorry. It sounded better in my head."

Sam felt strong enough to stand now and rose to join Dean. He wasn't back to his full strength yet, but he was getting stronger by the moment, and he knew his brother was, too. He took a quick glance around the battlefield that TechEdge's parking lot had become, and while many people still lay motionless, a number were starting to stir, and a few were even up on their feet.

Paeon's confusion vanished then, and a sly smile came onto his face. He lunged toward Adamantine, dropping his caduceus in the process, and grabbed hold of her spear with both hands. He yanked it out of her grip, spun it around, and drove the point into her chest. He shoved the spear deeper until it burst through her back, dripping with gray blood.

"I am the One!" Paeon shouted. His voice was no louder than a normal human's now, but it was strong and full of triumph.

"That's only a trophy," Geoffrey said.

Paeon frowned at Geoffrey. "What are you talking—"

His voice cut off as Adamantine sank the sharp fingers of her gauntlet into his throat. She released an electrical charge, and Paeon gritted his teeth as his body began jerking uncontrollably. The spear still jutted from Adamantine's back, but it didn't appear to bother her. Still holding onto Paeon's throat, she crouched, forcing him down with her, and with her free hand she snatched up the caduceus and plunged it into Paeon's right eye. The god shrieked in pain as Adamantine shoved the rod into his brain. Blood poured from the wound, and Adamantine released her grip on his throat, causing more blood to spill from where the metal tips of the gauntlet had pierced his flesh. Paeon staggered backward, clawing at the caduceus with both hands, but he was unable to dislodge it. He turned toward Lena and gave her a last unreadable look before his body began to glow with a white light. His form collapsed into a small sphere, and then shot forward and disappeared into Adamantine. Her skin regained its silvery luster, she seemed to stand taller, and her features became sharper. Once more, she looked like a god.

Grinning, she pulled the spear out of her chest and tossed it aside. The wound healed almost at once.

"So much for that fool," she said. "That was the real reason I kept Wyld's spear in the first place."

"It was a decoy," Sam said.

"Yes. But I no longer have need of it." She fixed her gaze on Renee. "There's only one thing I need now. Once I kill you and absorb your power, I shall be unstoppable."

The young woman took a step backward, and Lena and Geoffrey stepped to her side as if to protect her.

"So… you betray me in the end, Geoffrey?" Adamantine said. "No matter. Priests come and go, but I shall live *forever*." She bared her teeth in a cold, cruel, and above all hungry smile, and started toward Renee.

The brothers stepped in front of Renee, Geoffrey, and Lena, drew their guns, and fired at Adamantine. Sam feared their bullets would be useless against the god now that she was nearly at full strength, and he was right. A barrier of crackling electricity appeared in the air in front of Adamantine, repelling every round the boys sent at her. Within moments, their clips were empty, and when the last shot was fired, the electric shield vanished. The brothers tossed their guns aside, drew their knives, and rushed forward.

Adamantine laughed with delight as they came at her and spread her arms wide, as if in greeting. Sam aimed his blade at her heart, while Dean swept his toward her throat. But the knives had no more effect on her than the bullets. The blades struck her gleaming metal flesh and broke against it without leaving a scratch. The brothers tried to pull back before Adamantine could take hold of them, but she was too fast. She grabbed them by their throats and held them tight. Sam feared she would electrocute them, and as if reading his thoughts—and maybe at this point she was powerful enough to do so—she said, "I wouldn't waste the energy on you two." Then, as easily as if they were ragdolls, she tossed them aside.

The brothers flew a dozen feet in opposite directions and landed hard. Sam felt a rib or two crack as he hit the asphalt, and he wished he still had the healing powers granted to him by Paeon. The impact stunned him, and although he tried to get to his feet, his body refused to cooperate. The best he could do was push himself up on his hands and knees and watch through blurred vision as Adamantine continued striding toward Renee, Lena, and Geoffrey.

Lena and Geoffrey stepped in front of Renee, although what they hoped to do to protect the girl wasn't clear. Neither of them held weapons, nor did they possess the special abilities their gods had bestowed upon them. They were ordinary humans now, and while Sam admired their bravery, he feared it would only get them killed.

"Renee!" he shouted. "Run!"

If she heard him, she gave no sign. She only stood and watched, eyes wide and filled with fear, as Adamantine approached.

When Adamantine reached Lena and Geoffrey, she stopped and regarded them for a moment, upper lip curled in disdain.

"I can't believe that Paeon and I ever thought the two of you were worthy to serve us."

Then, before either Geoffrey or Lena could react, she flicked a hand toward them, as if shooing away a pair of insects. Tendrils of electricity shot from her fingers and struck the former priests directly between the eyes. Their bodies stiffened, convulsed, and then they collapsed to the ground. Sam had no idea if they were dead or merely stunned, but right then his primary concern was for Renee. Now nothing stood between her and the being she'd created. She had given Adamantine life, but the god—no, the *monster*—wouldn't be satisfied until she had taken every bit of energy housed in Renee's body, leaving her a drained and lifeless husk.

No way in hell was Sam going to let that happen. He forced himself to his feet and began staggering toward Adamantine and Renee, fighting the dizziness in his head and the pain in his body. He looked across the parking lot and saw Dean doing the same. The ground was littered with discarded weapons—guns, knives, and more—but Sam knew that none of them would do any good against Adamantine. There was only one thing that could kill her.

"Dean!" he shouted. "The gauntlet!"

His brother nodded grimly, and the two Winchesters ran toward Adamantine.

She seemed unaware of the brothers' approach. She gazed at Renee as if transfixed, and with her left hand she reached out and almost tenderly stroked the girl's cheek.

"I thank you for bringing me into this world," Adamantine said. "Your death shall give me everlasting life, and in the end, isn't that what any creator wants? For her creation to outlast her?"

Renee shook with terror and tears slid from her eyes. "Please don't," she whispered.

For the briefest of moments, it seemed Adamantine actually considered Renee's request. But then she said, "I must fulfill my destiny, just as you must fulfill yours."

She raised her gauntleted hand and reached for Renee's throat.

Sam and Dean came at Adamantine from opposite sides, and before she could take hold of Renee, they each grabbed her gauntlet by the wrist and, working together, bent her arm downward and plunged the sharp fingertips into her abdomen. The mystic gauntlet pierced her silver flesh with ease, as if her body was no more solid than water, and she shrieked with equal amounts pain and fury. The brothers jammed the gauntlet as far into Adamantine as they could, until a silvery substance gushed from the wound. Her shriek became a deafening scream of agony, and Sam and Dean let go of the gauntlet and turned toward Renee. They bore her to the ground and shielded her with their bodies as the divine energy stored within Adamantine exploded in a single blinding burst of light.

After several moments of silence, the brothers risked turning back to take a look, but Adamantine was gone, without so much as a single strand of metallic hair remaining to show she'd ever existed.

"Looks like the Apotheosis was canceled," Dean said.

Sam turned to look at Renee, who was sobbing now, her

face in her hands. He saw Lena and Geoffrey stirring and was glad they had survived, but he thought of all the men, women, and children who had been forced to fight in Paeon and Adamantine's war, too many of whom were wounded or dead. "Too bad it didn't happen sooner."

"Yeah," Dean said.

FIFTEEN

"I remembered how we killed the Lord of the Hunt by stabbing it with its own antlers," Sam said. "And we'd already seen how the gods could only be killed by their own weapons."

"So you figured Renee was still part of the gods she created—or they were a part of her—so she could be our weapon this time." Dean nodded. "Makes sense."

"Yeah. It didn't work out quite the way I thought it would, though. She wasn't able to destroy them."

"Hey, she was able to take Paeon and Adamantine down more than a few notches. If she hadn't weakened them, we might be singing hymns to one of those jumped-up monsters right now."

Sam and Dean sat at what had become their usual table in Doughnutz. It was after nine in the morning, and by this point they'd been up for more than twenty-four hours. They were both tired, but neither was particularly sleepy. Maybe it was all the excitement, maybe it was due to some residue of the power Paeon and Adamantine had given them, or maybe it was simply due to the amount of coffee they'd had since they'd returned here. Whatever the reason, they were both wide awake.

After Adamantine's defeat, Lena tried calling 911, but there was no one left in the Sheriff's Department to answer the call. So she called the Illinois State Police, told them that she was a doctor and there had been a riot outside the TechEdge store in Corinth. She said hundreds of people had been involved, there were dozens wounded—at least—and they needed every paramedic that the State Police could find, and they needed them *now*. It had taken some work to convince the State Police, though. After all, a riot involving hundreds of people in a small town like Corinth was a bit hard to believe. Sam and Dean helped Lena tend to the wounded until the first emergency vehicles began to arrive—followed closely by the first news vans—then they got in the Impala and headed for Doughnutz, where they'd been ever since. They'd asked Renee if she wanted to come with them, but she'd said she wanted to stay. *I may not have made this mess on purpose, but I did make it. I think I should stick around to help clean it up.*

Sam took a bite of his cruller and chewed slowly. "You're right. These things *are* awesome."

"Didn't I tell you?"

For a time they ate donuts and drank coffee in silence. After a while, Dean said, "What do you think will happen with Renee?"

"I don't know. I don't think she'll start another Apotheosis, though. They're rare events, or else there would be a lot more mentions of them in the lore."

"I hope so, for her sake as much as the world's. Can you imagine the guilt that poor kid must feel? And for something that wasn't even her fault."

"A lot of people were hurt," Sam said. "And a lot died, too."

"But a lot more lived. That's what matters."

"Easy to say, but not so easy to believe. We both know that."

"Yeah."

"While we were helping treat the wounded, Renee told me that she's going to quit art and change her major. She said she can't stand the thought of ever painting or drawing something again after what happened. And she said she doesn't want to take the risk of another Apotheosis happening."

"That sucks," Dean said, "but it's probably for the best. If nothing else, it'll help her sleep better at night."

"Let's hope."

"At least we know Geoffrey's going to be okay," Dean said.

Once Lena had learned that Geoffrey had been homeless for several years, she promised to help him find a job—once his shoulder wound had healed, of course. *We ex-priests have to stick together,* she'd said, and Geoffrey had laughed.

"And Lena's promised to stay in touch with Renee, too," Sam said. "Hopefully, the three of them will be able to get past this together."

"In the end, that's all we really have, you know?" Dean said. "Each other."

Sam smiled. "Now that's something I can believe in."

ACKNOWLEDGMENTS

Thanks as always to my agent, Cherry Weiner. Thanks to Natalie Laverick for lovingly shepherding this book from concept to finished product, and thanks to Hayley Shepherd whose sharp eye improved the final manuscript. And a very special thanks to the team at WB: Chris Cerasi, Amy Weingartner, and Victoria Selover—stalwart keepers and defenders of all things *Supernatural*.

ABOUT THE AUTHOR

Shirley Jackson Award finalist Tim Waggoner has published over thirty novels and three short-story collections of dark fiction. He teaches creative writing at Sinclair Community College and in Seton Hill University's MFA in Writing Popular Fiction program. You can find him on the web at www.timwaggoner.com.